MW01681108

Angel's Blues

Rhonda Tibbs

This book is a work of fiction. Names, characters, places, and incidents are the product of the author's imagination or are used fictitiously. Any resemblance to actual events, locales, or persons, living or dead, is coincidental.

ISBN: 0-9829-4412-8
ISBN-13: 978-0-9829441-2-7

Dedication

For Geri, Walt and Dennis, gone too soon, but never far from my heart.

Also by Rhonda Tibbs—Song of the Snowman
See all of our books at: www.rtibbs.net

Acknowledgments

This book simmered a long while before being written in the final form. There would be no book without the patience, love and support of my family and friends. I will be forever grateful to all of you.

I would also like to thank a Marine Corps sergeant who read this book on my husband's suggestion in Iwakuni, Japan, back in 1994. I never had the pleasure of meeting her, but the comments she shared proved I just might have something worth reading.

Peace and may God bless.

Chapter 1

Michael O'Mara's scream split the quiet hours of the morning, waking nearly everyone in his parents' Brooklyn home. He bolted upright in his upper bunk, scrambling backward until his back slammed into the wall.

Although his eyes were open, he was still entangled in his worst nightmare and didn't see the familiar bedroom he shared with his two brothers. He drew his knees to his chest and covered his head with trembling hands, willing the terror away.

His father burst into the room and crossed from the door to Michael's bed in just two steps. "Shut the hell up!"

The first blow from his father's big fist struck the side of Michael's head and he turned his face to the wall, taking three additional blows to his back.

"I'm sick of you screaming like a little girl every night!" His father shouted.

Michael held his position, hoping this episode was finished, but his father grabbed him by the ankle and yanked him from the bed. Before he finished bouncing off the hardwood floor, his father was gone again.

He sat up slowly, listening as his father's footsteps receded down the hall and his parents' bedroom door slammed shut. Though it was only a little after five, sleep was out of the question. He stood and the room spun in front of him. He grasped the upper bunk and leaned against the frame, closing his eyes for a moment before reaching for his clothes. He pulled an NYU sweatshirt over his head and a pair of jeans over his long legs then searched the darkness for his shoes.

Across the room, his older brother Bobby rolled over in bed and grumbled, "Asshole."

Michael didn't know if Bobby meant him or their father and didn't care right now. The only thing that mattered at this moment was surviving his father's latest assault.

The long stairway to the first floor swayed in front of his eyes. He gripped the railing and ascended carefully. As usual, the front door tempted him with freedom, but he turned and walked the long dark hall that led to the kitchen, stopping abruptly in the doorway.

The light over the kitchen sink revealed the slender figure of his mother seated at the table, an unlit cigarette poised between her fingers. She glanced up at him, met his gaze then dropped her focus back to the rosary lying near her coffee cup. Michael swung around and went out the front door after all.

He sat outside on the front steps of his parents' two-story brick home, one of the finest houses in their working-class neighborhood. His parents had purchased the house after his father returned from serving in the Marine Corps during World War II and this was the house where they raised their healthy Irish brood of seven children. His three older siblings had fond memories of life here in this house, of being an O'Mara, sharing amusing anecdotes about their childhood. Michael had none of those stories. All of his memories were snugly bound with barbed wire. Once again, he wished he was anywhere but here.

After sixteen years of living and twelve years of testing, such labels as "brilliant, gifted, and genius," meant no more to him than a ticket out. Those who assigned those labels never understood he was an impostor. He believed a real genius would have grasped the necessity of silence in an imperfect world, a lesson that for him had come at a very high price.

Despite the unusually warm spring morning, he shivered involuntarily and cursed the familiar aftereffect of the recurrent nightmare. Over the course of the day, the immediate misery would fade like always, but the cold, nearly palpable terror lingered like an extra-fine layer of skin and never really left him.

A sudden burst of red-gold light breaking through clouds overhead caught his attention and he lost himself in the beauty for a moment, reminding himself to focus on the hope of what lie ahead at the end of summer and not his misery. Only a final few weeks stood between him and a bachelor's degree from NYU and a transfer to MIT that fall. The goal had become his mantra, his song of freedom.

For years the promise of life outside his family was all he had and now that freedom was close. Unfortunately, the course of his existence never ran that smoothly.

The front door opened and he cringed, but did not turn.

"Mom says breakfast is ready," his youngest sister informed him.

His father glanced up from his morning paper then flicked a cigarette ash into the ashtray when Michael entered the kitchen. "After you eat, I want you to clean the garage, Einstein."

Michael understood this was merely the opening move of an old game. Unlike the rest of the family gathered around the kitchen table, he had no appetite. He moved around them all and headed for the garage.

He crossed to the workbench and switched on the radio to a station that played the top forty hits. A Beatles' tune floated out of the speaker as he reached for the broom. Each night, music filtered from his brother's plastic aqua-blue radio into their bedroom and

Michael passed many sleepless hours listening to the popular music of their generation, like the Rolling Stones and Dylan. The music threw him a lifeline, especially after the nightmare came.

His father eyed the interior of the garage then looked down at the dark stains on the concrete floor and shook his head. "I don't know why, but I actually expected better of you."

"I don't know how to get the oil out."

"Why, Mikey," his father said, moving closer, "are you admitting you don't know everything?"

Michael dared to look at his father while one more prayer for protection rose in his subconscious. Thus far prayer had proven to be a mostly useless appeal for divine intervention, but prayer was all the hope he had.

His father grinned. "Think you could lick it up?"

They stood, side by side for a moment, Ed O'Mara savoring his son's discomfort while Michael's spirit died just a little bit more. He hoped his father wouldn't actually insist he lap up the oil. The bitterness flowed between them and a nearly uncontrollable rage surged through Michael. The thought of picking up a shovel and smashing his father's head in actually crossed his mind.

Sighing loudly, Ed crossed to the workbench and grabbed a bag of sawdust tossing it at Michael. "Sprinkle that around, let it absorb the oil then sweep it up and get the hose and wash the floor down. It's simple, even an idiot like you can do it."

Michael followed the instructions then waited for the next phase to begin while his father examined the floor. He hoped to hear he had done enough, but experience cautioned his father was just getting started.

"I guess this will have to do." His father took out a cigarette and smiled thinly. "I've been watching you, Mikey. The closer you get to leaving us, the cockier you get."

He gave Michael a little shove. "You ready to take me on?"

Michael looked past his father out the door to the sunshine, his gut tightened and bitterness welled in his throat. He wanted to run. He shoved his shaking hands in his front pockets and took a deep breath looking back to his father, words failing him.

His father scowled and stepped closer, loosening his belt. He smelled like aftershave, cigarettes and last night's whiskey. "You got something to say to me?"

Michael shook his head quickly. "No, I..."

His father swung the big black belt and took the game the rest of the way.

Half an hour later, Michael eased through the kitchen, every step sending sharp pains up his back where the belt had landed. He passed the open door to the living room and saw his brothers and their father watching a baseball game. Bobby was the only one who looked up as he passed.

The stairs to the second floor loomed ahead and the climb seemed to take forever. After gathering some clean clothes, he crossed the upstairs hall to the family bathroom and flipped on the light. He opened the water tap in the shower and stripped then stood under the spray and let the water run over his back to cool the welts his father's belt left on his body.

The grandfather clock at the foot of the stairs chimed five times as he popped two aspirin into his mouth and crossed the upstairs hall from the bathroom to his bedroom. He picked up his book bag and sat at the desk he shared with his brothers, hoping to catch up on some reading, but footsteps on the stairs told him his mother was on her way.

She knocked softly, but entered carrying his brothers' freshly laundered clothes without waiting for a reply. He read one sentence eleven times while she slipped the clothes into the chest of drawers. She turned toward the door, but hesitated. She seemed to be searching for something to say, but he couldn't help her. Conversation never came easy for them. She had six children she loved and then there was him.

"Don't forget to ask to get off early for your sister's wedding rehearsal, it's at six-thirty on Friday," she said finally.

"I don't know if I can get off work early."

"They'll let you off if you just ask," she said, adding quickly, "do it for your sister."

Anger boiled in him. He didn't owe anyone in this family anything. He knew exactly how to get rid of her. He turned and looked directly at her, knowing any frank contact between them would send her running.

On cue, she turned and hurried away. He watched the door close behind her and turned back to his books.

On Monday his last class ended at two and he ran seven blocks to catch the subway back to Brooklyn then ran again in order to be on time for a job in a grocery warehouse where he loaded trucks four evenings a week and all day on Saturdays.

His advisor at school had strongly counseled against anything that distracted from his classes. Between a small inheritance from his uncle and scholarship programs Michael had enough for tuition and books. What he did not have enough of were the basic essentials like clothing and other things that his parents willingly provided for his brothers and sisters, but for him had fallen by the wayside.

Other than a quick sandwich every now and then he seldom ate at home. Mealtimes with his father were something he dreaded.

The transition away from the ordeal of sitting down for a meal with his family had begun the first year he started the commute to NYU and now no one even missed him.

He had purchased his own clothes for better than a year. Though his wardrobe was limited, the few things he could afford fit him better than Bobby's hand-me-downs, since Bobby was a good two inches shorter these days.

Another benefit was that for twenty-five hours a week working on the loading dock was the only time he wasn't expected to do mental cartwheels to prove his worthiness of scholarships and degrees of higher learning. Most importantly, the job was a place where every fiber of his being didn't fear his father's approach.

His advisor at school never understood much about him anyway. The man never questioned him about his occasional absences and certainly never seemed concerned regarding his parents' lack of involvement in his academic career. In fact, as long as Michael excelled, not one person in authority at any school he attended had ever asked questions.

That evening he arrived home fatigued, but still had hours of studying in front of him. Bobby called his name as he passed the living room so he stepped inside.

"Max Burnette wants you to call him," Bobby said.

Michael heard only the first three words. Across the room was the fireplace mantel, the place where his mother proudly displayed family pictures. Tonight there was a new addition, a picture taken of him just before his twelfth birthday. In the photo, he wore an altar boys cassock and held a single candle that lit his blue eyes. The photographer had urged him to smile, an impossible notion on that day or many since. He crossed the floor quickly, intent on snatching it from the mantel, but stopped abruptly, hand in mid air, unable to make himself touch the photo.

"Where did this come from?" He asked.

"Mom's been helping Grandma clean out her attic. They found a bunch of your stuff mixed in with Uncle Frank's old things," Bobby said, his attention still on the television. "Susan's got everything out in the kitchen."

Michael backed away from the mantel and found his sister Susan at the table in the kitchen. Before her was a box containing the trophies and awards he won in piano competitions years ago.

Susan lifted a framed award and looked up at him, her eyes narrowing to slits. She was his twin, but they had little in common and she resented him for the disparity. She didn't bother speaking to him much anymore and when she did the level of malice she exhibited rivaled that of their father.

Michael eyed the collection on the table. His assessment ended with a picture of him and his father's youngest brother, Frank. Uncle Frank had an arm draped casually around his shoulders and was holding a trophy. Each of them was smiling, but only Frank's smile was genuine.

"I never heard you play one thing," Susan said bitterly.

Michael's heart was pounding so hard the roar in his head made it difficult to hear anything she said. He took a step back just as his father rumbled in the back door fresh from a couple of customary shots of Irish whiskey at his favorite bar.

His father glared at the things on the table. "What's all this?"

"Michael's piano awards," Susan said, picking up a trophy. "They're all first place," she murmured as if speaking to herself.

His father glanced at a few awards then looked at Michael, "A faggot's idea of a good time."

His father turned to the refrigerator and pulled out a beer. "Get that crap out of my sight."

His father moved away to the living room where the sound of the TV grew louder as he turned the channel to a baseball game.

Susan turned back to Michael. "You got it all, didn't you?"

Michael grabbed the trophy from her hand, tossed it and all the others into the box, snatched up the box and turned toward the back door.

She ran after him, pulling on his shirt. "Mom wants those," she whispered.

He dumped the contents of the box into the stone barbecue pit and turned toward the garage. When he returned, he found Susan searching through the pile. Bobby had taken a seat on the back steps and watched the two of them with idle curiosity.

Michael nudged Susan with his foot, "Move."

He sprayed lighter fluid into the pit and dropped in a match. Flames leapt out at him, but he stood firm. He had to be close. He deserved to savor this victory.

Susan shoved him. "I hate you."

She stalked into the house and Michael watched the fire consume paper and wood, melting glass and twisting metal, until only the bitter memories lingered. When he turned toward the house he discovered his brother still seated on the steps.

Bobby eyed him for a moment before speaking. "She's jealous, you know." He looked across the yard to the smoldering barbecue pit. "I guess we all wish we had just a little of your talent and brains."

Michael stepped around him. "Be careful what you wish for."

His last class on Friday ended at noon. After grabbing a quick lunch, he walked to the admissions building for a final meeting with his advisor. His mother usually waited for him outside the office on a bench where she would be fidgeting nervously and watching the clock. She was always uncomfortable in these surroundings.

Her presence had allowed him to continue down the path that Uncle Frank had so carefully mapped out years before, inadvertently ensuring Michael's shot at leaving them all behind. His mother's participation was never fully involved, but for this one thing he was grateful to her.

Today, the bench where he usually found her waiting was empty. His mother had never been late before and he had a sinking feeling things were not turning in his favor. He waited until ten minutes after one then opened the door to the advisor's office and the secretary was surprised to see him.

"Oh, Michael, Dr. McCabe already informed your mother you didn't need to meet with him again. We mailed all the papers out a week ago. Didn't your mother tell you?"

"No ma'am."

"Well, I'm sure it must have slipped her mind. Just get those papers signed and back to us as soon as you can, all right?"

Michael thanked her and turned toward the door, his mind reeling. His parents had possession of the papers that would allow him to attend school in Cambridge. The fact that they hadn't bothered to mention this to him was not a good sign.

On Friday evening, Michael finished working and hurried to the church for his sister's wedding rehearsal, hoping his father hadn't noticed his absence. Things were backed up at work and his boss had been in a foul mood. Leaving early hadn't been an option.

Bobby stood in front of the church, smoking a cigarette with the groom's brother. Michael looked past them through the open doors and tried to catch his breath.

"Is the rehearsal finished already?" He asked.

"No such luck," the groom's brother said. "They haven't done much except stand around and talk."

Michael stepped inside the familiar church, calculating the odds on whether his father would have stopped by the corner bar on his way here. He quickly scanned the room and spotted his parents talking to Father Patrick. His father appeared sober and Michael breathed easier. Even when sober, the big man could be mean, but the odds for violence were usually lower.

He wanted to ask his mother about the papers but doubted she would make time for him until the wedding was over. If his parents were playing games, there was only one choice for him. He would need to find the papers, forge their signatures and take a long hike after finishing his finals. Whether he would succeed would be determined by his father's commitment to punish him.

He slipped into the shadows and sat facing the altar, hating the sights and the smells of this church. Being here forced him to think of Uncle Frank, his father's younger brother, a scholar, a priest, and the pride of the O'Mara's. For eight years, he spent endless hours here with Frank, learning chess, the dead language of Latin, practicing endless hours on the rectory piano, but most of all enduring Frank's idea of devoted mentoring.

The last time he had been in this building had been Frank's funeral four years ago.

Feeling the weight of this life, Michael closed his eyes and said a prayer. "Ite in pace" he finished with a whisper, a common phrase repeated often by an uncommon man who knew nothing of the nature of peace. Michael offered this plea for the spirit of his dead uncle and no more. The well of love had been boarded over long ago.

An elbow nudged him in the side, drawing him from the past, "You asleep?"

He looked up at Bobby then past him, locating his father quickly. "I don't know why I have to be here."

"Me neither, but you know the O'Mara motto, family sticks together, even if it kills us."

Michael managed a little smile and wished he shared his brother's sense of humor.

Bobby stretched his legs and yawned. "Want to shoot some pool after we're finished?"

He started to say no. The nightmare had come three times this week and he was exhausted. He glanced at his father, wondering what his chances were for an uneventful night at home. Bobby seemed to read his mind.

"I heard Dad say that he's going straight home after this," Bobby said casually. "You might as well give him a chance to get to sleep before you go home. If you're lucky, you won't see him the rest of the night."

The soft admission stunned Michael. No one ever directly referred to the violence between him and his father, but Bobby just came close.

For a change, he met his brother's direct gaze. "I guess a few games would be okay."

The toss of a quarter decided Bobby would shoot first. Susan and a couple of girlfriends were seated nearby, but she was busy flirting with a group of boys at the next table and didn't acknowledge their arrival. Bobby sank two balls before Michael cleaned the table.

Bobby cursed softly as the last ball fell. "Is there anything you can't do, Egghead?"

"He can't say no to me," a woman said.

Recognizing the voice, Michael swung around, glaring at him was a tall, sexually-charged blonde nearly eight years his senior and a friend of sorts. She flipped her long hair over one shoulder, revealing a deep V-neck blouse and generous bosom.

She walked a little closer and smiled. "I thought you were going to come by after you finished at the church."

"I said I might come by."

"Couldn't you call?"

Michael turned to his brother, intending to make an introduction, but she grabbed his arm.

"Don't turn your back on me."

Michael shook off her grip. "Stop it."

She smiled coolly, but she was clearly angry. "Come outside where we can talk."

"Why are you making a scene?"

"I haven't seen you all week. You haven't even bothered to call. What's going on?"

Michael shrugged and dared a quick glance at Bobby. His brother was watching with a curious, almost amused look on his face.

"Why don't you come over for a while?" Jean stroked his cheek with a fingertip and smiled wickedly at Bobby. "Bring your big brother."

Bobby grinned but turned away, feigning interest in the game going on at the next table.

Michael took a long, slow breath, again realizing how weary he was. "I'll come by tomorrow, after the wedding."

Jean studied him, probing for signs of weakness, but he never let her that close. She gently caressed one cheek and kissed the other softly. Michael shuddered involuntarily both out of anger and need. Affection was the one thing that kept him coming back to her and she knew it.

She wiped the lipstick from his cheek and smiled brightly, happy with her small victory. "You win."

Michael watched her walk away knowing when it came to Jean, he never won. He turned to face his curious brother.

Bobby eyed him for a long moment then nodded at the table, "Your turn to break."

Michael picked up a cue and bent over the table. As he slid the smooth wood back over his forefinger, his sister Susan sauntered over. He completed the break and straightened his back, watching the five ball teeter on the edge of a pocket before dropping silently.

Susan moved closer to him. "Doesn't that woman I just saw you with date Max Burnette?"

Michael studied his pretty sister for a long moment before deciding on the truth. "She dates me."

"She's at least ten years older than you."

"It's none of your business," he said, moving around the table for his next shot.

Susan threw a cube of blue chalk at him. "You think you're so much better than everyone else."

"Shut-up, Susan," Bobby cut in impatiently. "Go back to your side of the room."

Susan threw a cue stick on the table and scattered the balls. "You're such jerks. I hate both of you."

Bobby moved closer to her, "Go away."

She turned on her heel and stalked back to her friends.

The brothers didn't discuss their sister's behavior and Bobby asked no questions about Jean. They finished one more game, got a slice of pizza then walked home. Turning the corner of their block, they spotted Susan sitting on the steps in front of a neighbor's house. Susan and the neighbor, Danny D'Angelo, each had a beer in their hand.

"Great," Bobby muttered.

"Hey, look," Susan called, "It's Mikey, the wonder boy."

Danny D'Angelo snickered. He was short and muscular and had a father who drank more than Ed O'Mara and didn't bother to single out just one of his five kids to punch on. Just like his father, Danny D'Angelo never missed an opportunity to relish in the misery of others.

Most who knew Susan, knew she had already developed a penchant for alcohol. She stood as they drew closer and Michael sighed audibly. This had been a long day and he only wanted to go to bed, hopefully to sleep.

"Hey, Mikey," Susan said, "guess who I saw a little while ago? That woman you're *dating* was hanging all over your buddy Max outside Baxter's bar."

Michael kept walking, hoping she was done, but her viciousness trapped him. She poked him hard in the spine with her beer bottle.

"What do you think Uncle Frank would say about you sleeping with such a whore?"

He turned swiftly and in three quick steps put inches only between them. He grabbed her beer bottle and threw it in the air. The bottle arced high and fell to the street at the end of the block and exploded with a loud pop.

He cocked one eyebrow and smiled thinly. "Party's over."

Danny D'Angelo jumped from the steps and hit the sidewalk with both feet, ready as always for a fight. Even without this current display of bravado, Michael had suffered enough of Danny's ridicule over the years to know whose side the stocky Italian was on.

"Why don't you try picking on someone your own size, Mikey?" Danny asked.

Michael looked down at him, lost in the absurdity for a moment. Danny had given boxing a try the previous summer and was thrown out of the program due to his unruly nature. He stood at least four inches shorter and weighed about twenty pounds less than Michael. Nevertheless in Danny's mind three months of boxing made him tougher than most, especially someone like Michael.

"I should knock you on your ass just on principle you arrogant asshole," Danny said.

Michael's teenage body was long and lean, but working on the loading docks had developed the strong musculature inherited from his father. He could keep up with the older, well-muscled men at work without any effort.

He nodded shortly at Danny, his hands curling into tight fists thinking it might just feel good to punch back for a change. "Give it your best shot."

Bobby quickly stepped between them.

"Come on, Mike," he said quietly. "Let's go in the house."

"Yeah, you wouldn't want to break them faggoty piano fingers," Danny said grinning wriggling his fingers in Michael's face.

Susan laughed out loud and Michael punched Danny in the face, knocking him backwards three steps before striking again. The second blow put Danny on the ground. Michael grabbed the front of Danny's shirt just as his father appeared at the front door.

Bobby gripped Michael's arm firmly, "Dad," he whispered.

Ed glared at Michael. "What the hell are you doing?"

"They're just messing around," Bobby said placing his body in front of Michael's, blocking their father's view as Michael straightened up.

His father didn't switch focus. "You're grounded, Genius." He pushed the door open. "Get inside."

Michael moved over the threshold and every fiber of his body anticipated an attack. The sound of his father's footsteps climbing the stairs behind him turned his feet into lead weights.

He topped the stairs and his heavy feet delivered him safely to his room. He listened as his father kept walking down the hallway and when the door to his parents' bedroom closed, he began breathing again.

His left hand was throbbing as he crawled onto the top bunk. He had no regrets about hitting Danny. Danny had antagonized him since they were both seven years old and hitting back for a change did feel good.

His younger brother slept soundly on the bunk below. Michael envied such peace of mind. Right now, the only thing that would give him such serenity was to get far away from this house. He wanted to fly down those stairs, hit the street running, and never come back.

He didn't care that he was the only one of his father's seven children to receive punishment for staying out too late; being grounded was at the bottom of a list filled with high-risk events.

There was a mountain of rage and fear inside his body. For years, he had swallowed each bitter feeling, tamping the harshness down into every available recess of mind and soul. Lately, containing the volatile mix seemed more than he could manage.

"Three more months," he muttered.

He had been in a holding pattern all day until his sister mentioned Uncle Frank. He shouldn't have gotten so angry with her. She had no way of knowing Frank was the reason he existed on a sharp edge, clinging to one lean hope.

Bobby came in and approached his bed, holding up a bag of ice. "Here."

"Thanks, my hand is killing me."

"I didn't know you had it in you, Mike."

Bobby switched on the radio before undressing. A song drifted into the room and Michael shifted restlessly. Bobby lit a joint and opened a window. "Man, I don't see how you stand there and take Dad's shit."

Michael grunted at the absurdity. "It's not like I have a lot of choice."

For a few minutes, the only sound was the radio and their younger brother's even breathing.

Bobby sighed loudly and looked up at him. "I envy you."

Michael laughed shortly. "What?"

"I don't have any idea what I want to do now that I'm graduating high school. You're moving on to something better soon."

"Not soon enough."

"Oh, come on. You're only sixteen for crying out loud."

"I'll tell you what, the next time Dad wants to exercise his fists, I'll let you stand in for me then lets see how old you feel." He hadn't intended to let the bitterness escape but the family charade infuriated him.

"I'm sorry," Bobby said softly.

He rolled over and faced the wall. "Thanks for the ice."

Chapter 2

The moment Jean walked into his sister's wedding reception, Michael knew there was going to be trouble. Jean seldom indulged in conservative dress and today was no exception. Her bright yellow mini-dress and three-inch heels displayed all of her voluptuous assets.

Across the room, his sister Susan took immediate notice of Jean's entrance and said something to the group of friends and cousins near her, all of whom turned to stare at Jean.

Though Jean clung to the arm of their mutual friend Max Burnette, her eyes searched the room until she found him. She smiled widely and came straight for him.

Jean brushed an imaginary something from the satin lapel of his tuxedo. "I hope you don't mind that I came."

"Of course not," he said, shooting an irritated look at Max.

Max shrugged and looked around the room, "She wanted to come."

Max Burnette had been Michael's oldest brother's best friend since they were in second grade. After high school, both Michael's older brother and Max had attempted to join the military, but a physical revealed that Max had a minor heart condition and was unacceptable.

When Max's father died a few years ago, Max inherited the three-story building with six-family flats just three blocks from the O'Mara house. Max looked after his mother, acted as manager of the apartments, and lived comfortably on the income from the rent, and slipped into his father's role.

Max Burnette was an overweight, coarse-featured, lonely man and he was captivated by Jean.

Jean moved into one of Max's flats that previous September and Michael happened by only moments after Max had volunteered to carry her possessions up two flights of stairs. Max saw him coming down the sidewalk and waved him over.

"Hey, Mike, you're just the help I was looking for," Max said.

Michael paused and shifted his heavy book bag to the other shoulder. "What do you need help with?"

Just then, Jean emerged from the building. The mid-afternoon sun lit her long golden hair and blue eyes. Michael was certain he never saw a more beautiful woman. Seeing him, Jean stopped abruptly and eyed him.

"Jean, this is Mike O'Mara," Max said. "He's graciously agreed to help me move your things upstairs."

As Jean studied Michael, her eyes narrowed almost imperceptibly and her sunny expression shifted to something darker, something salacious and raw. Michael had almost no experience with girls and the unspoken message bewildered him.

"It's a pleasure to meet you," she said softly.

Blushing, Michael shifted his gaze to Max, but Max seemed unaware of anything except his new tenant. Jean laughed and bounced lightly down the steps to the truck parked at the curb and threw open the back doors.

Max grinned foolishly and lowered his voice, "I think I might be in love."

Over the course of that afternoon, Jean wrapped Max tightly around her finger. She teased him so much Max had difficulty executing the task at hand and Michael moved most of the smaller items alone. Finally, he prodded Max to finish.

Max frowned at him. "Why? Are you in a hurry to get back to your books?"

Michael stepped up into the rented moving truck and surveyed the remainder of her belongings. "I'm in a hurry to get away from the two of you."

"She's something, isn't she?"

"Want to take the couch now?"

"Hey, you understand don't you?" Max grinned at him. "I mean people with your kind of IQ get horny, don't they?"

Michael wiped the sweat from his forehead and looked at him directly. "I'll be here ten more minutes then you're on your own."

"Okay, slave driver. Let's get this over with then you get lost and I'll make my first move."

Michael sighed loudly, "I thought this was your first move."

When the last item was in her apartment, Jean offered them each a beer. Michael asked for water, planning to down it quickly and get out of there. Jean sat on the couch and crossed her long, tanned legs.

"Why don't you two have a seat?" She asked.

Max immediately took a seat near her on the couch. Michael stayed on his feet and she looked to him.

"Sit down, sweet thing," she said.

"I can't stay."

Jean cocked her head to one side and smiled wickedly, "Come on."

He found an empty spot on the hardwood floor. Jean smiled at him then turned to Max.

"Do you smoke pot?"

"Hell yeah," Max said.

Jean looked back to Michael and waited for a response from him. At the time, he still believed there was already enough risk in his life without the addition of an illegal substance.

"He thinks he's too smart to mess with drugs," Max said for him.

Michael shifted restlessly. "It's not a good time for me to gamble."

"Gamble?" She asked.

Jean's fierce concentration embarrassed and flustered him.

Max came to the rescue. "Mike's our neighborhood genius. He's been going to college since he was like fourteen."

Jean's eyebrows shot up in surprise. "You're only fourteen?"

Michael shook his head slowly, thinking she and Max were a good match after all. "I'm sixteen and I've been in college since I was twelve."

"Why, you're just a baby." She smiled slowly, appraising him. "You are going to be one hell of a good-looking man."

Michael glanced uncomfortably at Max knowing this conversation wasn't what Max had in mind.

Jean pulled the top of a tin off and frowned. "Damn, no papers. Max, do you have any?"

"Sure downstairs. I'll be right back."

Michael started to rise. "I'd better go."

"Oh, no, stay a while." Jean smiled brightly. "We'll barbecue up on the roof."

She turned her bright smile on Max. "That is, if my new landlord doesn't mind."

Max grinned like a fool, "No, of course not."

Soon Max had rolled out three neat joints. Jean lit one and knelt in front of him, "Just try it." She placed the lit end of the joint in her mouth. A healthy stream of smoke came from her pursed lips and Michael inhaled until he could stand no more. Jean rocked back on her heels and laughed while he choked and his eyes watered. Jean came at him again and he shook his head, holding up a hand to stop her, but she wasn't a woman who accepted no for an answer easily.

"One more, then I'll leave you alone."

That was the last time he believed what she told him. Half an hour later they were on the roof. Michael was sitting on the roof with his back to a vent pipe and couldn't seem to move. The music coming from a radio nearby sounded familiar yet the lyrics were in a language he didn't recognize. He could see Max and Jean across the roof laughing and talking while they barbecued. An overhead plane caught his attention and he stared at the sky, his thoughts drifting lazily.

Max knelt in front of him, blocking out the sun with his bulky body, "How are you doing, Mikey?"

"I don't know. My knees feel fuzzy."

Max laughed and patted his shoulder. "That will pass after you eat," he said.

"Yes," he said, nodding. "I'm hungry."

After a meal of barbecued chicken, garlic bread and salad, things made more sense and the lingering euphoria felt like a blessing. He smiled to himself and leaned back against Jean's living room wall, stretching his long legs in front of him.

Jean was across the room, sitting on the floor in front of the coffee table, lighting another joint. She smiled at him through the haze and crawled across the floor on her hands and knees. The loose linen blouse swung away from her body and he could see firm white breasts.

"Stop looking down my blouse you little pervert."

Somewhere in the back of his mind, he knew he should be embarrassed, but the playful reprimand did not distract him. She got to her knees and straddled his legs, the joint poised before her mouth.

"Close your eyes and inhale."

"I have to go."

Jean laughed. "Relax, will you?"

"Where did Max go?"

"He is looking after one of his tenants."

Jean leaned forward and offered his mouth a woman's ripe kiss sending a spasm down his body and he looked up at her in surprise.

A slow smile lit her face. "You have got the most beautiful blue eyes I've ever seen. I don't even know what color to call them."

"Blue," he managed to say.

"Honey, mine are blue. Yours are...I don't know kind of purple and blue together, like violet. They're just unbelievable." She leaned close, lips near his ear. "Call your Mama and tell her you're spending the night with a friend."

Max rapped on the door and Michael jumped. Jean rose and Michael took the opportunity to get on his feet.

"I've got to go," he said, pushing past a bewildered Max.

For the next week, Michael walked a different path home from work, but on Saturday it was raining so he took the quicker route and turned the corner just as Max parked his car at the curb. Max climbed out and waved to him.

"Come inside for a minute."

Michael followed him into the kitchen and Max started putting away a few groceries.

"You made quite an impression on Jean," Max said.

"I didn't do anything," he said quickly.

"What are you getting defensive about? I didn't accuse you of anything, did I?"

"No, but I know what you're going to say."

"Shut up," Max snapped, throwing a box of crackers into a cabinet. "She's having a little party tonight. She made me promise to ask you over."

Max folded his arms over his chest and fixed him with a cold stare. "So, will you go?"

"I know how you feel about her, Max."

Max leaned against the counter. "What do you want?"

"I want to keep my body intact."

"I'm not going to hurt you because Jean prefers boys."

Michael shook his head. "Tell her no."

Max snorted. "Tell her yourself."

Michael climbed to the second floor and tapped on Jean's door and took a deep breath. Jean opened the door and smiled.

"Sweet thing," she drawled.

Without warning, she did the one thing that still had him coming back. She reached out and embraced him tenderly. The gentle, foreign touch, hurt almost as much as his father's fist.

"I'm so glad you're here," she said in his ear.

That is how his affair with Jean began, with a genuine embrace and words whispered tenderly. Jean's keen instinct for reeling him in was her talent. There were occasions when she was capable of genuine tenderness and moments when she let him see her own vulnerability. There were times when they fell into a long conversation and he found her knowledgeable and refreshing. In the quiet moments after sex, he simply enjoyed the touch of her soft skin against his as they lay side by side. Though inconsistent, Jean had offered some of the kindest moments of his life.

Unfortunately, the little good there was between them was rapidly slipping away. He was poised to move forward, while she was moving on to nowhere and resented him. Her indulgence in drugs and alcohol was growing worse by the day. Now, here they were eight months later, at his sister's wedding reception, each of them pretending.

Despite Max's little speech about not standing in the way, Michael knew Max still had a powerful attraction to Jean. Jean still gave Max only enough bait to manipulate him. Michael knew how adept she was with manipulation and empathized with the bigger man.

He smiled at Max. "You look pretty good in a suit."

Max grimaced and looked around. "I need a beer."

"Oh, a slow dance," Jean said, pulling Michael to the dance floor.

Michael did his best to keep a respectable distance between their bodies. He caught his sister Susan's fixed stare from the edge of the dance floor and cringed.

Jean grinned. "Worried Mama and Daddy might see?"

He dropped his gaze to her and her teasing smile disappeared.

"Jesus, you hurt me so much when you look at me like that with your runway-blues."

Michael's smooth brow creased in irritation, "My what?"

"Your damned eyes, right now, they are the color of those violet runway lights at the airport. They remind me of the short time you'll be mine before you fly out of my life."

Sighing, he looked away in time to see Susan approaching their father and his heart began to beat faster. Jean chose that very moment to press closer to his body.

Michael stepped away. "Don't Jean, not here."

She stared for a long minute, swung around, cursing him under hear breath and started for the door with Michael on her heels until they were outside at the corner of the church where he grabbed her arm.

"Wait, please."

"No! I don't know why I let you treat me the way you do. Go on back to your precious family, obviously you prefer the abuse."

Michael released his grip on her arm and her mouth spread into a mean grin.

"That's right," she said. "I know where you get all the bruises."

He inhaled quickly and looked down the street. "I can't do this anymore," he said.

"What the hell does that mean?"

He looked at her directly, now solid in his resolve. "We're done."

He found Bobby and Max smoking a joint behind the reception hall and gratefully took a long, deep drag. He was shaking from head to foot. A day with his family always left his tolerance paper-thin, but with Jean added to the mix the discomfort was unbearable.

Max eyed him suspiciously. "Where's Jean?"

"She left."

"Damn it, you hurt her feelings again, didn't you? You're such a little shit."

Michael eyed him for a minute. "There's nothing I can do about it, Max," he said quietly.

"Well, you're the genius. I'm sure if you really cared you'd figure a way."

Michael was fed up with Jean and sick of Max's jealousy. "Why don't you go comfort her? She always appreciates your attention."

Max exhaled dramatically. "I'm going to have to hurt you one of these days."

"You don't have to hurt me, Max. She's all yours."

No one saw his father come around the corner, but all heard him bark Michael's name. Michael obeyed immediately, walking on legs that begged to run the other way.

"Who's the whore in the yellow dress?" His father asked.

Michael flinched at the crude question. The smell of bourbon flooded the cool night air and Michael had no doubt what was coming.

"A friend," he said, forcing the words out of a constricted throat.

His father moved closer, within inches of Michael's face. He grinned and lowered his voice. "I hear you're screwing her, is that right?"

The stench of the alcohol robbed Michael of fresh air and he swallowed hard then tried to catch his breath.

"I…yes," Michael managed.

"Well, well, so you're not a faggot after all." His father shook his head and sighed. "Unfortunately, it looks as if you've found another way to embarrass this family. I'm only going to tell you this once, Einstein," his father stepped right next to him and poked him in the chest with a beefy finger. "Stay away from that piece of work."

Deep inside, the rage stirred. Michael turned away, hoping his father wouldn't see his flash of anger. His father grabbed his arm and spun him around and Michael's raw fury met his father's fierceness head on. The exchange clearly set his father back for a moment then he struck so fast Bobby and Max only saw Michael hit the ground.

"You little son-of-a-bitch!" his father roared, kicking Michael in the back. "Go ahead, come across to me like that one more time, I promise it would be my pleasure to put you six feet under."

He hovered only a moment before mumbling another expletive and returned to the reception.

Bobby and Max reached Michael as he struggled to sit upright.

Bobby knelt in front of him. "Are you all right?"

Dazed, all Michael could do was nod. Bobby reached out and touched the swelling knot on Michael's jaw but Michael jerked away and managed to stand. He looked around reorienting himself then started away on legs that did not want to cooperate.

"Are you going home?" Bobby called.

Michael lifted a hand and waved without looking back. He managed to walk only half a block before nausea swept over him and he ducked into an alley to vomit before heading for an old safe haven, a neighborhood park just three blocks from his parents' home. He left the sidewalk to sit in the shadows under a favorite tree. The dizziness took over an hour to diminish, but the buzzing in his head stuck around. He heard church bells signal midnight and knew he should go home, but found himself knocking on Jean's door instead.

Music and the familiar smell of marijuana drifted through the door. Jean opened the door and eyed his face.

"I see you and Daddy had another talk."

"Can I come in?"

She stood back and waved him into the room. "Want some ice for the swelling?"

Michael shook his head and dropped onto to the sofa. Jean turned down the stereo and lit a joint, then handed it to him and touched his tender face.

"Is this because of me?"

Michael laid his head back on the sofa, took a deep draw on the joint, and closed his eyes. After a moment, she began to unbutton his shirt.

"I can't stay," he said.

She kissed his bruised cheek. "That's what you always say."

At five that morning, Michael woke with a start. He glanced at the clock and groaned.

Jean rolled over and squinted at him. "What's wrong?"

"I've got to go."

Jean reached for him and Michael moved beyond her touch. She jumped out of bed, grabbed his shirt, and threw it at his feet. "Get out. I'm sick of your little boy games."

Michael drew in a shaky breath and picked up the shirt. Jean hovered over him.

"You think you can just use me and walk away, don't you?"

He shrugged his shoulders into the tuxedo shirt then peered up at her, still sleepy. "What?"

"I never know when you'll come around and when you do, I'm supposed to just drop everything."

Michael got to his feet and looked around for his pants.

She stared hard. "I'm going to Cambridge with you in August."

That got his full attention. He studied her for a moment and saw she wasn't kidding.

"I thought this was just about sex," he said quietly.

It was a mean thing to say, and certainly not the truth, but he didn't want her entertaining notions of coming to Cambridge. Her eyes filled with tears and she slumped onto the edge of the bed. In the past eight months, she had never shown this much vulnerability. Now, here it was, staring him in the face at five in the morning with his father's fists waiting.

Her need was too much. He had nothing to give this woman. He sat down next to her and his shoulders sagged under the weight of this life.

"Stay here, Michael. Stay with me."

"I have to get home before my father gets up."

She pulled back and took his chin in her hand, forcing him to look at her. The moment of vulnerability had evaporated.

"I mean, live here, with me," she said.

"I can't do that."

"Why not? Your parents certainly don't care about you."

The words might have hurt more if he hadn't come to the same conclusion a few years ago. He pulled away and stood.

"I'm not trading one nightmare for another," he said.

Jean jumped to her feet. "What the hell is that supposed to mean?"

He grabbed his shoes. "I've got to go."

She attempted to put her arms around him, but he stiffened and backed away.

"I love you," she said. "I thought you loved me too."

He looked at her squarely. "This isn't love, Jean."

Jean slapped him. "No wonder he beats the hell out of you."

The rage in him rose so strong he trembled. He pushed past her and headed for the door. Jean, of course, had to have the last say. She followed him into the hall and leaned over the railing as he descended.

"We're through! Do you hear me, Michael? Don't come back!"

The nightmare rode his shoulders all the way home. He could feel the end coming. Every step felt like a separate act of self betrayal. He slipped in the door of the screened-in back porch and found the door locked. He didn't have his key and curled into a corner of the porch to stay warm.

He woke with a start a few hours later and found his mother standing over him, a strange, almost concerned, expression on her face. She turned away quickly, as if embarrassed.

"It's almost time for breakfast. Hurry and get changed."

He was the last one to the table and took the only available chair next to his father.

His father eyed him with typical loathing, "So nice of you to grace us with your presence."

With the big man so close, Michael had no interest in food. He sipped orange juice. His father had other ideas.

"Bobby, pass the eggs to your brother." He pointed a butter knife at Michael. "Your mother went to a lot of trouble to make us a nice breakfast. You will eat."

Michael swallowed the first bite of scrambled eggs and choked. He didn't see the fist coming and his left cheek and temple took the full impact. The blow knocked him off the chair to the floor. His father jumped to his feet, grabbed Michael by the hair, and threw him back into the chair.

"You will sit here and eat like a normal human being. Do you understand?"

Michael managed a slow nod and picked up his fork. While he swallowed eggs, blood, and fear, his father allowed nearly three minutes to pass without torment.

"Hey, Mikey, did I mention you're grounded until September?"

Michael forced his body to remain completely still when every fiber of his being wanted to flee. His mother and siblings had stopped eating and waited in silence. Maybe they felt the same inevitability he did.

"I suppose you're thinking let him ground me. I'll be gone soon then he can kiss my ass." His father leaned closer, chuckling. "Better think again, Einstein. You're not going anywhere. That scholarship you worked so hard for is useless."

Michael's chest constricted. "What do you mean?"

"I'm not signing the papers and without our permission," his father smiled and poked him in the chest with a fork, "you ain't leaving home."

Michael's mouth moved, but his throat was so tight he could only manage one word. "Why?"

"Because, altar boy, you owe this family."

Michael's eyes filled with tears and he inhaled sharply.

His father laughed. "I love it when I get you by the balls, you arrogant little son-of-a-bitch."

"It wasn't my fault," Michael murmured.

His father grabbed him by the throat and shoved him backward. Michael fell to the floor, his foot striking the table, dishes and utensils clattered to the floor. His mother and siblings backed away from the table and his baby sister began to cry.

His father kicked him in the ribs with a steel-toed work boot. "I hate you for what you did!"

The big man grabbed a handful of shirt and jerked Michael to his feet, shoved him against the wall and punched him in the abdomen before backing away. Michael bent over and struggled to catch his breath. Bile raced to his throat and choked him.

Finally, he straightened his back and eyed his father with open contempt. "If you hate me so much, why not sign the papers? I promise I won't come back."

"No, Genius, that's what you want. What I want is more important." His father moved close again, shoving him into the hallway. "Downstairs."

The basement was the worst his father had to offer. Michael decided there was no way he was going down there without a fight this time. Fury was in charge of his destiny now. He was finished playing this game. He swung around in the hallway and punched his father squarely in the face.

His father fell back two steps, but recovered quickly and actually smiled. Michael understood he had just given his father the very thing he wanted all along. The first counter blow was so hard it broke Michael's jaw in two places.

Chapter 3

Martin Edger frequently wondered why he chose a profession that could, without warning, remind him that man was the most cold-blooded of creatures. Usually, these moments occurred when he was tired, which happened a lot as a resident here in one of Brooklyn's busiest emergency rooms. There were those moments when he faced something so vile he found no excuses for the rotten way people behaved.

The paramedics wheeled in a sixteen-year-old boy and they transferred the patient to an exam table. Martin forced each eyelid open and had a look at each pupil while a burly paramedic ran down the vital signs.

Martin glanced up at the seasoned medic, "Car accident?"

The man held up a clenched fist, "Father."

Martin spent the next twenty minutes assessing injuries, stitching wounds, and waiting for x-rays. After looking at the films, Martin turned the case over to an orthopedist and went looking for the mother of this unfortunate patient. He stepped into the crowded waiting area.

"Michael O'Mara's family?"

A pretty, slender woman looked his way and the young man sitting next to her stood.

"Could you follow me please?"

He turned to the busy hall and waited in the doorway, watching the boy's mother stand wearily. She moved slowly as if underwater. Once they were in the hall, she straightened her back and looked Martin in the eye, a look of half defense, half shame. Martin had seen this behavior before. His mother had used the same stance when preparing to lie for his father.

"Is he all right?" The mother asked.

"I suppose that depends on your definition of all right. If you mean, will he live? Yes. Will there be any permanent injury to his body? Probably not. The places I stitched back together, the bruises, cuts, abrasions, broken jaw, ribs, fingers, and arm will all probably heal well. Do you want to tell me how this happened?"

"I'm not sure."

The young man next to her exhaled sharply and took a step away from her, his face flushed red.

"Come on, Mrs. O'Mara. The police received a call that someone was beating the hell out of their kid. Are you telling me you didn't see or hear anything?"

She immediately bristled, all defiance now. "Michael and his father always butt heads. I stopped investigating every little argument between them long ago. I want to see my son."

She started to push past Martin, but he stepped in her way.

"I can't allow you in there right now. They're setting his broken arm right now."

"How long before you let him go?"

"I want to run some tests tomorrow and I'll need the results of those before I'll release him."

"What kind of tests?"

"There's blood in his urine. I want to check his kidneys." That was the truth or part of the truth. He really wanted social services involved and that took time.

"So you're admitting him?"

"Yes."

"Then I'll come back tomorrow. Excuse me."

She took three steps and turned back to look at the young man who hadn't moved.

"Bobby, come on."

Bobby shoved his hands in the front pockets of his jeans. "I'll wait here," he said

She hesitated, glanced at Martin quickly, turned and left without another word.

Martin turned to the rebellious teen. "Are you Michael's brother?"

He nodded. "Can I see him for a minute, please?"

Martin thought of the bloody face he just put stitches in and wondered if there was any resemblance between these two when one wasn't a battered mess.

"Did your father do that to your brother?"

Bobby nodded, his shoulders slumping a little.

"Does he abuse any of the rest of you?"

He shook his head, "Mostly just Mike." He looked away, down the hall. "It's never been this bad before."

"Was he seen for other injuries? Would there be any record?"

"I know he had a broken arm. I guess our doctor would have records."

Martin decided to stop pressing him. "Come on, I'll let you see him for a few minutes before the oral surgeon gets here. They're casting his arm and fingers right now."

Michael tried to concentrate on breathing. He could only see out of one eye, but kept it closed to keep out the blinding light coming from overhead. Every inch of his body hurt so badly he wished he would pass out again. A doctor manipulated the bones in his right hand and pain shot up his arm, into his chest and he moaned softly. They had promised he would receive pain medication before they started wiring his jaw, but right now he was close to begging.

He had no idea his brother was standing next to the stretcher until Bobby cleared his throat. Michael opened the eye that wasn't swollen closed and turned his head slowly until Bobby was in his line of vision.

Bobby took a breath and moved a little closer, "Hey, Mike, I, ugh, just wanted to tell you how sorry I am. I wanted to help you, but I was scared he might turn on me." Bobby lowered his head, fighting for control. "The only thing I could think to do was call the police."

Michael reached out and patted his brother's hand lightly. A small gasp escaped Bobby's lips and a tear slid down his cheek that he wiped away roughly.

"I'm sorry," Bobby said again then turned and fled from the room.

The final procedure was wiring his jaw together. Michael received Demerol for pain and floated off in a haze.

In the morning, the young doctor from the emergency room came by with a small pad of paper and a pen.

"Have you ever tried to write with your left hand?"

Michael picked up the pen and wrote neatly. "I'm left handed."

The doctor nodded. "I guess that's a plus for once. I don't know if you remember me from yesterday. My name is Martin Edger."

Michael drew a finger across the stitches just above his left eyebrow.

Martin smiled warmly. "Yep, that was me. Your brother, Bobby, tells me you received a scholarship to MIT, but your father won't give you permission to go. Is that right?"

He nodded slowly.

"You don't have to go back home, you know. You can be made a ward of the state and we can get you to Cambridge. I have contacted social services and they are already making the arrangements. You'll be here for at least a couple of days and I think we can get this done in time."

Michael pulled the pad back and wrote again. "Is my father in jail?"

"I don't know. Are you afraid of what he'll do now?"

Michael nodded shortly, though he was beyond afraid. He knew he either got out of his parents' house now or he was dead. The young doctor watched him closely, waiting for a moment before speaking again.

"If we handle this right, he won't be in a position to ever hurt you again. Please don't discuss this with anyone until it's finished."

As if on cue, Jean pushed the door open and stepped in. She smiled slowly at Martin and Michael recognized her numbed state of mind. Jean couldn't make it past ten in the morning without a joint to soften the edges of the real world. She turned her attention to him and gasped. Judging by the look on her face, this morning's joint wasn't going to be enough to get her through this situation.

"Baby what did they do to you?"

Martin seemed a little stunned by the blonde beauty. "We were just finishing," he murmured.

She turned back to Martin. "I'm Jean Davies, a close friend."

Martin nodded and looked at Michael. "I'll check in on you later."

When the door closed behind Martin, Jean moved closer and touched Michael's swollen face. Tears rimmed her eyes. "I feel like shooting that son-of-a-bitch."

Michael closed his eyes and didn't bother with a response. He was too exhausted to deal with her right now.

Jean tapped his forehead with a sharp fingernail. "Talk to me."

Michael forced himself to look at her. Jean stroked his face then bent and kissed his cheek. She wiped the lipstick from his cheek and offered a sad smile. "Aw, that bastard bloodied your pretty eyes."

The relief of the Demerol was ebbing away and every inch of his body was starting to hurt. He wished they would give him something else for the pain so he could sleep and leave this world behind for a while.

Jean stroked the top of his hand, demanding his attention. "I want you to come and live with me when you get out of here. Okay?

She brushed a lock of hair from his forehead. "I promise when the times comes, I'll personally take you to MIT."

He shook his head and Jean stepped back, shaking her head in disbelief.

"You don't have a choice. He could kill you the next time."

Michael picked up the pad of paper and quickly wrote "NO", then underlined it three times.

Jean stuck her hands on her hips and frowned at him. "You think it's better to go home and run the risk of that son-of-a-bitch killing you than moving in with me?"

There was no safe response to such a question. He stared and waited for her to go away.

"So, we're through then? Is that it?"

Michael's steady gaze didn't waver. He nodded slowly and hoped she would finally get the point. She glanced around the room, her eyes filling with fresh tears then back to him for what seemed an eternity. Finally, she bent over, her lips near his ear,

"I'm always going to love you," she whispered softly. She kissed his cheek tenderly, turned on her heel and left.

He closed his eyes and took a deep breath. Sharp pain stabbed his rib cage and he gripped the sheets with his good hand, groaning in frustration.

After a liquid lunch, he received pain medication and slipped into sleep. Hours later he heard a voice echoing from above. The voice called soothingly and he felt like he was floating up from a gentle, deep place. A hand stroked his arm, providing surprising comfort for one of his dreams.

Someone kissed his swollen mouth, which hurt as much as it stunned him. He groaned and forced his eyes open, expecting Jean, shocked to find a new living nightmare. His sister Susan's kiss tasted like whiskey. He growled and pulled away as best he could. Susan drew back her hand as if to hit him, but grabbed his bruised face instead and squeezed until he groaned in pain.

Michael sucked in a breath and tried to push her hand away, but lost the battle. She had a firm grip and the one hand he had to fight with had an IV needle imbedded in a vein.

"I found Uncle Frank's suicide note in that box with your trophies," she said. "He loved you so much. He asked so little in return," she leaned down, close to his face again, "but you're incapable of love, aren't you?

She leaned close to his ear now, her whisper driving the stake all the way in. "You killed him. You killed a priest."

She released his face with a toss and walked out the door.

Michael sat up quickly and a sledgehammer of pain shot through his chest. He fell back to the bed, ripping out the intravenous line in the process. He cried in deep, choking sobs, fighting for each breath through the narrow opening the jaw wiring allowed.

In the next bed, his elderly roommate pushed the call light until a nurse appeared.

Martin entered the room and a nurse quietly filled him in on the details before withdrawing to get the Valium Michael's attending physician had ordered.

Michael stared at the ceiling. Tears had stained his bruised face and his body still trembled uncontrollably.

"Want to tell me what happened?"

Michael turned his face away.

Martin made a decision to reveal part of his own past, a past he had thus far shared with no one. "Mike," he began quietly, "I need for you to understand, I'm not pretending to sympathize. I truly understand because I've been right where you are. I know all about the fear. I still deal with the shame that I don't deserve. Sometimes the anger still creeps up on me."

Michael shut his eyes tightly and rebellious tears slipped from beneath closed lids. He covered his face as best he could with his hand. For the second time that evening, his body shook. The events of the past two days had weakened his defenses. He was no longer capable of containing the misery.

Martin patted his shoulder. "We're going to give you a little something to take the edge off things for tonight and allow you to get some sleep. Tomorrow morning someone from Social Services will be here to talk to you. I'll be here if I can."

Martin turned to leave and Michael grunted at him, reaching for the note pad, scribbling desperately.

"No visitors," Michael wrote then underlined it three times.

"I can't do that yet with your parents. Let's see what Social Services tell us. Okay?"

Michael nodded and looked away again. He closed his eyes and sighed wearily.

Gail Cummings was waiting for Martin as he entered the nurses' station where she had been reviewing Michael's chart. They had worked together a few times, but she was fairly new to the Social Services staff and before today their encounters had been brief. She had a reputation as a fierce patient advocate, especially when it came to children. Some of the staff found working with her difficult. Martin welcomed her passion and was confident she would do whatever she could to protect Michael O'Mara. He had given her a brief rundown on the situation over the phone yesterday and as he filled her in on the incident with the visitor last night her pretty smile slipped.

"We have to get this done now," she said quietly. "I'm certain there would be no problem making Michael a ward of the state and that could get him to Cambridge for that scholarship if we can find a guardian who is willing to take on the challenge for a few months while we get him emancipated. From the history you gave me it sounds like he can manage on his own up there with a little help from his friends."

Martin laughed quietly, "To quote the Beatles."

She managed a tight little smile. "Well, we don't want him high, just safe."

"What if I volunteered?"

Her eyes narrowed slightly, on guard now. "Why would you do that?"

Martin held her gaze, a little distracted by his sudden attraction to her. "I understand his life."

She absorbed the quiet statement and smiled sweetly. "Can I buy you a cup of coffee?"

Later that afternoon, Martin returned to Michael's room and found him sitting up in bed. Today he could see both of the young man's eyes, although the white of the left eye was still bloody.

He pulled the curtain around Michael's bed and stood next to the head of the bed, "I have a proposition for you. How would you feel about my being your guardian for the remainder of time you're here in Brooklyn?"

Michael picked up his paper and wrote *why?*

"Because I think you deserve a chance."

He studied Martin for a minute before looking away.

"Before you consider my offer, I think you'd better know what I expect," Martin said. "There will be no contact with your family without my prior approval, no alcohol, no drugs, and no girls in the apartment without my presence."

When Martin added nothing else, Michael nodded soberly.

Martin forced a smile. "Okay then. It's a deal. I've got to run, but I'll come back later."

At eight the next morning, just as he was finishing his night shift, Martin received a page to Michael's room, where he found Michael seated on the edge of the bed, staring at the floor. Martin got the impression Michael wanted to run and understood exactly why when he came all the way into the room and saw the large man arguing with Michael's attending physician about releasing him. Michael's mother stood next to her husband gripping her purse so tightly her knuckles were white. She looked from her husband to Martin as he entered then quickly looked away again.

A nurse hovered at the other side of Michael's bed watching the loud man with intensity, obviously losing any objectivity she brought with her that morning. She glanced over at Martin, a bitter edge in her voice, "These are the parents."

Michael's father stood over six-feet tall and weighed in the neighborhood of two hundred pounds. His upper body looked powerful. He stopped yelling at the attending physician and looked first at the nurse then brought angry, bloodshot eyes to bear on Martin. "Who are you, another one of his doctors?"

Martin caught himself recoiling from the menace of the large man. "I admitted him."

"Tell me why you're keeping him here. He looks fine to me."

Martin bit back a response to the absurd observation just as Gail, the social worker, joined them.

"What's going on?"

"These are Michael's parents. They want to know why we're keeping him here."

Gail looked from mother to father then stepped closer to them and in a soft, no-nonsense voice, explained they wouldn't be taking Michael home. Martin watched the big man's reaction shift from annoyance to rage.

The mother glanced at Michael once, but his focus remained locked on the floor and he missed the absolute misery in her eyes. Martin felt a twinge of pity for the woman he had judged so harshly in the emergency room two days ago.

The social worker finished her brief speech. "Do you have any questions?"

"Yeah, I got a question," the father said, stepping closer to Gail. "What gives you self-righteous bastards the right to make these decisions for my family?"

Finally, the nurse moved, pushing behind Martin. "I'll see what is taking security so long."

The social worker stood her ground. "You gave us permission, Mr. O'Mara." She now stepped closer and looked him in the eye, her voice strong, angry. "When you assaulted your child, you gave us your express permission."

The father turned to Michael. "I hope you're happy, you little bastard."

Michael raised his head, looking directly at his father. The big man stepped toward him and Martin heard the attending suck in a quick breath and stepped between father and son.

"I want you to leave now, Mr. O'Mara, we can talk in the conference room," the attending said.

Michael held rock steady, seemingly frozen with fear.

"You want out?" The father shouted at Michael. "You got it. I don't ever want to see you again. Do you understand me?"

Michael looked to his mother who straightened her back and shifted her eyes to the door. After a moment, he brought his gaze back to his father. "Yes," he managed to hiss through his teeth.

Martin saw the flash of anger cross Michael's father's face and for a moment Martin thought the man was going to attack his son, but he swung out the door, his wife a few steps behind.

Gail exhaled loudly and turned to Martin. "Can we talk later?"

"Anytime, just have me paged."

She gave him a quick smile and moved to where Michael sat, staring at the floor again. She placed a hand on his shoulder.

"I'd like to set up some counseling sessions for you."

Michael shook his head.

Gail spoke softly, gently now. "Let them help you, Michael. They might be able to give you a slant you haven't considered yet."

Michael finally lifted his head and Martin saw familiar convictions etched in the battered face. This kid had survived an education that had nothing to do with a fine mind or mathematical principles.

Martin heard the social worker using the appropriate words that were intended to soothe, but his focus remained riveted on this boy. Although he had enough facts to justify what he saw, instinct insisted Michael O'Mara had some pretty hideous secrets.

The social worker finished and patted Michael on the back, offering a soft, sympathetic smile. "Promise to think about it?"

Michael nodded and glanced Martin's way, immediately registering the doctor's intrusion. Those expressive eyes flashed an angry message before he slammed a steel wall between himself and the world again.

Chapter 4

Michael chose to skip his graduation ceremony at NYU. He hadn't really connected with many from his class on more than a superficial level and the few classmates he knew better would have family and friends there to congratulate them for a job well done and share in their accomplishment. When he finished high school four years ago, no one in his family seemed aware he had graduated except his mother and she only took notice because she had to trek with him to Manhattan to start his undergraduate courses. After that process was complete, he undertook the daily trip to Manhattan by himself at only twelve years old.

Now with his bachelor's degree behind him he began a few summer classes. The hospitalization and recovery had cost him the job on the loading docks and he had more free time than at any point in his life. Martin's long shifts at the hospital left him alone a good majority of the time and he passed the time cleaning the apartment, studying, reading, and thinking too much.

Finally free of the wires in his jaw, he could eat solid food again and began to regain a little weight. For the most part, his body had healed well. However, the emotional damage from the last beating lingered and he felt fragile, brittle even, as if he just might shatter if one more unpleasant event came his way.

The nightmare had intensified and drove him awake nearly every night. On the nights when Martin was home, he slept with a gag in his mouth to muffle the screaming if it came. There was nothing he could do to prevent the horror that waited and he experienced an even deeper dread for the endless nights.

Tonight was no exception. Martin was working until the wee hours and he was ahead on his class work, so he read until his eyes grew too tired then drifted to his small bedroom where he stared at the ceiling and his thoughts took a downward spiral back to the day he made the first mistake.

On Easter Sunday, just a few weeks before his fourth birthday, he sat next to his older sister on his parents' living room floor and stared at the pages of the newspaper spread before her. She looked over her shoulder at him and smiled at him, for he was a welcome member of the family back then.

"Hi, Mikey, want me to read to you?"

He nodded eagerly. "I want to know about the tiger."

Karen giggled and rubbed the top of his head playfully. "What tiger?"

He pointed an index finger at a heading and read each word aloud. "Zoo gets rare white tiger."

Karen gasped and jumped to her feet, "Mom!"

Of course, that was just the beginning. He had acted out of ignorance, completely unaware that most people learned to read in school when they were older. For that oversight, he forgave himself.

Frank, his father's brother, immediately insisted they have him tested. Frank was the youngest of Michael's father's siblings and the shining star of the family, earning his doctorate by age twenty-five before choosing the priesthood. Naturally, the family scholar's opinion on what to do with Michael was given great merit.

On the day they learned the results, Frank took him back to his private quarters in the rectory. He sat Michael in a straight-backed chair and gave him a saucer of cookies and a glass of milk.

Michael remembered nibbling a cookie, swinging his feet over the polished marble floor and studying the reflection. Frank watched impatiently, allowing him to consume only part of a cookie before kneeling in front of Michael. He brushed the crumbs from Michael's small hands then gripped each hand tightly.

"What I'm going to tell you is very important. You must pay attention."

The church school was across the yard from Frank's residence and a bell resounded off the stone walls, announcing recess. The happy voices of children rang out as they burst from the building onto the playground. Michael lifted his head and gazed at the stained glass windows set high in the wall. Sunlight streamed through, providing warm light. Unfortunately, the glow didn't reach down into this cheerless room.

Frank squeezed his hands harder. "Pay attention."

He started to complain about the pain, but a bright, feverish look in Frank's eyes suggested it might be best to keep quiet. All Michael wanted suddenly was to be out there with those other children. He could still hear their happy voices; Frank couldn't take that away from him.

"God," Frank began solemnly, "has placed an extraordinary gift in your hands."

Michael wanted to turn his hands over to see what God had placed there. Unfortunately, Frank had increased the pressure and pain was traveling up Michael's arms, making his eyes water.

"You must never disappoint God, Michael. Do you understand me?"

Outside the kids were laughing, playing, calling to each other. Oh, to be out there, instead of in this uncomfortable chair with a zealot breaking his hands. There was no choice but to nod in compliance.

Tears slipped down his cheeks and a little moan escaped his lips. "You're hurting my hands."

"Hush now." Frank pulled him from the chair, forcing him to kneel. "Let's thank God for this wonderful gift."

The prayer seemed endless and Michael was in significant pain when he finally heard the word amen. Frank pulled him into his arms and hugged him enthusiastically.

"Let's go tell everyone our good news."

If only he had followed his instincts, used the gift God placed in his hands to find a way out, Frank would still be alive and he wouldn't be out here on the periphery of life, disconnected from everyone. Of course, all that was unchangeable and the role of pariah was his penance.

Night after night, this was the course of his thinking while he lay awake in Martin's apartment. Still, one truth shined brighter than all the others, he was desperate to move on. He had withdrawn all the money from his savings account and kept the cash in a spare book bag beneath his bed.

The alarm woke him at six-forty-five. The day was already sunny and birds chirped in the tall tree near his window, but he pulled the covers over his head. The third time the alarm rang Martin tapped on the door.

"Are you going to class today?"

"I'll be out in a minute," he said.

He sat up slowly and looked out the window. Today was the second day of June, a date that always brought more misery than joy.

Michael was at the kitchen table writing a paper on math variables when the phone rang that afternoon. He jumped at the sound. So far, the day had been kind.

Martin had the day off and was napping on the couch. Michael had no choice but to answer the phone before the sound woke him.

"I hope I'm not interrupting your new life," Max said without preamble.

The sarcasm hit him squarely and Michael felt the shift of fate in his day. "What do you want, Max?"

"I thought you might want to know what you're doing to Jean is tearing her up."

He sighed loudly. "It's for the best."

"You're such a cold hearted little bastard," Max said. "I found her outside crying on the steps this morning and had to carry her inside. We had a long talk, Michael. She told me all about the baby."

Michael wasn't sure he heard correctly, "Baby?"

"Yeah, as in yours asshole."

Michael sank into a chair, his mind turning over a hundred thoughts at once. "I guess I'd better talk to her."

"You're out of time. She's leaving for Connecticut tonight."

Jean's door was slightly ajar and he tapped lightly.

"It's open," she said.

Her back was to the door and she didn't turn. She sighed deeply, listening to someone on the other end of the telephone. "Mother are you going to pick me up, or not?"

Michael hovered near the open door. There were packed boxes everywhere.

Jean slammed the receiver down and turned to him. Surprise registered on her face, then malice. "What are you doing here?"

"Max called."

She nodded and patted her abdomen. "I guess he told you all about this little bundle of joy."

She picked up a partially smoked joint from the ashtray, lit it then offered it to him.

He shook his head. "Is the baby mine?"

She took another draw on the joint and blew the smoke in his face. "Of course it's yours."

Michael choked and took a step back. "You shouldn't be smoking that stuff now."

"Mind your own business, Mikey." She spat his name out like a bitter grape seed.

"Let me raise the baby."

Cold frosted her blue eyes. "You're never going to see this child."

"So you plan to keep the baby?"

"Of course, it's my revenge."

Suddenly, he found it difficult to breathe. He swallowed hard. His throat was nearly too dry to speak. "What happened between us was inevitable, Jean. Don't take it out on a child."

"Falling in love with you wasn't inevitable. I hate it."

He looked her in the eye, his own anger rising. "You're not in love with me."

Jean charged arms outstretched and rammed him in the chest with her hands nearly knocking him off his feet. "Get out!"

Michael backed out of the room, into the hall, where he turned for the stairs.

Jean followed as far as the rail and leaned over. "This child will never know who you are. You are nothing, Michael."

She continued in a string of spiteful words that followed him down the two flights of stairs. Michael burst through the front door of the building and ran to the end of the street where he had to pause for a breath. Without warning, the dark sky dumped cold, summer rain, soaking him quickly. He crossed the street just as a car resembling his father's turned the corner. He panicked and ducked into the shelter of a doorway. As the car slid by he realized the car looked nothing like his father's.

Across the street, a cab stopped in front of Max's building and honked. After a minute, Max emerged, carrying Jean's bags. She slipped into the back seat and Max kissed her cheek quickly. As the cab did a U-turn, Jean spotted Michael. She lifted her hand and blew a kiss off the tip of her middle finger.

He didn't get back to Martin's flat until a little after seven. His clothes were soaked. His hair was wet and clung to his head and neck. He was cold all the way to his core.

Martin was supposed to have a date with the social worker from the hospital, but was waiting for him when he stepped inside the door. Martin looked angry. This day had drained Michael's energy and he didn't think he could take another confrontation.

"Where have you been?" Martin asked.

"Talking to Jean."

"Who's Jean?"

Michael slipped off his wet shoes near the door. "The blonde you met in the hospital," he said.

Martin stared for a minute. "Go change. We'll talk when you're finished."

He walked to the hall, but turned back. "I'm sorry, Martin. I know you were looking forward to your date."

Martin still looked angry, but his tone softened. "She gave me a rain check."

Michael took a seat on the couch and accepted the hot cocoa Martin offered him. He was still cold from his hike through the rain and the warm mug eased the chill from his hands.

Martin studied him for a minute. "So, tell me."

"A friend called this afternoon and told me Jean's pregnant, so I went to talk to her."

"Why didn't you tell me you were leaving?"

Michael pointed at a piece of paper near the lamp. "I left you a note."

Martin picked up the paper and glanced at the words. "I'm sorry, I didn't see this." He folded the note and considered Michael for a minute. "How old is Jean?"

"Twenty-four."

Martin took a moment to digest the fact that Jean was eight years older than Michael. "Do you believe this child is yours?"

Michael nodded slowly. He couldn't explain it. Jean might lie about a lot of things, but somehow he knew this was the truth.

"What are you going to do?"

"She doesn't want anything to do with me. She's on her way back to her family in Connecticut."

"So, do you think she's going to keep the baby?"

Michael sighed and nodded again.

"How do you feel about all of this?"

He let his head fall back on the couch, giving thought to ignoring the question or lying. Still, Martin was doing so much for him. It would be rude to not answer.

"Lousy," he said.

"What bothers you most?"

Sudden tears stung his eyes and one errant, crystal drop slid down his cheek before he had a chance to blink it away. He wiped the traitorous tear away roughly with the back of his hand. Under better circumstances, he wouldn't have let Martin see, but lately he just couldn't keep his emotions in check.

"I, uh…" he paused, clearing his throat. "Jean as the mother of any child bothers me the most, I guess."

"You do come out of left field some times. I didn't expect that," Martin said.

"She'll be a terrible mother."

"This baby may be important enough to change her."

Michael grunted and gave Martin a sidelong look. "She just invited me to smoke a joint with her."

"I see your point."

Michael sat up quickly, rubbing any remaining moisture from his treasonous eyes. "I'm such an idiot."

The phone rang and he jumped to his feet as if the sound had an electric charge. He walked toward the kitchen just to discharge the energy as Martin lifted the receiver and talked for a few minutes.

"Hey, would you mind if Bobby comes over?"

Stunned, Michael shrugged and shoved his hands in his pockets.

Martin concluded the call and smiled. "He'll be here in about half an hour. I'm glad at least you and your siblings get along."

Taken aback, he frowned at Martin. "What gives you that idea?"

"Well, Bobby seems to really care about you." He looked directly at Michael now. "And one of your sisters visited you in the hospital, didn't she?"

Michael sensed Martin was fishing and didn't respond, forcing him to press the point. Martin promptly obliged.

"Is your sister the one that upset you that night?

"She has problems," he said, turning away.

"Is alcohol one of them?"

Michael managed a slight nod before moving out of Martin's direct line of sight. He leaned against the refrigerator and wiped his mouth roughly, as if his sister's kiss still lingered.

Bobby stepped inside and held out a black guitar case with a big smile. "I couldn't stand seeing your guitar lying on your empty bed anymore. I bought the case down at Marconi's pawnshop. It's used, but in pretty good shape."

Michael sat on the sofa and opened the case, running his fingertips over the polished wood of his twelve-string. He smiled and looked up at Bobby.

"Thank you."

Martin settled back in his chair. "Well, play something."

Bobby sat on the other end of the couch and watched him, just like Martin was doing. Waiting, expectant, nothing cruel or demanding in either of them, yet an old panic stirred to life in Michael.

"I haven't played since my fingers were broken," he said.

"You never know until you try," Martin said. "Just see how it feels."

Cornered by a well-meaning brother and Martin's nudging, Michael took the guitar from the case and tuned it. He warmed up his fingers with a simple song and when he moved into a more intricate piece, Martin moved to the edge of his chair and listened intently.

Michael was aware that the others exchanged looks a few times, but concentrated on the music. This wasn't his best effort, but as always music was his best escape. Finally, he finished and put the guitar aside. Some of the pressure of the day had dissipated and he breathed easier.

Martin smiled widely. "Wow. Where did you learn to play like that?"

"I used to play the piano..."

"He's being modest." Bobby interrupted. "I only heard him play the piano once and it was the prettiest music I've ever heard."

Surprised, Michael looked at Bobby. "When did you hear me play?"

"When Grandma O'Mara had her first heart attack, Mom sent me to the church to get Uncle Frank. You were there in the rectory practicing for that competition in Boston, so I sat outside in the hall and waited until you finished. I completely forgot why I was there until I heard Uncle Frank yelling at you."

The color drained from Michael's face. He got to his feet and walked to the window, putting his back to them.

"Who's Uncle Frank?" Martin asked.

"My father's youngest brother, a priest," Bobby murmured, looking toward Michael.

Before leaving, Bobby hesitated awkwardly at the door. "I'm behind what you're doing, Mike. I just hope we don't lose touch when you go to MIT."

Bobby threw his arms around him and hugged him tightly. Bobby's hug produced a sharp pain in Michael's still healing ribs. He sucked in a quick breath, but said nothing. This was the first time his brother ever touched him and that was much more important than the pain.

Bobby pulled back and grinned, "Happy birthday."

"Thanks, Bobby."

Michael closed the door behind his brother and eased himself onto the couch aware that Martin studied him.

"What's wrong?" Martin asked.

"I think he may have cracked my ribs again."

"Want me to look at them?"

"No, thanks, I think I'll just go to bed."

"Why didn't you mention this was your birthday?"

Michael glanced at him, then away. "This is the day my father hated me most," he admitted softly. "It kind of set a precedent."

"Do you know why he singled you out?"

Michael stared at his outstretched legs and mulled over a decision. He decided long ago to never tell the truth or any part of it to another person as long as he lived. He had learned that judgment, not understanding, was the result of telling his darkest secrets. He didn't want to eliminate Martin from his life.

"It's a long story," he said.

"Then you don't believe you're a scapegoat to him?"

Michael moved to the edge of the sofa. "Look, I just need to accept the facts and move on."

"Hey, if you can do that, more power to you. Like I told you, my father was abusive. I had to get some counseling to get through some of my issues."

Martin only wanted to help, but Michael had no desire to probe old wounds. He looked directly at Martin.

"Please stop," he said.

Martin nodded and patted his arm. "I forget I'm talking to someone with the capacity to figure all this out on their own."

Michael's right eyebrow arched slightly. "Are you being sarcastic?"

"I was referring to your IQ."

He laughed shortly. "My IQ doesn't have anything to do with this."

"How high is it by the way?"

"Oh, come on. You don't really believe in the validity of that system, do you?"

"Actually, I believe it has a great deal of merit."

"Well, I don't."

Martin watched him for a minute. "It looks like they pegged you pretty well."

"But it's not what matters, not really."

"How can you say that? Look at all you've been able to accomplish. An ordinary mind wouldn't have taken you as far, so fast."

Michael looked away and drew in a long, weary breath. "I wish I'd never been tested."

Martin nudged him playfully. "Come on, I'll tell you mine."

Michael shook his head. "I'll tell you the day I'm ready to leave. Okay?"

"Deal. Of course, you won't really be escaping me. I don't intend to lose track of you."

Michael stood and stretched. "You're a masochist, Martin. I'll see you in the morning."

He closed the bedroom door and relaxed against it, feeling old beyond his years. Another birthday had come and gone in style.

Michael shifted his heavy backpack and turned the key in the front door of Martin's apartment. He dreaded the hours of studying that lie ahead. For the first time in his life he could not escape his life by burying himself in school. Every step of the summer classes took enormous effort and he had to push himself to get anything done. He tossed the book bag on the couch and headed for the kitchen.

The phone split the silence and he answered on the third ring.

"Hey, are you busy?" Bobby asked.

"No, I just walked in." He opened the refrigerator door and peered inside looking for anything to make a sandwich. "What's up?"

"I enlisted in the Army."

"The Army? Haven't you heard about Viet Nam?" He realized he was nearly shouting and softened his tone. "Why don't you go to school, Bobby?"

"I don't have what it takes for college."

"Then learn a trade or something else."

"Look, you got the brains in the family, not me. Besides, even if they send me to Nam, it will be saner than living here. Since Dad found out I was the one who called the cops, I moved to the top of his list."

"I'm sorry."

"Don't be sorry, Mike. It's his fault, not yours."

Michael closed his eyes suddenly out of breath, his head spinning as Bobby continued.

"Anyway, it's too late. I leave in two days."

"It isn't too late not until they swear you in. Think about this."

Bobby laughed. "You worry too much. Listen, Max is throwing a going away party for me. Want to come?"

"I don't know if I can. I have to ask Martin."

"Bring the doc along, he's really cool. Come on, you have to say good-bye. Oh, and bring your guitar."

This was the second time in two weeks Michael had ventured near his parents' home and being back in the neighborhood made him feel like he might just jump out of his skin. He wasn't at Max's long when Susan arrived and tripled his anxiety level.

She paid very little attention to the guest of honor and zeroed in on Michael instead.

"Can I talk to you for a minute? Please?"

Michael followed her to Max's spare bedroom and watched as she closed the door. Susan's calm demeanor tricked him into believing this might be a civil conversation.

"You look better. I guess getting away from Dad was good for you."

She sat on the foot of the bed and studied him before continuing. "No one ever speaks your name at home anymore. It's like you never existed."

She slipped off the bed and came a little closer. "Don't you see? All that went on between you and Dad was so meaningless. Everyone would rather forget the whole thing."

"I don't care, Susan."

"Why not? Don't you feel things like the rest of us? Did all that priestly attention make you superior? She stepped closer, her voice soft now. "Uncle Frank never really loved you."

Michael turned toward the door. "I'm not listening to any more of this."

Susan moved around, in front of him, blocking his path. "I want to talk about what happened between you and Uncle Frank."

"No."

She reached up to touch his cheek. Michael pushed her hand away and she moved even closer. "Forgive me, but I can't help needing you."

"Susan, stop."

Michael reached for the doorknob and she grabbed his hand. He jumped back and his back struck the wall. Susan moved forward until her body pressed against his.

Michael closed his eyes and turned his face away from her. He couldn't breathe. Susan cupped his chin in her hand and tried to turn his face toward her. An involuntary shiver began deep in the base of his spine and rocked his body.

"It's natural," she whispered, pressing her lips against his.

Michael shoved her hard and sent her flying to the floor. Before Susan finished falling, he was out the door, running for the bathroom as bile rose in his throat.

Michael turned on the shower to drown out the sound of the party. Steam rose and slowly softened his reflection in the mirror, but he saw enough to smash the shadow with his fist, cutting his hand in the process. Blood dripped from his hand onto the tile floor and he watched it fall, fascinated by the contrast of red on white. Next to the droplets lay a slice of mirror reflecting the ceiling light.

He bent forward and snatched up the jagged glass and dragged it over his right wrist in several swift movements. The pain was merely the price of the ticket out. He switched hands and cut the other wrist and dropped the glass to the floor where it lay bloody and whole. He stepped over the side of the tub and eased his body down into the hot water and offered his wrists, forearms up to the hot water, willing the flow to draw the blood and take his life quickly.

Martin arrived at Max's apartment after a hellish thirty-six hour shift. He had seriously considered going home to bed, but Michael's apparent apprehension about coming back to this neighborhood drew Martin to the party instead. He expected the party to be in full swing, but heard silence as he knocked. A big man pulled the door open, revealing a quiet apartment.

"I'm not sure I have the right apartment. Are you Max Burnett?"

"I sure am. You must be the doctor. I'm glad to see you. Mike may be in trouble."

Max pulled Martin to an interior hallway where Bobby sat on the floor. He got to his feet and pointed at the bathroom door.

"Mike's in there, but I think we should talk before you do anything else."

Martin followed Bobby down the hall to Max's bedroom. Max stood guard outside the bathroom and lit a cigarette. Bobby closed the door and seemed to be searching for something to say. Martin couldn't stand the drama anymore.

"What in the world is wrong?"

"Our sister, Susan, came here tonight. She told Mike she wanted to talk to him alone so they came in here. A few minutes later, I heard her screaming so I came to see what was going on." Bobby shuddered and ran a hand through his hair. "Susan said they were just talking and Mike got all crazy. He punched her and ran to the bathroom. He's been in there for the last half hour."

"Where's Susan?"

"Passed out in the other bedroom. She'll be all right. She may have a black eye, but something tells me she deserved it."

"Have you tried to get in the bathroom?"

Bobby shook his head. "Mike locked the door. Max thinks we should break it down. He's afraid Michael's going to do something stupid."

"Let me try to talk to Michael into opening the door, but if I don't get anywhere, that's exactly what we'll do because I'm afraid of the same thing, Bobby."

Max ceased nervous pacing and swung around as they approached. Martin knocked on the door.

"Michael, its Martin, come on, open the door."

After a minute ticked by and there was no response, Martin looked to Max. "Break the door down."

Max shoved on the door twice before it gave, raining splinters of wood in all directions. Immediately, steam poured into the hall. For a moment, it was impossible to see anything. Finally, the air cleared a little revealing Michael sitting in the tub still fully dressed.

Michael heard the door splinter, but kept his knees tight against his chest and his head face down on his knees. His wrists were submerged in the hot water that had turned red from his blood.

Martin grasped his forearms just as a violent tremor shook his body. Martin lifted his arms and gasped at the jagged cuts then turned to someone behind him.

"Get me some towels or anything to wrap them!"

Martin applied pressure to his wrists and dropped his tone, speaking softly now. "Listen to me, Michael. You've got to keep fighting."

Martin wanted to save him, again. Michael couldn't speak, couldn't plead to be allowed this one decision. He didn't want a savior. He looked at Martin and shook his head.

Martin shook him roughly. "Yes, damn it."

He put his head back and a low eerie wail, a last plea, escaped his lips.

Martin pulled him close. "Sweet Jesus, what did they do to you?"

Martin first hoped the suicide attempt was a cry for help. He consulted with an orthopedic colleague and good friend about possible ligament damage, which didn't seem to be a concern, but the orthopedist cautioned that the gashes were potentially fatal and advised admittance to the psychiatric ward. In his opinion, Michael wasn't a dramatic teenager; he really meant to put an end to his life.

Martin knew his friend was right and that he should have admitted Michael right then, but feared it might open the door for Michael's parents to walk back in, so he broke all the rules.

Martin gave him Valium, stitched his wrists and took him home. At the apartment, he helped Michael change clothes and guided him to the couch where Michael sat limply, staring at his bandaged wrists resting in his lap.

Martin knelt in front of him. "I want you to listen to me carefully. I don't know what makes your family so sick, but I do know you're not responsible."

Michael raised his eyes and looked at him. Tonight there were no steel walls to keep the world at bay and the chasm of pain appeared endless. The impact was so powerful Martin was at a loss for words for a moment.

"I can't live like this anymore," Michael said.

"You don't have to."

Michael's eyes filled with tears and he lowered his head. Martin sat close and put an arm around his shoulders.

"This is not your fault. You didn't cause this."

"You don't know what I did," he whispered.

"Tell me."

Tears fell on the white bandages as he shook his head.

Martin wrapped his arms around Michael for the second time and didn't push anymore.

Sunday morning dawned bright and sunny. Martin rolled over and glanced at the alarm. It was only seven. He rubbed his eyes and listened carefully for sounds of Michael. Silence wasn't unusual, but instinct warned something was different.

Martin threw back the covers and crossed the hall to the smaller bedroom. The covers on the bed were smooth. Martin opened the closet and found it empty. He hurried to the bathroom, living room and then to the kitchen. Michael's schoolbooks and airline ticket to Cambridge were in the trashcan. A brief note and cash waited on the table.

Martin picked up the note and prayed Michael hadn't thrown everything away.

Martin,

I'm sorry to leave this way after all you've done, but I have to go. The money is for the wasted ticket to Cambridge. Thanks for letting me feel safe for a while.

p.s. IQ last clocked at 183 and slipping.

Chapter 5

Eighty miles west of Flagstaff Kevin Thomas ran into a snowstorm, but didn't slow his eighteen-wheel truck until sleet began pelting the windshield. Adjusting to the curves of life was nothing new for Kevin. He downshifted, slid in an eight-track tape and cranked the volume up.

Around noon, he pulled the semi over near an overpass and walked around the front for overdue bladder relief. The goal had been to make it to the next rest area, but driving so slow had forced him here instead. Out of habit, he looked down at the ground and found footprints in the slush. He peered up into the darkness at the base of the overpass and made out a human silhouette.

"Hey! Buddy don't you know it's only about thirty degrees out here?"

His deep voice rolled off the concrete, but there was no response. Kevin climbed the steep incline and paused next to the person. He couldn't see a face. The legs were tight against the chest, arms folded over the knees, and head resting on the arms. Dark hair cascaded over the knees. Surprisingly, the guy had no coat.

He had never been afraid of much, but this guy was so still, Kevin was afraid he might be dead. He reached down and shook the shoulder nearest him. After a moment, the person lifted his head, revealing the pale face of a young man.

Kevin breathed a little easier. "Can I give you a ride?"

The stranger looked away, out at the driving sleet then laid his head back on his crossed arms.

Kevin bent forward and slipped an arm around him, gripping his cold, wet shirt and lifted him. He had to half-carry him down the slope to the truck where he pulled open the door to the sleeper portion of the cab.

"Can you climb up there?"

The young man looked up at the open door blankly.

Kevin pointed up to the interior, "There are some clean clothes up there in that overhead drawer. Take off those wet clothes and put on anything you can find."

After a gentle nudge, the stranger gripped the bar next to the door and pulled himself up with Kevin's assistance. Kevin closed the door behind him, got back in the driver's seat, turned up the heat, and hit the road again.

Fifteen minutes later, a glance into the small compartment brought a disquieting surprise. The guy lay curled into a fetal position with a blanket wrapped tightly around him. Of course, this wasn't unusual for someone thawing out after a stint in freezing weather. What disturbed Kevin was the stranger had packed the corner of the blanket into his mouth, almost like a gag.

Near sunset, Kevin stopped for dinner and roused his passenger. The guy sat up slowly and slumped against the wall of the sleeper compartment.

"I thought you might be hungry," Kevin said.

The stranger ran a hand through his tangled hair and squinted out at the lights of the truck stop.

Kevin waited for him to say something and when he didn't Kevin's patience ran out. "Would you rather stay here and sleep?"

He finally looked directly at Kevin. His eyes caught the exterior neon light and their blue sparkled brightly.

"Please," the young man said.

The soft-spoken word reminded Kevin why he didn't mind helping a stranger now and then.

"When was the last time you ate?"

The guy closed his eyes. "I'm not hungry."

"All right, go on back to sleep. I won't be long."

After eating his dinner, Kevin purchased some soup and a chocolate shake, thinking it would be the easiest for his passenger to digest.

Once back at the truck, it again took some time for his passenger to wake up. Finally, he opened his eyes and blinked slowly. He glanced around the compartment then stared blankly at Kevin.

"Why don't you ride up here for a while?" Kevin said.

It took a minute or two, but he managed to climb into the front. He eyed the two containers Kevin held out, but shook his head.

"I don't have any money," he said.

Kevin put the containers into his hands, "Happy Thanksgiving."

"Today is Thanksgiving?"

Kevin put the truck into gear. "It's tomorrow."

His passenger coughed hard as they crossed the parking lot, bounced over a speed bump then paused at a stop sign. Finally, the coughing abated and he leaned back in the seat and took a deep breath.

Kevin glanced over at him. "My name is Kevin Thomas."

The young man shifted the containers in his hands. "Michael O'Mara."

Neither spoke again until they were on the highway and picking up speed.

Kevin had the impression that if he didn't ask questions, this guy would never say a word. "So where are you from?"

"Brooklyn."

"Is that where you were headed?"

"Yes," Michael said softly as he carefully peeled back the lid on the soup.

Kevin prided himself on having good instincts and took a chance. "You supposed to be someplace for Thanksgiving?"

Michael focused straight ahead. The dashboard lights lent an eerie, greenish tone to his pale skin. He shook his head, "No."

"Well, I think you should join me and my sister, Beth. We have a little place that used to belong to my parents over in West Texas. You can eat some turkey, rest up and get warm all the way through. I might even be making a run east pretty soon and you can ride along."

Beth Thomas waited anxiously all day for her brother to arrive. Kevin had been gone for over a week and this had been her first time to stay at the house alone since her eighteenth birthday. Their place was about twenty miles outside of town and Kevin was concerned about her safety. Beth was less anxious about being alone. She was a good shot with a rifle and there were three protective German shepherds roaming their property. The worst experience had been missing her good-hearted brother.

Finally, Kevin's rig turned off the blacktop and the lights illuminated their private road. She grabbed a jacket and hurried to greet him.

"I thought you'd never get here!" she called, as Kevin swung the truck door open. "Did you bring me anything?"

Kevin climbed down and hugged her. "Do people count?"

She laughed and kissed his cheek. "You brought me people?"

"Well, actually, it's one person. I picked up this guy a little west of Flagstaff and he got sick on me. Can we deal with a sick stranger on a holiday?"

Kevin had to half carry Michael into the ranch-style home. Beth hurried ahead and pulled down the covers on a bed in the spare room. Kevin lay him down carefully and her eyes widened in surprise.

"He's young," she whispered.

"I figure he's about your age," Kevin grunted. He began to unbutton Michael's borrowed shirt. "His fever must have broken, this shirt is soaked."

He hurried away to his own room to get a tee shirt and sweat pants. Beth couldn't help staring at the stranger.

"What's his name?" she whispered when Kevin returned.

"Mike something. He's from Brooklyn."

He pulled the shirt over Michael's shoulders, eased a sleeve down one arm, and stopped abruptly.

"Sweet Jesus."

Beth edged closer. "What?"

Kevin turned one of Michael's forearms up for her inspection. Beth traced one of several fresh scars on his wrist with the tip of a finger.

Kevin turned over the other wrist and found similar scars. "Maybe I shouldn't have brought this one home."

Beth considered Michael's young, pale face for a moment then rubbed her brother's shoulder. "You did the right thing."

Kevin started to remove Michael's pants and looked over his shoulder at her, frowning. "You gonna stand there until he's buck naked?"

Beth blushed and hurried away for some aspirin, water, and an additional blanket. She knocked softly before entering.

Kevin slipped the tee shirt over Michael's head and glanced at her. "He's burning up."

Beth touched Michael's hot forehead. "Do you think we can get him to swallow some aspirin?"

"I'll try." He took the two she had in her hand and sat on the edge of the bed. "He hasn't really been with it since last night."

Kevin shook Michael several times and called his name. Michael slowly opened his eyes and Kevin pulled him to a sitting position. "Swallow these."

Michael grasped the tablets, got them into his mouth, and downed the glass of water Beth handed him. He lay back and looked directly at her for a few heart beats, before his eyes closed again.

"Incredible," she whispered.

Kevin pulled the blankets up to Michael's chest. "What?"

Her brother prided himself on being a practical man and had little patience for abstract ideas. In one glance, this sick stranger had shared a shocking confidence with Beth, one she grasped with her spirit rather than her brain. Even if she could find the right words to explain, Kevin would never understand.

"His eyes," she said.

"They are kind of weird, aren't they?"

"I'll never forget," she murmured.

During the night, Michael's coughing woke both of them. Beth rose and found some cough syrup in the medicine cabinet. When she came back to the spare room, Kevin was just going in.

He scratched his head and yawned, "Sounds like he's getting worse."

"I thought I'd give him some cough syrup."

Michael started coughing again and they turned, listening to the deep hacking for a moment.

Beth grimaced. "Maybe we should take him to the hospital."

"If his fever is still high in the morning, I'll call doc Taylor and see if he'll come by."

They got Michael awake enough to swallow the syrup, but he immediately choked and lurched sideways, coughing so violently his face turned a dark purplish-red. Kevin pounded him on the back until he sucked in a breath and collapsed on his side, half-in, half-out of the bed. Kevin rolled him back to the middle of the bed and sighed.

"If the flu doesn't kill this kid, our good intentions just might."

Beth pulled a chair close to the bed and sat. Kevin shook his head.

"I'll stay," Kevin said. "You go on back to bed."

Beth met her brother's gaze levelly. "You're tired, I'm staying."

Kevin looked down and directed his next comment to their sleeping guest. "It's best not to argue when she's like this."

Beth sighed and folded her arms over her chest finding little humor in Kevin's quirky sense of humor at three in the morning.

The doctor pressed a stethoscope to several places on Michael's back. After listening carefully for a few minutes, the doctor turned to Kevin and Beth.

"Pneumonia."

Beth watched as he plunged a hypodermic into the flesh of Michael's upper hip and Michael didn't react.

"I'll give you an oral antibiotic for him. Get him to swallow one every six hours. I'll come back tomorrow. If he's not better, you might have to take him to the hospital."

Kevin paid the doctor and thanked him for making a house call on Thanksgiving and walked him out. Beth took the opportunity to examine Michael's handsome features in the light of day. His dark hair was a sharp contrast to the white pillowcase. Thick lashes outlined his closed eyes. His full mouth seemed relaxed, almost serene. He had fine eyebrows and wide, high cheekbones. There was a hint of beard on his upper lip and jaw line.

She didn't have a lot of experience with boys. There weren't many choices in their small West Texas town and being shy didn't help. This mysterious boy intrigued her.

After dinner, Kevin settled into his easy chair to watch television and fell asleep. Beth drifted by the spare bedroom and peered in at their guest. Michael was thrashing around and mumbling. She tiptoed across the floor and the instant she placed a hand on his forehead to check his fever, he cried out and threw up his hands, as if warding off a blow. Beth sat beside him on the edge of the bed and rubbed his forehead lightly with the tips of her fingers.

"Hush, everything is all right. It's just a dream."

Michael turned his face into her caress. "I'm so sorry."

He hadn't opened his eyes and Beth decided he was speaking to the dream. She continued to caress his forehead and whisper reassurances. Slowly, his breathing returned to normal and his face relaxed to a more peaceful expression.

Chapter 6

Distant voices filtered through the veil of illness, drawing him toward conscious thought. Michael opened his eyes and glanced around the unfamiliar bedroom. Sunlight filtered in through simple white curtains and highlighted a patch of wooden floor. There was a sewing machine and a dressmaker's mannequin against one wall, near the door.

He had no idea where he was, but the peace of his most recent dream lingered. In that dream, a brown-eyed angel appeared and drove the darkness away.

"Terra firma," he murmured then laughed at himself. He had no idea where he was, but he was so certain this place was firm ground that he was spouting Latin.

"Always the genius," he said to the mannequin.

He allowed his heavy eyelids to drop and focused on the discomfort within his body. While the reality of the last few days might elude him, there was a familiar pressure in his chest and his joints ached. He shifted his weight, bringing on a fit of coughing, confirming the malady in his lungs—pneumonia, again. This would be his third round since the first time his father locked him in the basement.

He should get up and thank the kindhearted strangers that took him in and move on before they were affected by the darkness plaguing him. He sighed wearily. Just one short nap then he would go. Maybe, the angel with the oval face and soft brown eyes would come again. As usual, the land of dreams had another entertainment in store for him.

He turned to his side and moaned.

"Everything is all right," a voice whispered gently. "It's just a dream."

The angel, just when he needed her most. He wanted to look at her, but couldn't. It was too soon. He knew from experience that the misery was in his eyes. He needed a few minutes to will the affliction back to the dark recesses.

Her weight pressed into the edge of the bed as she sat next to him, but his patient angel didn't speak again. The only sound was his labored breathing. Finally, he looked up, into the kindest eyes he ever witnessed. The angel smiled and her face glowed in the muted light of a late winter day. He managed to return a weak smile. If God sent this angel, maybe he was forgiven after all. Maybe the days of torment were over. The thought brought tears to his eyes.

"Thank you," he said.

The sympathetic angel reached out and the moment she touched him, he gasped. This was no angel. There was no reprieve. This pretty girl had witnessed his weakest moments.

"I'm sorry," he murmured.

"Hush, now. Go back to sleep."

Saturday morning, Beth slipped into the room and touched his forehead for the first check of the day. The instant her cool fingers touched his skin Michael opened his eyes. Beth jumped back and almost fell.

He blinked slowly, looking around the room, but brought his gaze back to her and her heart raced harder.

"Can I have a drink of water?"

When she returned with the water, he was sitting up with the covers gathered around his waist. He took the water and drained the glass quickly then handed her the empty glass.

"Thank you."

"Want some more?"

"No, thanks." He pushed at his tangled hair. "Where are my clothes?"

She pointed across the room. "On the dresser, but I don't think you should get up until the doctor sees you. He'll be here in about an hour."

"Doctor?"

"You have pneumonia."

A phone rang down the hall and Kevin picked it up on the third ring. He looked that way for a minute before treating her to another dose of his intense gaze.

"Who's that talking?"

Beth smiled, "My brother, Kevin. He brought you here."

He studied her for a moment and his eyes widened suddenly, as if he remembered her. "What's your name?"

"I'm Beth." She dared to meet his gaze straight on and giggled nervously. "Well, actually, my name is Elizabeth, but everyone calls me Beth. I was named after my mother and grandmother. They were both named Elizabeth, only Grandma went by Betty and Mom was called Elizabeth. Of course, Kevin insists on calling me Bethie, which makes me feel like I'm still five years old."

She stopped abruptly. He made her nervous. She made herself nervous. His even gaze hadn't shifted and a hot blush spread over her cheeks and down her neck. Now, she had the fever.

"Most people call me Michael," he began slowly. "Some call me Mike and I have been called Mikey a few times." He paused and smiled a little. "But you, Beth, can call me whatever you want."

Today, the depths of blue danced with mischief and offered no deep message.

"Michael has always been one of my favorite names," she managed.

The doctor pressed a cold stethoscope against his back and listened carefully as Michael took a deep breath and the coughing began. Finished, the doctor folded the stethoscope and turned to Kevin.

"Better bring him into the office for a chest X-ray this afternoon."

After the doctor left, Michael took a shower and joined Beth and Kevin in the kitchen for lunch. Except for their generosity of spirit, dark eyes and hair, Kevin and Beth were nearly direct opposites.

Beth was petite with small, delicate features and those incredible brown eyes. She seemed so sweetly shy, blushing every time he looked directly at her. Yet, it was her hands, her voice and tenderness that had reached through the fevered dreams and lifted him to a province he seldom visited. Beth Thomas made him feel safe.

Kevin, in contrast to his petite sister, was a giant. He was about six inches taller than Michael and outweighed him by at least eighty pounds. There was nothing shy or uncertain about Kevin, certainly nothing angelic.

Kevin ate quickly then sat back and studied him. "So, Brooklyn, tell me how you wound up all the way out in Arizona in the middle of winter without a coat."

Michael had expected them to ask questions. Talking about his life wasn't exactly a habit, but he probably owed them some explanation.

"I was up in San Francisco, but things were getting too crowded and weird so I decided to go south to LA with a couple of guys I met in San Francisco. We spent a little while in LA and when they told me they were headed to Chicago I decided to go along." He paused for a short coughing fit before continuing.

"I was asleep when they pulled in at a rest stop in Arizona. It was warm and they were in a hurry, so I got out and didn't bother to put on my coat. When I came out of the bathroom, there was a state police car in the parking lot and my ride was gone."

"Why did the cop spook them?"

He took a sip of hot tea before answering. "They had five kilos of pot in the trunk."

"Did you know they were hauling drugs?"

Michael met Kevin's gaze evenly. "I mind my own business most of the time."

Kevin chuckled. "Maybe that was a mistake in this case."

Michael toyed with the handle of his cup, "Probably."

"When did this happen?" Kevin asked.

Michael glanced at Beth then turned his attention back to Kevin who was studying him. "Saturday morning."

Kevin shook his head. "You're lucky you're not in jail or dead kid."

Michael picked up his sandwich and took a bite. He had no appetite, but Beth had gone out of her way to make the lunch. Besides, he hoped Kevin might stop questioning him if he had a mouth full of food.

After watching him pick at the sandwich for a while, Kevin shook his head. "You're a stubborn one, aren't you? Hell, I can see you feel terrible. Go back to bed for crying out loud. We'll wake you when it's time to go to the doctor's office."

"I can't pay for all this."

Kevin held up a hand, stopping the protest. "We'll worry about that later."

When it was time to wake him, Beth found him sleeping peacefully. She placed her hand on his forehead and found it hot to touch. She placed a cold washcloth on his forehead and called his name.

Michael shifted in the bed then squinted at her. "What?"

"You need to get up to go to the doctor."

He pushed the covers away and swung his feet to the floor, sitting up too quickly. The room spun before him. He gripped the edge of the mattress and closed his eyes. "I've got to shake this."

"Pneumonia is serious. It's not like you have a common cold. It can take weeks to recuperate."

Michael sighed. "Are you considering a medical degree, Beth?"

"How did you know?"

He looked up, his gaze holding her in limbo for what felt like an eternity.

"I'm a genius," he said evenly.

Only when he broke contact and reached for his shirt did she resume breathing. She watched as he shrugged his shoulders into the shirt. He was so thin each rib was visible and his jeans hung loosely around his waist. He pulled the shirt closed and his slender fingers fumbled with the buttons. Beth realized she was staring and forced herself from the indulgent reverie.

"Let me help you," she said.

"I can do it."

She brushed his hands out of the way. "Your hands are shaking."

When she finished, he stood, towering over her small frame.

Beth tilted her head back and looked up at him. "You're really tall."

He tucked the shirt inside the loose jeans and shrugged. "I imagine everyone looks tall to you."

She pulled herself to her maximum height. "I'm five-two."

He glanced at her sideways, one fine eyebrow lifted slightly and he smiled, unwittingly stealing another piece of her heart.

"A giant," he said softly.

Kevin rapped on the bedroom door, "Quit yappin' at him, Bethie. We have to go." He held out a Navy peacoat to Michael. "It will be a little big, but it's the best I can do."

Michael took the coat. "Thank you."

"Well, it's just an old coat I can't wear anymore. Don't think anything of it." He turned and headed for the door. "I'm going to warm up the car. Come on out when you're ready."

Michael sat on the edge of the bed and slipped on his worn shoes. When he was finished, Beth picked up the coat and held it out for him to slip on. He stooped down in order to slip his arms in.

"Thank you," he said straightening his back again.

"It's just an old coat of Kevin's."

Beth opened the front door for him and he passed through, but paused on the porch, turning back to look at her, nailing her to the spot.

"I meant thanks for everything you've done," he said.

Beth nodded slowly. Kevin honked the horn of their old station wagon and Michael obediently moved on. A few minutes later, Beth realized she was still standing in the open door, staring down the road after them.

The results of the chest x-ray pleased the doctor. He told Michael to continue with the medication, rest, and return in one week. Michael wasn't strong enough to argue.

That evening, Kevin and his girlfriend made dinner. While they cooked, Beth offered to teach Michael a card game. He watched in fascination as her small hands shuffled the cards with precision. Beth rattled off the rules of the game and the tiny part of his brain that was fully functioning only recorded bits of the instruction. She dealt and the game got off to a rocky start.

"You go first," she said.

Michael tossed the ten of spades on the table.

Beth shook her head. "You can't throw that card yet."

He picked up the card and tried to concentrate on his hand. Beth leaned over and eyed his hand. The soft, sweet scent of her drifted on the air and he took a deep breath.

"Open with clubs," she said.

He had the king and ace, so he threw down the king and she topped it with the three of spades. She scooped up the two cards and tossed down the six of hearts.

Michael sat back in the chair a little perturbed, mostly with himself. "Why did you do that?"

"That's the way you play if you don't have any cards in the suit. It's called a trump."

"I think it's called cheating when you look at my cards first."

She smiled. "If we were playing for real, it would constitute cheating. However, since this is a practice game, it's called instruction. Now pick up your cards and play."

Michael topped her six of hearts with the seven of spades.

Beth sighed loudly and handed the seven back. "I know you have hearts. You've got to use those first."

He took the card from her and tossed down the ace of hearts. She handed it back.

"Use your ten."

The tips of her fingers brushed his hand and drew away the last shred of his concentration. He stared at the cards and took a deep breath.

Beth laughed at him. "What's so hard about this?"

He didn't dare look at her and a hot blush crept up his neck. "I can't focus."

Her expression fell. "Oh, I'm sorry."

She came around to him and put her hand on his forehead, his neck and face and Michael slipped further into the mental breakdown.

She patted him on the back. "You're running a fever again. I'll get you some aspirin."

He watched her walk away and tapped his heels on the floor, expelling nervous energy. Every time she came close, his senses seemed heightened to unbearable proportions. One word from her pretty mouth, one touch with those kind hands, just one look from her soft brown eyes and the world was spinning out of control.

Michael started on a second helping of lasagna and Kevin chuckled.

"Looks like this boy can eat when he's feeling better, Bethie."

Hearing the word Bethie, Michael glanced across the table and grinned at Beth, who stuck her tongue out at him.

"What?" Kevin laughed looking from Michael to Beth and then to his girlfriend. "Did I say something funny?"

Rising, Beth put a hand on her brother's shoulder and kissed his cheek. "I told him you call me Bethie, like I'm still in first grade or something."

"So shoot me." Kevin shrugged, lighting a slender cigar. "You'll always be my baby sister. If Mike doesn't like it, he can kiss my..." he laughed at the expression on Beth's face. "Aw, Bethie, I wasn't going to use the word ass, I promise."

"Take your sweet girlfriend and nasty cigar to the other room," Beth said. "I'll do the dishes."

After the other two had gone, Beth sat across from Michael and watched him finish a salad. He caught her staring and offered a little smile.

"What?"

"I was just thinking how odd it is...I mean, I feel like I know you so well."

He met her eyes and his little smile faded. An odd expression flickered across his face. He cleared his throat and pushed his chair back. "I'll help you with the dishes."

Beth got to her feet. "The dishes can wait. Feel up to a little walk?"

"Sure."

"Do you like horses?"

He shook his head. "I don't know. I've never seen a real horse."

"Well, it's about time you did. My horse, Dove, is going to deliver next month. She's beautiful, wait until you see her."

He followed her out the back door, but had to slow his pace considerably to walk next to her. He took the opportunity to look around at the open land, amazed that he could see so far.

Beth paused, following his gaze. "I guess this must seem to be a pretty dull place to you."

"Not really. All this open space feels liberating."

She laughed. "You don't talk like a teenager, Michael."

Michael took a deep breath and released it slowly. Sometimes he felt older than all of West Texas.

Chapter 7

Michael looked out the window at the town and wondered how anyone could survive in a place like Silverpail, Texas. This was a one street, one store, one gas station kind of place that could have dropped off the face of the earth without notice.

Kevin grunted as they passed the sign announcing they were now in Silverpail. "Don't let that sign fool you, we call this place Rustbucket and just one look around will tell you why."

Michael shifted his weight. Beth was sitting between him and Kevin, far too close for comfort. Her knee kept touching his thigh. She was wearing a wonderful, spicy perfume and he inhaled, savoring the fragrance. Kevin swung the old station wagon into the semi-circle drive in front of the high school in a larger, neighboring town and Michael opened the door and got out.

Beth slid across the seat and looked up with sparkling dark eyes as she stood, taking his breath away. Quickly, clumsily, he stood aside, allowing her to pass.

She walked a few steps and turned, walking backward, smiling and so beautiful it took his breath away.

"I'll see you after school," she said.

He wanted to say something, but at the moment the best he could do was stand there and nod. Beth turned back and joined a group of girls going into school.

"Get in, Romeo" Kevin said. "You're letting in all the cold."

Michael waited in the car while Kevin went inside the trucking company he worked for and received his next over-the-road trip. Michael couldn't keep his mind off Beth. If she didn't stop touching him, looking at him with her big brown eyes, and drawing her to him with her sweetness and joy, he was going to make a fool of himself.

Everything about her was perfect. He especially enjoyed the soothing sound of her voice and those affecting dark eyes. He smiled at those thoughts. There was so much more he liked, such as the way her long hair swayed against her back as she walked her almost bouncy girl walk. Of course, there was also the music in her laughter and the tender way she had touched his face when he was so sick.

Kevin pulled the door open and interrupted his reverie. Kevin put the car in gear and turned the car around. "Now, you're in for a treat. I'm taking you to a place that has the greatest food a hungry man could hope for."

They took a seat in a booth and Michael asked where Kevin's next assignment would take him.

"Little Rock." Kevin nonchalantly scanned a menu. "Why?"

"Can I catch a ride?"

"Why?" Kevin repeated.

"I need to go east."

"I'm hurt. I kind of thought we might convince you to hang around a little while."

"We?"

"Yeah, Bethie and me." He grinned broadly. "She likes you, Mike. She likes you a lot."

Michael chose to address only one portion of this revelation. "Thanks Kevin, but I don't think I should stay."

"Excuse me, but I think you better have a look around. In case you don't recognize this, it's winter. If I recall correctly, you don't own a coat and you're not taking my ultra-sentimental, irreplaceable Navy coat on some hitchhiking madness from Little Rock to New York City in the dead of winter. No one wants to pick up a hippy in a military coat."

Michael looked away quickly. Kevin had a point. "I can't continue to mooch off you and Beth."

Kevin replaced the menu and picked up a cup of coffee. "Well, what if you got a job? You could make some money. Buy a coat that fits and head east if you still want to in the spring."

Catching on, Michael smiled slowly. "Do you know of a job that's available?"

"Yep, but they want to know if you finished high school."

"Yes."

"College degree?"

From Kevin's tone, he understood this was a joke, Kevin had no idea.

"What kind of job is it?" He asked.

"Well, this requires a lot of smarts. It's a high-class kind of job." Kevin laughed, amused with himself.

Michael sat back. "What is it? Sweeping streets? Digging ditches?"

"Damn, Boy, you're good at this." Kevin grinned. "This friend of mine owns a roadhouse bar about three miles out of town. He needs somebody to help in the restaurant, stock the bar, and clean the place up after closing. You can live in an extra room upstairs. It won't pay big bucks, but with room and board included it's not a bad deal."

"Let's go talk to your friend."

"I like your style, O'Mara." Kevin nodded. "Soon as we've filled up on fatty delicacies, we'll slide on over and see if he's there."

After ordering, Kevin started reading a newspaper. Michael looked out at the rainy day and lost himself in thought. So far in this life, the kindest people had all been strangers. He hoped that someday he would be in a position to pay some of that kindness back. First, he had to dig himself out of this hole.

"What are you looking so serious for?" Kevin asked.

"I don't understand why you're going out of your way like this for me."

"Well, as a rule, I'm not someone who likes to meddle in other peoples business. It's just that I figure something must be wrong somewhere along the line or you wouldn't be out hitching rides with drug dealers and sitting under some underpass, so broke and sick you can't hold your head up." Kevin sat back and looked at him soberly. "Everybody deserves a break."

Michael watched him, waiting for the other shoe to drop.

"Now that you're feeling better," Kevin continued, "there are a couple of things I'm a little curious about."

Michael tensed. "Like what?"

"Well, how old are you?"

"Seventeen."

"Seventeen! You mean Bethie's older than you?"

"I don't know."

"What were you doing in San Francisco, trying to be part of the hippie crowd?"

Michael lifted a strand of long hair in response.

Kevin shook his head, "All right, so you have the long hair, but otherwise you just don't seem to fit the mold." Kevin leaned closer and lowered his voice. "Did you drop acid like they're always talking about?"

Remembering how crazy it really was in San Francisco and not the media hype, Michael shook his head. "No, I was too afraid to try it."

"What about the free love part?"

"There's no such thing as free love."

Kevin sat back and considered that statement for a moment. "Well, Mr. Cynical-about-love, how long were you there?"

"Just a few weeks."

"Why'd you leave?"

"It was just time to move on."

The waitress approached and they fell silent as she set their food on the table. Michael eyed the stack of pancakes and eggs with distaste. He really had no appetite. Kevin had inadvertently nicked an old wound. He was cynical about love, no doubt about it.

Kevin attacked his food with relish. "So, are you saying you left some kind of heartache there in San Francisco?"

Michael shook his head and picked up the syrup bottle as Kevin continued.

"What about home? What about your family?"

He shot a look at Kevin. "What about them?"

"Is that why you are in such a hurry to get back east?"

Michael sighed and looked back to the rain. He had no interest in talking about his life in Brooklyn, not now, probably never. "No," he said softly.

The humor about Kevin vanished. "Boy, you are one hell of a conversationalist."

Kevin parked in front of a big, two-story, wood frame building that sat near an interstate access road. The building was divided into basically two rooms. The biggest room had tall ceilings, a large wooden dance floor, tables, booths and a long L-shaped bar. Stairs to the left of a small stage led to an office and some storage rooms upstairs. On the other side downstairs was a smaller, oblong room that served as a restaurant with a few tables and booths. The restaurant served lunch every day and on Thursday, Friday, and Saturday nights had a short-order kitchen with hamburgers, fries, simple sandwiches and such.

Kevin grinned at Michael and slapped him on he back. "Your new home."

The owner was a man named Kelsey. He pumped Michael's hand eagerly.

"I hear you're in need of a job."

"Yes sir."

"Well, I won't lie to you. This place is a loud, rowdy, crowded, hard-working joint Thursday through Saturday night. You will work long and hard on those days. Every other day the bar isn't quite so full, but it is still a six-days-a-week job. I can't pay much, maybe forty or fifty a week. I still have to figure that out. Of course, if you figure your room and board in…"

"I told him all that," Kevin interrupted impatiently. "He says the job sounds great."

The bar was open on Christmas Eve and surprisingly busy. Michael worked hard all night then cleaned and restocked the bar, and managed to get a few hours of sleep before the alarm rang. He took a shower and drove Kelsey's old truck to Kevin and Beth's for breakfast at seven.

After breakfast, Kevin left to pick up his girlfriend and Michael did the dishes while Beth started a turkey. Michael dried his hands and sat at the kitchen table, watching Beth prepare a sweet potato casserole. The oven had warmed the kitchen and his lack of sleep caught up with him. He leaned against the wall and slept until Beth nudged him.

"Why don't you go take a nap back in the spare bedroom?"

He rubbed the sleep from his eyes and sat up straighter. "I'll be all right."

She reached for his coat and held it out. "All right then let's take a walk."

He didn't feel like moving, but got to his feet anyway. It didn't matter that it was twenty-eight degrees outside and the wind was coming out of the north at a steady clip. If Beth wanted to go for a walk, they walked.

The light dusting of snow on the ground crunched beneath their feet. The wind seeped through his second-hand coat and stung his face.

Michael shivered and shoved his hands into the coat pockets. "Wouldn't you rather stay inside and beat me at cards?"

"Don't be such a baby. I want to show you Dove's colt."

He tramped along behind her to the barn and kept his mouth shut. The interior of the barn was heavenly comfort after the walk. Beth walked to a corner stall and motioned him to follow.

She knelt in the straw and smiled, "Hey, little one."

Michael's stiff knees smarted sharply when he knelt beside her for a peek. Inside the stall, Beth's horse stamped a forefoot and reared her head.

"Settle down, Dove, its just Michael." She nudged Michael in the side and pointed into a dark corner of the stall. "See him?"

A tiny colt peered under Dove's belly and blinked slowly.

Michael smiled, "Wow."

"I'm calling him Brooklyn."

Michael frowned at her. "Give him a decent name."

"I named him that because of you."

"I figured that part out, Beth."

"I'm not changing my mind. He's got beautiful eyes, just like you."

Michael switched his focus to her. Their faces were only inches apart and suddenly he couldn't breathe. He never wanted anything more than to kiss her mouth. Beth reached up, caressed his cheek with her unforgettable, gentle touch and drove him over the edge. He leaned forward and kissed her soft lips. Beth's instant response took him even higher and the kiss slipped to a more important plane until Michael's sense of self ruined the moment. He had crossed the line. He had no right to enjoy the precious gift of this girl. He jumped to his feet.

"I'm freezing," he said. "Can we please go back to the house?"

They opened presents and sat down at the dining room table. Kevin opened a bottle of wine and poured a glass for everyone.

"My father always made homemade wine for this holiday. Each of us would sip a glass and toast the new year. When our parents died five years ago, Beth and I decided to keep the tradition alive in our own way. We don't make the wine and we changed the toast to honor our parents. We'd be honored if you'd join us."

Affection toward parents was a foreign sentiment, but Michael figured the parents of such fine people such as Beth and Kevin probably deserved the tribute, so he lifted his glass and joined the toast.

After dinner, Michael took a seat in an easy chair and tried to watch football with Kevin, but he was never a fan of the sport and was overly tired. Within minutes, he fell asleep and the old nightmare came calling.

He was back in the cold cage, peering out into the blackness, waiting for his worst fear to slither out of the dark. Too late, he realized the worst was already with him. The clever, icy hand came from behind and slipped over his mouth and nose. Thick fingernails dug into his face, cutting his flesh.

"I've been looking for you," the voice said.

The sound of someone calling his name pulled him from the dark world. Michael opened his eyes while his own voice echoed in the cozy room.

Kevin shook him roughly. "Buddy, you need to wake up."

Kevin, Beth, and Kevin's girlfriend, Audrey, stood around him, staring. The alarm on Beth's face said it all. Humiliated, he sat forward and covered his face with his hands.

"I'm sorry," he said weakly. Nausea rolled in his stomach and he jumped to his feet hurrying toward the front door.

He closed the door and dropped to the top step, sucking in cold air, tamping down the bile in his throat.

The screen door squeaked and Beth wrapped his coat around his shoulders. "You're shaking," she said softly.

One of her small hands stroked the back of his head and he jerked away.

"Don't baby me, Beth."

"Do you want to talk about it?"

He shook his head and got on his feet. "I need to go."

"Wait, I'll go with you."

"No," he said sharply. He dared to look directly at her and softened his tone. "I'm so sorry."

He floored Kelsey's old truck and flew down the back roads, gripping the steering wheel so tightly his hands began to ache. He tried to focus on the road ahead, but the past had slipped over him like a net. His heart pounded fiercely and he realized he was holding his breath. Quickly, he turned on the radio, hoping for a distraction, and forced himself to take deep, even breaths. He refused to look in the rearview mirror, afraid of what he might see behind him in the night.

Back at the bar, he got a bottle of his father's favorite bourbon and took it upstairs to Kelsey's office where he stared at the phone and thought about Kevin and Beth's tribute to their parents. He could call his family, but that would be a waste of time. Although he had been gone for nearly seven months, he was certain nothing would ever soften their hearts toward him.

Finally, he tilted the bottle to his lips and saluted family the only way he could. Near midnight, drunk and unable to fight sleep anymore, he dropped to his knees next to his bed, praying the nightmare wouldn't come again on this day.

As usual, God seemed to be preoccupied with other requests.

He spent every Sunday afternoon with Beth. Sometimes, they drove twenty-five miles to the next town for a matinee and lunch at what Beth deemed a decent restaurant. Usually, they spent the day at the Thomas home. His skill at spades improved, unless he allowed his attraction for his opponent to interfere.

Beth's skill at reading him was uncanny. At times, she seemed capable of slipping into the darkest recesses of his heart. Once there, she was privy to his most intimate pain and all he wanted to do was run in shame. Keeping her at arm's length was a constant battle. Still, he couldn't stay away.

She taught him to ride a horse and they spent some afternoons exploring the countryside. If it was warm enough, they took a picnic lunch to a cozy place next to a pond and spent the afternoon talking.

Beth's quiet beauty seemed to intensify each time he saw her. Her sweet nature loosened the ties binding his spirit and lifted him above the pain. She had a way of catching him off guard. Sometimes, when she looked at him her expression shifted from pleasant to concern. Remarkably, she never questioned him.

Her approach was consistently subtle, but she managed to make her expectations perfectly clear. Like him, she wanted more than matinees and card games, more than long talks and a little handholding. To his astonishment, he realized she was falling in love with him too. When this realization came, he knew he should move on before he hurt her, but couldn't. Her love was so precious he wanted to cling to the pleasure just a little longer.

One Saturday afternoon, as he and Kevin sat at the kitchen table playing cards, Beth stood nearby, talking on the phone to a friend. Michael watched her wrap a strand of satiny black hair around one finger and forgot all about the game.

Kevin reached across the table and tapped his hand. Michael pulled away from the daydream and turned to him.

Kevin grinned broadly. "You were a million miles away. I've been talking to you for twenty minutes."

Michael blushed. "You were not."

Kevin grabbed him by the shirt collar and pulled him to his feet. "Let's talk."

Michael followed him to the front porch where Kevin laughed openly at him. "Man, you got it so bad."

Michael sat on the porch railing and hoped Kevin would be brief for a change.

"You should've seen your face," Kevin said, sitting beside him. "When are you going to let her know how you really feel?"

Michael shifted uncomfortably. "I'm not planning on staying here. It wouldn't be fair for Beth to get involved with me."

"Where you gonna go?"

"There are some things I have to work out before I even think about a serious relationship."

"Who said anything about a serious relationship?"

Michael shrugged. "It couldn't be anything else with a girl like Beth." He said the words with more passion than he wanted to display and immediately blushed crimson. "Beth deserves more than I can ever give her."

"Shit, you sure go from A to Z in a hurry." Kevin patted him on the back. "Tell me did she enjoy any of this life with you? Were there affairs? Any serious arrests?"

Michael grunted at him and looked across the yard.

Kevin studied him, probably noting the added flush of color to his face. "I guess you think I should shut up."

"Something like that."

"Well, I'll say this then I promise not to say anymore. Okay?"

Michael looked back to him and waited, disbelieving the promise. He knew Kevin too well by this time.

"I say let Bethie choose for herself whether she wants to get involved or not. If you're interested, then say so, damn it. You owe her the truth. Lay all your cards out on the table. If she has a say then she can't get pissed when you say adios."

Michael rolled his eyes toward heaven and groaned. He stood and looked down at the big man. "I have to go to work. Are you coming by tonight?"

Kevin folded his arms over his chest and stared at his feet.

Michael needed for him to understand. "Kevin, she deserves better than a guy like me."

Kevin kicked his heel against the wooden step. "Bethie's never had a serious boyfriend. Do you know she can't even say your name without a big sigh?" He finally looked at Michael. "My sister's in love with you."

Michael turned to hide the tears that sprung to his eyes. "I'm sure she'll get over it."

He parked Kelsey's old truck behind the bar and entered through the back door. Two cooks were preparing the usual fare Kelsey's customers complained about, but still ordered time after time. The cooks told him Kelsey wanted to see him immediately.

Kelsey was at the long bar, pounding the keys of the adding machine with his fist and cursing.

Michael shook his head. "No wonder it won't work."

"I might as well save myself the time and add it up on paper. It takes me twice as long to figure this thing out."

"I hear you're looking for me."

Kelsey glanced away from the plastic beast, but was too distracted. He still couldn't comprehend what Michael was saying.

Michael leaned casually against the bar and watched him with the calculator. "What do you want?"

"Why don't you shut up and help me? I don't have time for a chat right now. I was supposed to be gone by three."

"Where are you going?"

Kelsey's head came up with a snap. "Oh, yeah! I wanted to talk to you. I won't be back until after eleven or so. I want you to take care of things back here and keep the bar stocked. Okay?"

Michael sighed loudly and tried again. "Where are you going?"

"Never mind that." Kelsey waved his hand. "If anybody asks, tell them I went over to Clayton. I'll be back before closing time."

He finished Kelsey's books in fifteen minutes then sat at a table in the kitchen to eat as the waitresses began coming in to work. A couple of them joined him at the table, catching up with each of their lives before the night began.

Of all the waitresses, Michael liked Ellen best. She was a no-nonsense, world-weary, divorced mother of three, with a dry sense of humor. She squeezed his shoulder affectionately before sitting next to him. After stealing a few fries from his plate, Ellen lit a cigarette.

A man stuck his head through the open door and looked around.

Ellen eyed him through a puff of smoke. "Can we help you with something?"

"I'm looking for Linda. Is she here yet?"

"She called in sick."

The man's face reddened, he offered a curt thank you to Ellen, and left. Everyone there knew about Linda and her jealous, abusive spouse.

Michael looked to Ellen. "Was that Linda's husband?"

"Yep," Ellen blew out a long stream of cigarette smoke, "and I'd hate to be Kelsey when Mr. Charm there figures everything out."

Michael was shocked. "Kelsey and Linda?"

"Yeah," Ellen laughed. "Don't try to picture it. You don't want to spoil your dinner."

Chapter 8

Beth asked Michael to escort her to her senior prom in May. Michael expected the date to be agony, but couldn't turn her down. He used a considerable amount of his savings to rent a black tuxedo and buy flowers for Beth. He then went to a barber for the first time in over a year and got a regular haircut.

Kelsey offered Michael his most prized possession for the occasion, a shiny gold Cadillac complete with a set of cattle horns on the hood. Michael accepted the offer only because he believed Beth deserved to ride in something dependable and the truck Kelsey usually lent him was anything but reliable.

Kevin answered the door and a big smile spread over his face. "Well, hell, you clean up pretty good." He followed Michael into the living room and slapped him on the back. "Better be careful, you could be accused of resembling a date."

Beth didn't keep him waiting. She smiled shyly and walked toward him in a floor length gown. The pale lilac dress was the perfect accent for her dark coloring. The airy material flowed softly around her feet, giving the illusion that she was floating.

Her long, black hair hung loose about her shoulders. Beth seldom wore makeup but tonight she had applied a little rouge to her cheeks and moistened her lips with a little gloss. She had enhanced the almond shape of her dark eyes with a little mascara and eyeliner. Stunned, Michael's heart caught and then skipped a beat before lurching into action again.

Kevin nudged Michael. "She made that dress herself."

Michael couldn't take his eyes from Beth. He smiled and dared a glance in her eyes. "You're beautiful."

"Thank you," she said softly.

Kevin took each one of them by the elbow. "All right kiddies, let me see if I can capture the magic of you on film."

Until a few weeks ago, Beth had no experience with dancing and expected to stumble over Michael's feet, the way she had when Kevin tried to teach her. She planned to say no if Michael asked her to dance, but he didn't ask. He took her hand and guided her to the dance floor.

"Kevin told you, didn't he?"

"Told me what?"

"That I've never danced with a boy before. I've never even had a..."

When he looked down, his eyes caught the light from the mirrored ball overhead and flashed in a burst of blue. Beth stared up at him with her mouth half-open.

"Wow, you are so handsome," she managed.

His face tensed and he looked away, an edge in his voice. "What were you saying?"

"Oh, right. Well, I've always been a little on the shy side."

He looked back, his expression softening. "You don't seem shy to me."

She smiled broadly. "With you it came easy."

"What do I have to hide from you? We started out with you seeing me naked."

"When did I see you naked?"

"Kevin said the night he brought me home, when I was so out of it, you stood right there while he undressed me and even commented on certain parts of my diminutive anatomy."

Beth rolled her eyes. "He's teasing you."

Michael grinned at her then kissed her cheek softly. "Dancing with you is a pleasure," he whispered in her ear.

After the prom, they attended a private party with some of Beth's friends. Finally, around three that morning, Beth announced she was ready to go home.

In the Cadillac, she slipped off her shoes and slid close to him, laying her head on his shoulder. Michael agonized in silence when she snuggled even closer and placed a hand on his upper thigh.

"Boy, I'm tired," she sighed, "but I guess you're used to these hours aren't you?"

Michael's mind wasn't on the road or conversation. Her warm hand was creating waves of desire and his body seemed to be short-circuiting.

"When will you have time to clean the bar?" She asked.

He stared out the windshield weighing his own desire against what was best for Beth.

"Michael?"

"What?"

"The bar, Michael."

"What about the bar?"

"What's the matter with you?" She pulled back to look at him now and her hand inched further up the inside of his thigh. "Are you tired? Do you want me to help you with your work tonight?"

He shook his head and took a deep breath. His body throbbed from his toes to the top of his head.

A love ballad came over the speakers and Beth gave up staring at him to sing along. The song finished as he pulled into the driveway and cut the engine. Beth pressed her soft lips against his.

"Thanks for tonight," she whispered. "I'll never forget it."

Her words launched a shiver near the base of his skull. The sensation sent a basic message racing toward the lower regions of his body. He let his gaze wander to her deep brown eyes and desire rocked him, leaving his heart pounding against his ribs. He shifted his weight and took another deep breath.

Misreading his reaction, Beth broke away and stared at him. "So, what's wrong with me?"

He laughed softly. "There's absolutely nothing wrong with you."

He tapped on the steering wheel, wishing he were someone else, someone worthy. "It's just that when I've saved enough money for a bus ticket, I'm leaving. I don't think we should start something we can't finish."

"Stop making decisions for me," she snapped.

A long, painful silence reined until she spoke again. "Are you telling me what I see when you look at me isn't desire?"

"What I'm trying to explain to you is..."

Beth grabbed her shoes, purse, and the door handle. "Stop it! You don't have to explain things to me like I'm a child. If you don't want to touch me, fine. The hell with you." She got out of the car, slammed the door, and stalked into the house.

"If you only knew," he sighed, starting the engine.

Back on the highway, he rolled the window down, letting the cold morning drain the heat from his body. His thoughts were still on Beth when he glanced in the rearview mirror and saw a pickup bearing down on the Cadillac at an alarming speed.

There was no shoulder to pull onto, so Michael pushed the accelerator to the floor and the heavy car began to move faster down the deserted blacktop, but the effort wasn't enough. The pickup edged up and over, attempting to force him off the road.

Michael hit the brakes and the pickup passed quickly then disappeared over a rise.

A few miles down the road, the red pick-up waited in the middle of the road, facing him. He took his foot off the accelerator and tapped the brakes. With screeching tires, the truck started toward him. Michael swung the big car over as much as possible. The truck adjusted and veered toward him, slamming the Cadillac in the left front panel and driving the car into the ditch.

The force of the impact threw Michael forward and his face struck the steering wheel. He sat back and shook his head, hoping to clear his vision. Someone pulled the door open, jerked him from the car and threw him to the pavement. He braced for more, but nothing happened. He looked up and recognized the waitress's husband towering over him.

"I thought you were Kelsey," the man said then he turned, got in his truck, and left.

Kelsey was in his office when Michael walked in that morning. It had taken hours to get the Cadillac out of the ditch with the aid of a nearby farmer's tractor. Michael was muddy, bloody, and in a foul mood.

Kelsey didn't look up from his paperwork. "Hey, Kid, how was the prom?"

He dropped in a chair opposite the desk. "We have to talk."

Kelsey raised his head then jerked awake at the sight of him. "What the hell happened to you?"

"Linda's husband ran me off the road," Michael said. "He thought I was you,"

"I didn't know he found out," Kelsey murmured, rising, hunting through his pockets for his keys. "I'm sorry he hurt you, Mike."

"He'd have to be deaf, dumb, and blind not to find out. Everybody in town knows."

Kelsey paused mid-stride. "My God, my wife may know."

"Did Linda work last night?"

"No."

"Maybe someone should call and see if she's all right."

Kelsey pushed the phone across the desk toward him.

"I was thinking of Ellen or one of the other waitresses," Michael said, pushing the phone back.

"I guess you're right," Kelsey nodded. "Come on, let's go."

"Go where?"

"To the doctor, it looks like your nose is broken."

It was early afternoon by the time they returned from the hospital. Michael took a quick shower and fell into bed to catch a few hours sleep. He called Beth later that evening during the band's intermission.

He could hear the television in the background; otherwise there was silence from her end.

"It's Michael," he said.

"I know who you are," she snapped. "What do you want?"

"Do you want to go to the matinee tomorrow?"

"Are you sure you'll still be in town?"

"Beth, please, I'm sorry I hurt your feelings."

"Forget it, Michael. I'd rather pretend last night never happened."

"Okay," he drew the word out slowly. "Want to skip the movie and just talk?"

"I don't think so. In fact, don't bother to call anymore. Let's just pretend you're already gone."

Michael woke to a pounding headache and Beth on his mind the next morning. After swallowing a couple of aspirin tablets, he made a sandwich and sat at the baby grand on the stage. He played nearly every morning, when no one was around to hear or ask questions.

He took a bite of his sandwich and ran a fingertip over the cool white keys. Soon he became absorbed in the resonating waves from the piano and completely lost the world around him. He slipped into a favorite song and sang the lyrics written on his heart.

He didn't see Don, the leader of the weekend band enter the room. The man froze, captivated in the doorway, as Michael's voice articulated the mood of the music flowing so effortlessly from his fingertips.

Michael finished and sat back, taking a deep breath. Don burst into applause and startled him. He lurched backward, pulling the piano bench to the floor with him.

Don jumped onto the stage and helped him to his feet. "Damn, you're good! How come you didn't tell anybody you could do a thing like that kid?"

Michael shrugged and started to push the bench under the piano, but Don wagged a finger at him.

"Oh, no you don't. Sit your butt back down. I got to hear more, after you tell me what happened to your face, that is."

"Linda's husband thought I was Kelsey."

Don shook his head. "Everyone is talking about those two. Come on now, sit down and play me a tune."

Reluctantly, Michael righted the bench and sat as Don leafed through a stack of sheet music. He pulled a few sheets from the stack. "I assume you read music?"

"Yes sir."

"Stop that sir stuff and call me Don." He handed Michael the few pages. "Here, play this little ditty."

Michael took the sheet music from him and ran through the song once. The band always played this song and he had heard it many times while he worked.

"Okay," Don said picking up a guitar, "Now do it again, but sing this time."

"I'm not a singer."

"Baloney, kid, I just heard you and even with that broken nose you gave me goose bumps."

Don stood close by and the need to run bounded out of the past and hammered Michael so hard he nearly fell off the bench again.

He placed his trembling fingers over the keyboard and willed them to play. The keys, so cool and smooth, again fell beneath his touch and he relaxed. Compared to classical piano, this was recreation.

Don smiled at him. "Why don't you join me and the band on Wednesday for rehearsal? If things work out, you could join us for a set this weekend."

The thought of playing in front of an audience set off a deep-seated panic. "I can't."

"Kelsey won't mind. I'll talk to him."

"It's not Kelsey."

Don waited for him to explain so Michael took a stab at a half-lie.

"I just can't play in front of people."

"Well, suit yourself, but it's a damned shame to let all that talent go to waste."

Chapter 9

On the second day of June, Michael was working the grill when Ellen tapped him on the shoulder.

"How come you didn't say this was your birthday?"

He groaned. "How did you find out?"

"Kevin's coming by with a cake."

"Great." He sighed and flipped a row of burgers.

Ellen set a shot glass full of clear liquid and a slice of lime on the counter. "Have some tequila, birthday boy, just don't tell anybody."

He looked at the drink for a minute then picked up the glass, shot the liquid back in one swallow, and choked when it burned his throat.

Ellen laughed and patted his back. "I'd better get back to the animals."

During the band's first break, a crowd gathered in the kitchen and Kevin lit the candles on a sheet cake. They sang a chorus of Happy Birthday and someone shoved another shot of tequila in Michael's hand. Michael looked at Kelsey for his reaction and the boss shrugged.

"Go on. You don't have to work anymore tonight."

"Hell if he don't," Don said. "Y'all wait until you hear this one make music. I heard him playing and singing a few weeks ago," Don said. "This boy knows his way around a piano," Don said.

Everyone looked at Michael with curiosity and the panic returned. Michael downed the shot and Linda refilled the glass.

"You gonna play for us, Sugar?"

Michael shrugged and half-smiled. "I don't really want to."

Kelsey nodded at the full shot of Tequila in Michael's hand. "Be careful of liquid courage."

Michael shot the tequila down without flinching. He wasn't sure if it was his third or fourth and didn't care.

Kevin nudged his side. "Cut the cake."

After everyone else went back to work, Kevin helped himself to another slice of cake. "You're handling all this attention better than I expected."

Michael grinned. The alcohol was beginning to move through him, relieving some of the anxiety that was his constant companion.

Kevin considered him for a moment. "I was going to invite Bethie, but she had to work. You know she got a job out at the truck stop, don't you?"

Michael's eyes narrowed. "You let her work in that place? What's the matter with you?" He asked loudly.

"Hey! There's not a damn thing wrong with truckers," Kevin shot back.

"Maybe there's nothing wrong if you're six-five, weigh two-fifty, and you're name is Kevin, but we're talking about Beth." He threw up his hands in frustration.

Kevin wiped his hands on a napkin and shrugged. "She wouldn't quit, even if I told her to. If I tried, she'd only get mad at me. Right now, she's concentrating on you, which suits me just fine."

"Michael?" Ellen's voice called from the doorway. He turned to her, just as another rush of the tequila pulsed through him.

"Don says they'll be ready for you after this song's finished."

Michael picked up the bottle of tequila and placed it to his lips. He swallowed three times before putting it down again. He wiped his mouth and stared at the bottle in his hands.

"I hate my birthdays."

The band was finishing a fast song when Michael entered the bar. Don spotted him and waved him to the stage. "Come on up here."

Michael climbed to the stage and sat on the piano bench. The room swayed slightly and he realized he had too much to drink. He hoped he wasn't about to make a fool of himself.

Don leaned over, close to his ear. "Do your song first."

Kelsey dimmed all the lights except for the stage and Michael began to play. The song Don requested was most appropriate for his birthday. Michael closed his eyes and the song took him back in time, to all the darkness, pain, and fear, but he was just drunk enough to be brave.

After determining he had not passed the mashed potatoes quick enough, his father backhanded him out of the chair then hauled him down the stairs to the basement and instructed him to strip. It was the usual ritual. His father preferred to strike bare skin. While Michael gripped a support post, his father pounded his back and legs with a thick, leather strap. When his knees buckled and he collapsed on the floor, his father dragged him to the storage area in one corner, tossed him inside, closed the doors and snapped the padlock. At the top of the stairs, his father switched the light off and locked the basement door.

By that time in his life, he was beyond tears. To keep his mind off the pain and things that waited in the dark corners, he stuck his hand in a hollow spot between two blocks and pulled out a flashlight, notebook and pen he had stashed there for nights like this. The song began as a plea for clemency and he added the music later when he bought the twelve-string.

Tonight, Michael finished the tribute to pain and opened his eyes to the present time. Looking around, into the faces of these silent strangers, he realized he had taken these innocent people to a place they didn't deserve to go.

He took a deep breath and placed his fingers back on the keys, picking up the tempo with a parody of country songs about drinking, cheating, and losing love. He finished with a piano boogie and the crowd exploded into applause. Don slapped him on the back and Michael left the stage, making his way through a mob that wanted to congratulate him, but he heard them at a distance. The past clung to him and he felt like he was swimming through dark murky waters with his flesh burning from the beating. Apparently, there wasn't enough tequila in this world to keep him brave for long.

Kevin had watched the performance from the doorway of the kitchen. Unlike others, what froze him in place wasn't Michael's incredible talent. The first song reminded him of scarred wrists and screams on Christmas. He had saved this soft-spoken teenager from the weather and illness, but didn't know how to help with this kind of sorrow.

He stood aside now, holding the door for Michael to enter. Michael picked up the bottle of tequila with a trembling hand and swallowed eagerly.

Kevin stepped inside, letting the swinging door close behind him. "Want to get away from here?"

Michael nodded and was out the back door before Kevin finished cutting a piece of cake for Beth.

"You're certainly full of surprises," Kevin told him in the car. "Maybe you should consider a career in music."

"I did once, I'm over that now." Michael rolled down his window, inhaled some fresh air then glanced at Kevin. "Where are we going?"

"Want to go out to the lake?"

"Sure."

At the lake, Kevin sat on the hood of the car sipping his beer, quiet for a change.

Michael eyed the water and considered a quick swim to clear his head. "Do you think the water has warmed up enough for a swim?"

"Hell no, but the shock might sober you up before we go get Bethie."

Michael bent down and picked up a few rocks to toss at the water. "You didn't say anything about picking her up."

Kevin shrugged indifferently and shoved a sandwich at his young friend. "Here, you need to put something in your stomach."

Michael hadn't eaten dinner yet and food did sound like a good idea. He picked up the sandwich and ate it quickly.

Kevin shifted his weight on the hood and threw a rock out into the lake. "So, tell me about you and music."

"There's not much to tell."

Sensing Kevin's steady gaze, Michael glanced at him then looked out to the moonlit water. "What?"

"You've got a God-given talent, Michael. It's a shame you don't use it."

"God-given," Michael repeated, shaking his head. "Why don't people ever think it might be the other way around?"

"Like how? Like you giving something back?"

Michael slid off the hood. "More like a price tag nailed to my flesh."

Kevin sat back quickly, stunned by the bitterness of Michael's tone. "What the hell is the matter with you?"

The contents of Michael's stomach churned and he ran a few steps before the whole thing came up. Finished he wiped his mouth, popped the top on one of Kevin's beers and took a few swallows to get rid of the taste in his mouth. He turned and walked to the water's edge, shoving his hands deep into his pockets. Kevin let him stand there for a while before he followed, unsure what would be helpful or harmful at that point.

"Everything I love always ends upside down and crazy, Kevin" Michael explained after a moment. "I can't dream about music anymore."

Kevin decided to drop the subject that obviously brought so much misery to his young friend. "We need to go, Mike. Bethie's gonna kill you as it is."

"Me?"

Kevin grinned at him. "I intend to blame our tardiness on you."

Michael's eyes narrowed and he gave Kevin a sidelong glance. "How late are we?"

"She's been waiting for half an hour."

"Why didn't you say something?"

Kevin patted his shoulder. "You were more important at the moment."

"So," Kevin began as they turned back toward the interstate, "I proposed to Audrey. We're planning to get married on July Fourth as kind of a joke on Independence Day. Now that Beth's on her way to college, I figure it's time."

"I like Audrey," Michael said, relieved that Kevin had found a neutral subject to discuss on their way to Beth.

"I guess I'll have to watch you two then because she thinks you're about the cutest thing that ever fell off the turnip truck. She and Bethie talk about you, but I'll spare you the meticulous assessment of your cute little butt and purtie blue eyes."

Michael laughed and relaxed a little. "Good."

The minute they pulled into the all-night truck stop parking lot they spotted Beth standing near the entrance, arms folded over her chest and peering into the night with an angry scowl on her face.

Kevin moaned, "Uh-oh."

Kevin deliberately placed the passenger side of the car closest to the curb. Beth looked down prepared to let loose until she saw Michael's bruised face. She hadn't seen him since the incident with Linda's husband.

"Oh my God," she said.

Kevin leaned across Michael, grateful for the distraction from her anger. "You should've seen him a week ago."

She bent over, peering inside at her brother, suddenly remembering he was there. "I've been standing here for forty-five minutes. Where have you been?"

"I swung by and picked up Mike."

"Yes, I know, I called the bar. Ellen said you left about nine-thirty. That was over two hours ago."

"We went to the lake," Michael said.

Beth's eyes flicked over him quickly then turned her attention back to Kevin and pointed at Michael. "Is he the reason I had to stand here for over an hour?"

Kevin sighed, "Oh Bethie, come on, just get in the car."

She walked around to Kevin's side and opened the door. "Get in the back. I'm driving. Good grief, I can smell the beer from out here Kevin."

"That's the birthday boy. He's drunk as a skunk."

"No, I'm not," Michael said. "That sandwich sobered me up."

"Yeah, right, like it could happen that fast."

Beth slid into the driver's seat as Kevin climbed into the back. "Both of you shut up. Kevin, I can't believe you'd be this stupid."

"But Mom, it's Mikey's birthday," Kevin whined then cackled loudly.

Beth slammed the car into gear, the tires squealed and they jerked forward. At the intersection, she turned toward town rather than home.

Kevin leaned forward resting his forearms on the front seat between them. "Let's take Mikey home with us."

"Sorry, but I promised to bring him back to the bar for a private party. I hope you're not all partied out."

"It really hasn't been much of a party," Michael said.

Kevin moaned. "Who did you invite, your teeny-bopper, high-school crowd?"

"I called Audrey. Kelsey and the people who work at the bar are staying." She looked over at Michael and smiled for the first time. "I hear you knocked them dead tonight playing the piano and singing. Would you play for me?"

Michael smiled slowly. "Are you speaking to me?"

"Yes," she smiled. "Would you play for me, please?"

He shrugged. "It will cost you."

"What?"

"Stop hanging up on me."

Beth laughed, "Deal."

"Yea, peace," Kevin said quietly.

They stayed up all night playing the jukebox, drinking, and dancing. While Michael played the piano, Kevin ran an impromptu singing contest then pronounced himself the winner. Michael didn't drink anymore, but smoked a joint with Ellen outside behind the bar to calm his uneasy stomach.

Around four, the party finally broke up and Audrey took Kevin home. Beth wanted to stay so Michael promised Kevin to drive her out later rather than her trying to drive. After stocking the beer cases, he walked over to the table where Beth sat. A little drunk, she leaned on her elbows watching him with sleepy eyes.

"Why don't you go upstairs and get some sleep, Beth?"

"Where?"

"My bed."

She yawned, reminding Michael of a little girl.

"I'm not going to take your bed," she said.

He took her hand and pulled her to her feet.

"Come to bed with me, Michael." She leaned against him and he lifted her in his arms. She closed her eyes and put her cheek against his chest. "I need to cuddle."

They reached the second floor and he set her back on her feet. Beth didn't move. She stood there looking at him with a silly grin while he caught his breath.

He waved toward his room. "It's that way."

"I want another kiss." She moved toward him and Michael groaned. Beth laughed, enjoying the game, and pressed against his body.

The soft crush was so pleasurable he hesitated for a second before backing away, but it didn't help. Beth kept in step with him.

"No," he said, but laughed.

She wagged a finger at him. "Your mouth's saying no, but your body just told me yes."

"I'm eighteen, my body always says yes."

"Then why does your mouth keep saying no?"

"Because, Beth, I'm not staying. Don't you understand? What do you want, a temporary thing?"

"Excuse me, Mr. Know-it-all, but we both know we have already passed temporary."

This night had been like a ride on a roller coaster and Michael's resistance was thin. "You don't know me. I have a whole life you know nothing about." He paused, looking away from her and started toward the stairs. "Trust me, you wouldn't like the truth."

Beth jumped in front of him, blocking the hall.

"You have to admit there's something strange between us. We have this weird energy thing."

Michael laughed tiredly and stepped around her. "Please go to bed."

Beth gripped both of his arms, forcing him to stop. Her gaze held him. "Michael, I know it's not my imagination. You feel the same way I do. It's just that you're afraid of something, some big, ugly thing that has nothing to do with us, with now." She straightened her back and stood taller. "Tell me I'm wrong."

"Beth, I don't have a choice. I have to finish something I started a long time ago."

She hit him on the chest. "That is such garbage! You can't let the past run the future! She threw up her hands in frustration. "What happens to the present? What happens to right now?"

Beth watched as he blinked slowly then looked away, breaking eye contact. Clearly, her questions had taken him by surprise. When he stepped around her, she let him go, watching him descend to the first floor and disappear into the storeroom.

She turned on the overhead light in his small room and looked around for the first time. The old blankets on the twin bed had tight, precise corners. An upturned wooden crate next to the bed served as a makeshift bookcase and night stand. Inside, was a stack of used books on subjects ranging from tax law to the poetry of Yeats. One of the pictures Kevin had taken of her on the night of the prom rested against the base of a lamp on the top of the crate.

There was a small dresser against one wall and she found a T-shirt in the top drawer. After removing her clothes, she slipped the large shirt over her head and crawled under the covers. She snuggled her face against the feather pillow and fell asleep breathing in the scent of him.

The phone rang in Kelsey's office precisely at ten. Michael was in Kelsey's big swivel chair, facing the outside window with his legs stretched out and his bare feet resting on the windowsill as he mulled over the decision he had come to a few hours ago. He had cleaned the bar, taken a shower and settled here instead of waking Beth to take her home. He was tired, but sleep would not come. His time here was over.

He picked up the receiver knowing it was probably Kevin.

"Where's Beth?" Kevin asked without preamble.

"Sleeping."

There was a long pause before Kevin spoke again. "Did she sleep alone?"

"Yes, Kevin," he sighed. "I'm sorry, I should have called. I'm sure she'll come home as soon as she wakes up."

He dropped the receiver back onto the cradle and looked back at the new day.

"I suppose that was my brother looking for me," Beth said.

He swiveled around to face her. "He's concerned about you. I was supposed to take you home, remember?"

Michael wasn't in the mood for another drama. He stood and stretched his stiff body.

"He should know there's nothing to worry about," Beth said.

Michael finally looked at her directly, about to respond to her sarcasm until he saw her standing there in just a white T-shirt. After allowing himself a quick appraisal, he forgot what he wanted to say. He could see a great deal though the thin material and blushed. She cocked her head to one side, reading his reaction, and he expected her to nail him for his boldness.

Instead, Beth waved her hand at the chair. "So this is what you preferred over sleeping with me last night?"

Michael shrugged. "I got up here around eight-thirty this morning, so I wouldn't call it last night."

"You must be exhausted."

"Actually, I'm hungry." He moved past her to his room. "Want to go out for some breakfast?"

Beth followed and watched as he put on a clean shirt. "Why don't we make something here?"

"That would be too much trouble. Let's just drive to Gert's."

"I thought you wanted to talk."

He stopped tucking his shirt in and met her eyes. "I'm through talking. You refuse to take me seriously."

"That's because you don't make sense."

"You don't want me to make sense," he snapped. "You want me to say what you want to hear."

Beth stepped closer, angry now. "And what is it that I want to hear?"

She was too close. Suddenly, it was difficult to breathe. His face was on fire and he wanted to run. Instead, under the guise of sarcasm and the weight of his decision to leave, he finally told her the truth. He leaned down close and looked her in the eye, leaving only inches between his face and hers, his voice soft.

"I want you so much I ache all the time. I never want to face one more day without you." He had to pause for a deep breath. His heart pounded hard against his ribs. His voice was nearly a whisper as he told her the final truth he wouldn't admit any other way. "I love you, Beth."

He stood tall again and cocked an eyebrow, "Happy now?"

For a moment, Beth stood perfectly still. Slowly, her eyes filled with tears and without any warning, she attacked. He grabbed her arms, trying to stop her, but she swung wildly, striking his still tender face.

Michael dropped to his knees and placed his hands over his face, she had managed to hit him squarely in the nose.

Beth immediately knelt beside him. "Oh damn it, what did I do?"

She tried to move his hands, but he brushed her away.

"I'm so sorry," she said. "I'll get some ice."

She raced to the kitchen and soon returned with a towel full of crushed ice. Michael put his head against the wall and closed his eyes tightly, carefully laying the ice against his throbbing face.

"Does it hurt much?" Beth asked. "Do you want to go to the hospital?"

"No," he grunted at her, wishing she would leave him alone.

Beth knelt on the floor next to him. "I'm sorry."

Michael hated the hurt in her voice. He didn't want her to feel responsible for what happened. He never should have let things get this far. He knew the end would be painful. Unfortunately, falling in love with her was never a choice.

He lowered the towel and looked up at her. "Could you please just go home?"

Beth stared for a minute where he died a thousand times. Finally, she rose and went to his room without speaking.

Michael heard her crying softly and cringed. He wiped the blood away with the wet towel and hoped she would stop soon. When the crying continued, he went to her.

Beth was dressed now, but sitting on the bed, clutching his T-shirt.

"Beth…" He said.

She raised her head, looking at him. She seemed so young and vulnerable he wanted to wrap her in his arms and protect her. He shook his head at the absurdity of protecting her from himself. Yet, in two quick steps he stood in front of her. He took her hand, pulled her to her feet, and wrapped his arms around her, laying his cheek on top of her head, hoping she wouldn't break away. He desperately needed to hold her.

Beth relaxed in the comfort of his embrace, resting her cheek against his chest and they stood together for a long while. Finally, she moved back a step, looking up at him.

"Why won't you give this a chance?" She asked.

"Beth, please," he paused, swallowing the need to give in. "It's taking all the strength I have to do this."

"Maybe it's not the right decision. The right decision should be easy, shouldn't it?"

He shook his head. "It would be a disaster for you."

"No matter what, the way I feel about you is not a disaster."

He took a deep breath and shoved his hands into his pockets. "Look, you're going to college in two months. You'll find some guy with a future and know I did you a favor."

She stared at him for a long minute, walked back, stood on her tiptoes, and kissed his mouth. This kiss wasn't tentative or shy, Beth lingered, offering her heart. Michael's will to resist dissolved and he responded passionately, finally offering her a straight answer.

She touched his honest lips with the tip of her index finger. "Don't go."

"I don't have a choice," he said softly.

She looked up at him and trapped him with her acute perception. She stroked his cheek tenderly and took a few steps back. "Do what you have to do then come back to me."

She folded his T-shirt neatly then tucked it inside her purse and when she reached for her shoes, Michael walked back to Kelsey's office.

He heard her pause in the office door behind him, but stood with his back to her staring at the rolling hills, holding his breath. He shoved his hands into the front pockets of his jeans. There was no turning back, he had to go now. They had crossed the line.

"I love you," she whispered.

He heard her turn and her quick footsteps grew distant. Each syllable of her, "I love you" carved an initial into his heart and each footstep on the stairs sounded like a cannon signaling doom. When the door closed behind her, Michael exhaled sharply and dropped his head.

A thunderstorm darkened the sky as he hurriedly stuffed his few belongings into an old duffel bag. He wrote a note to Kelsey, locked the back door, and placed the key under the mat. Rain soaked him as he walked the three miles to Gert's diner where he bought a cup of coffee and a ticket for the only bus coming through that day.

Chapter 10

Rain followed the half empty bus all day. Michael sat next to a window and watched miles of Texas roll by numbly. He rolled up his coat for a pillow and tried to sleep, but the luxury of rest wasn't to be his. He was too near the bathroom and a crying baby, and each time he closed his eyes Beth was all he thought about.

They stopped for dinner around five and Michael was the last to emerge. He stepped down and turned his eyes to the sky. A blanket of dark clouds told him the storm wasn't finished. The weather mirrored the turmoil inside of him; the resolve to keep moving and his heart were at war.

He shifted the strap of the duffel bag on his shoulder and headed into the crowded diner. There was an empty stool at the counter next to a pregnant young woman. Michael put his bag on the floor behind the stool and sat, reaching for a menu, accidentally knocking her purse on the floor.

He handed her the purse and offered a weak little smile, the best he could do today. "I'm sorry."

The woman pulled a red flannel shirt tighter about her swollen abdomen and turned her attention to the waitress.

"Can you tell me where I can get help with a flat tire?"

"There's a gas station down the road about fifteen miles, but they won't be open until tomorrow morning."

The woman put her face in her hands and started to sob. The waitress looked to Michael with a tired expression.

"Are you going to order anything?"

"I need a minute." The waitress made a sour face before turning away. Next to him, the pregnant woman dabbed her eyes with a paper napkin.

"How far is your car?" Michael asked.

She pointed out the plate glass window, "About half a mile."

Michael glanced at the clock on the wall behind the counter. If he hurried, he could probably change the flat, and make it back before the bus left. He wasn't hungry anyway.

He put the menu back. "Do you have a spare?"

She nodded and blew her nose on a napkin.

"My bus is leaving in forty minutes," he said. "I could change it for you if you'll drive me back."

She couldn't keep up with his long-legged strides and he slowed for her. They walked down the blacktop, around several curves, and at least a mile before he understood the woman wasn't a good judge of distance. By the time they reached the car, he had the sinking feeling he wasn't going to get back in time to make his bus.

The rusted jack looked unreliable and there was no handle, so Michael made do with a lug wrench. The spare was bald, but he slapped it on as rain began to pour down on him. He jumped in the car and glanced at his watch. He had three minutes.

The woman did her best. She drove faster than she dared on the oily blacktop with smooth tires. Unfortunately, the bus was gone.

Michael went back inside the restaurant and ordered a sandwich and coffee. He watched the rain through the plate glass window with a growing sense of defeat. He didn't have enough money for another bus ticket. Hitchhiking was the only choice, but he lacked a direction. All he could think of were the places he couldn't face again. He went out into the rainy night and started walking.

The two-lane road had no traffic and the night was too dark to see much around him. He kept his head down to avoid the driving rain. There were no trees, rest stops, or overpasses to use as shelter. All that was available was wide-open land and cold rain.

He had no idea how far he walked before the first car approached. He turned and stuck out his thumb. Headlights blinded him as the car pulled to the shoulder. All he could see were the lights mounted to the roof of the car and he lowered his hand.

The man next to him leaned against Michael's shoulder to sleep. Michael eased away and moved to the floor of the crowded cell. The room smelled like old booze, vomit, urine, and body odor. He leaned against the bars and closed his eyes.

The heavy metal door opened at the end of the hall, and three deputies escorted a drunken giant of a man to the holding cell. He stumbled inside, bumping into people, cursing them, and waking everyone in the crowded cell. No one challenged him. The giant sat on the edge of a bench mumbling unintelligibly for a few minutes before falling over onto the poor fellow sitting next to him and starting to snore.

The cell was nearly empty the next morning when the big man finally stirred. Michael was stretched out on a wooden bench, taking a shallow nap. Hearing the sudden noise, he immediately sat up and waited to see what would happen when his cellmate was semi-sober.

The man brushed a strand of long black hair from his eyes and focused bloodshot eyes on his obviously wary cellmate. He laughed then winced in pain. "Ugh, I must have been three shades of ugly last night."

The man rose carefully, went to the urinal then washed his hands and face. He dried his hands on his jeans and held one out to Michael.

"Red McDonough."

Red's hand dwarfed his own. Awed by the size of the man, Michael managed to mumble his name.

Red eased himself back onto the bench and grinned. "So you're an Irish lad. Tell me, Michael O'Mara, what do you think I am?"

"McDonough sounds Scottish."

He pointed a finger at Michael and winked, "Daddy was in fact a Scotsman, kilt and all, but Mom was full-blooded Shoshone. Mom had stronger genes when it came to us kids, all except my sister, Nellie, who inherited Dad's red hair and full beard."

Michael grinned, grateful for the diversion from his grim situation.

Red's expression didn't change. "You think I'm putting you on, don't you? Hell no. That sister of mine has to shave twice a day."

Michael got up from the hard bench to stretch his back while Red searched through the pocket of his shirt and found a broken cigarette. He stuck a match to the end and held the break between his fingers, sucking gently. He blew out a stream of blue smoke and eyed Michael.

"So, how'd you wind up in here, boy? You been out raisin' hell?"

Michael shook his head, "I've been out being stupid."

Red's deep laugh rumbled off the concrete blocks. "Well, I guess there's a lot of that going around. Last time I was through this way I met this sweet little woman named Rita. She told me if I was ever in the neighborhood again to give her a call. I went down to Houston on some business and finished a couple of days early, so I decided to take a little detour on my way home. I gave her a call, we met for dinner and drinks at this little bar, and, as you saw, I indulged a little too much. We were having a fine time, until this rude little son-of-a-gun comes up to me and says to get my hands off his old lady. I told him if he didn't have enough respect to call her his wife, he could kiss my ass."

Red took another draw on his cigarette and shook his head. "That's when I discovered he was a deputy sheriff."

Michael and Red remained in jail for two days waiting for the judge. Unless he was sleeping, Red either had a story to tell or spent his time interrogating Michael. On the third morning, they took Red before the judge. An hour later, a guard opened the door for Michael.

"You're free to go."

Michael didn't raise any questions. He walked out into the late morning sun, grateful to be free, and heard someone call his name. Turning, he spotted Red leaning against a black pickup, puffing a cigarette.

Red squinted at him then slipped on a pair of dark sunglasses. "Ever spend any time on a horse?"

"A little."

"Well, that's good, because I've got just the place for a foot-loose boy. I live with my sister and her husband up in Wyoming. They're always looking for an extra hand if you're interested."

Michael looked out the window of Red's truck in pure wonder as they drove the long, straight blacktop from a town only slightly larger than Silverpail. The rolling hills sloped straight into the Rocky Mountains and a clear blue sky.

Red swung the truck onto a gravel road and waved an arm out his open window at the rolling land. "From this point, you're on Parker property for as far as your eye can see and then some.

My brother-in-law's great-grandfather started this place back in eighteen-eighty-nine. The Parker's have run cattle on it ever since."

The long gravel road led to the front of a simple ranch house. A plump, red-haired woman came out of the house and scowled at the truck as they parked.

Red switched off the engine and nudged Michael. "That's my sister, Nellie. Guess she's already shaved this morning."

"Where have you been?" Nellie asked, descending the stairs.

Red pushed Michael toward the passenger door. "Hurry, get out."

Michael slid out and Red came around the end of the truck and hunkered down behind him though he was hardly hidden. "Look what I brought you Nell, a nice little kid to fatten up."

Michael stepped away quickly, trying to look back at Red, but the big man jumped right back behind him.

Nellie laughed. "Stop hiding behind that boy, you devil." She reached around Michael playfully swatting her brother with a wooden spoon. "Where have you been, Red? Sam needed you here two days ago."

"I was in jail."

"Jail! What for?"

"Well, I got drunk."

Her hands went to her hips. "You promised you were through with all that."

"I know, but it snuck up on me, Nell. Can we talk about all of this later? Let me introduce you to Michael."

Nellie opened her mouth to say more, but changed her mind and turned to Michael. Her sky-blue eyes were possibly the kindest he'd ever seen.

"Please, excuse my manners. Your name's Michael?"

"Yes, Ma'am."

"I'm Nellie Parker and though we're kin, I'm nothing like this heathen. What's your whole name?"

"Michael O'Mara."

"Welcome to Wyoming, Michael O'Mara." She smiled brightly, reached out, and patted his cheek before turning toward the house. "Ring the bell, Red. Let's see if Sam's in the mood to hear it today."

Red held the front door open for her then waved Michael through and gave him a wink. "Looks like you get to stay, jailbird."

He let the screen door slam behind Michael and started ringing the bell attached to a post on the corner of the porch.

The inside of the house had a lived-in charm. The living room fireplace was so large he could have stood inside it. Old photographs of the Parker's and this ranch rested on the mantel. Unlike the pictures on his parents' mantel, these people looked content.

Bookshelves lined the walls on either side of the fireplace, but he didn't take the time to read any of the titles. The windows, covering nearly half the rear wall, drew his attention. Just below the windows was a wide deck. The house sat on a high plateau and the land behind it sloped to a long valley. Beyond the valley, the sky and land seemed to go on forever.

"Come on in here, Michael." Nellie called from the kitchen.

The aroma of homemade biscuits and fried chicken made his empty stomach twinge. She motioned to the kitchen sink. "Wash up and have a seat."

As he was washing his hands, the back door opened and a small, wiry-looking man wearing faded jeans, worn boots, and a brown cowboy hat entered. He didn't seem surprised to find a stranger in his home. He glanced at Michael then turned to Nellie. "Who's ringing that damned bell?"

Nellie placed a basket of hot biscuits on the table. "Red finally made his way back. Sam, this is Michael O'Mara."

Michael quickly dried his hands on a dish towel and looked down into intelligent, brown eyes set in a weathered face. Sam shook his hand quickly then took off his hat, revealing a full head of silver hair that touched his shoulders.

Sam tossed the hat on a small table near the back door. "Well, Michael, I suppose that fool out there dragged you up here with the promise of work, is that right?"

"Yes sir."

Sam's eyes narrowed a little. "Did he tell you its hard work?"

"I'm not afraid of hard work."

"I can't pay much."

"That's fair, Mr. Parker. I don't know much."

Sam examined him for a minute then nodded. "You can share the bunkhouse with Red. We supply three meals a day. Nellie will more than likely want to drag you to church on Sunday. Don't even try to resist, just consider it part of the job."

"Wouldn't do anyone here any harm to join us," Nellie said.

Sam winked at Michael and a smile played at his lips as he moved to the sink to wash his hands. "Boy, would you please go out there and tell the fool I'm here before he wears the bell out?"

Everyone that knew Nellie Parker knew that being childless left a hole in her life, but no one felt her loss more acutely than her husband, Sam. Over their twenty-year marriage, he watched as she babied all the animals, took in the unfortunate, and saw to most of the lonely and elderly for a fifty-mile radius. Still, nothing satisfied her desire for a child.

When Red delivered Michael to the ranch, he handed over someone who needed her as much as she needed him. Sam watched as Nellie began to take careful steps, reeling Michael in closer.

"Now, don't get all wrapped up in this boy, Nell," Sam cautioned over their early morning coffee before the workday began. "He's probably just passing through."

"I know that. There's just so much hurt in those pretty eyes."

Sam shook his head. "He looks spooked to me."

"He's a boy, not an animal," Nellie said.

"You know what I mean. He's injured, I'd say deep."

"I've got to try, Sam. God put him in our hands for a reason."

Sam smiled at her and nodded. He didn't share her belief in fate. Red simply brought the kid here because he saw a way to make his sister happy.

"Last time I looked, that brother of yours looked more like a full-blooded Shoshone warrior than the Almighty himself."

Nellie grunted at him and rose to check on her biscuits.

Michael's first visit to Nellie's church was quite an experience. He took a seat in the pew next to Nellie and listened in growing shock as the preacher began to shout about sin and damnation. However, when the man turned stormy, accusing eyes in his direction and pounded his pulpit, an acute resentment rose in Michael.

Red and Sam were on the front porch when he returned from this first trip to Sunday morning services. Nellie went inside to prepare lunch and Sam motioned Michael to sit with them.

While Michael unbuttoned the collar of his shirt and loosened his tie, Red grinned at him.

"So, how was today's sermon?" Red asked.

Michael shrugged and looked out across the land. "I think the reverend had you on his mind this morning."

"Going straight to hell, am I?" Red laughed and looked past Michael to Sam. "Guess we should've warned this boy about hell-fire and brimstone."

Sam nodded and pointed his pipe at Michael. "You just remember that no matter what he says that preacher wouldn't know a sinner from a saint. God doesn't tell his secrets to such a judgmental loudmouth."

"Samuel Parker!" Nellie called from the doorway. "You stop telling that boy such things. Preacher Barnes is a good man."

"I'm sure that's his belief, Nell. While I admire your loyalty to your pastor, I have to remind you the man ought to be teaching about God's love, not his anger. That preacher tries to make every soul he meets feel ashamed and unlovable. I don't believe that's what our Lord had in mind."

"We all have to face our shortcomings," Nellie said, in a softer tone.

"That we do. No doubt about it." Sam nodded then smiled at her. "Want some help with lunch?"

Nellie brightened at the offer. "I got everything ready before I left. I just need to finish. Thanks for asking."

Sam was always more reserved than either Red or Nellie. He usually took his time getting to know people, but when it came to Michael he made up his mind nearly as quickly as either Red or Nellie. When told to do something, the boy went to work without hesitation or argument. The rest of the time he kept to himself. Occasionally Michael met his gaze directly and Sam respected a person that wasn't afraid to look him in the eye, even if there were a few barriers present.

Most of the books on the shelves that lined either side of the fireplace were Sam's. One afternoon while Nellie finished making lunch, Sam found Michael standing in front of the bookcases, slowly scanning the titles.

"Which ones are you interested in?"

Michael hadn't heard Sam approach and took a quick step backward.

Sam laughed and patted his arm, "Didn't mean to startle you. Feel free to read any of these that you'd like. Just don't fold the corners of the pages."

Michael looked to the books, reading a few titles. "I'd enjoy reading The Long Valley."

"I didn't think kids still read Steinbeck."

Michael glanced at him. "I really enjoyed The Red Pony," he admitted shyly.

Sam waved a hand at the bookshelves. "Help yourself."

Michael read every day when their work was done. He finished Steinbeck then went to the top shelf and read every row until he completed the entire bookcase to the right of the fireplace then started with the books on the left side.

One evening, as he started to leave the dinner table Sam asked him to join him in the living room.

"Do you play chess?"

"I used to."

Sam sat in his favorite chair near the fireplace and smiled at him. "Feel like giving it a try?"

Michael hated the game. Uncle Frank taught him to play and like everything they did, Michael either played to be the best or he suffered. Holding his palm over the flame of a candle until he corrected an oversight was certainly an inducement to play well, but dulled the pleasure of the game immeasurably. Remembering the burns, he lifted his left hand and rubbed the palm over his knee quickly.

Sam watched with his wizened gaze, waiting for an answer.

Cornered by the need to conquer old fears, Michael nodded. "Sure."

Sam placed an old wooden chessboard on a small table and placed hand-carved wooden pieces on the squares. Michael sat across from him and fought the uneasiness in the pit of his stomach.

"I'll let you move first," Sam said.

Michael moved a pawn forward. It was a quick game, over in just under fifteen minutes.

Sam grinned at him. "Boy, I've been looking for someone to play for years. Nobody around here will play me anymore. Let's see if you can beat me again."

Michael shook his head. "Don't get your hopes up, Mr. Parker. That was just luck."

Sam laughed softly and shook his head. "Luck had nothing to do with it."

Michael glanced at him then to the chessboard and took a deep breath. Just when he finally had the opportunity to be an ordinary human being, he acted like a fool. Old habits were hard to shed.

"I'm kind of tired," he said. "Could we play tomorrow?"

Sam sat back in his chair and sighed. "You need some space?"

Michael ran his fingertips over the beveled edge of the table. He could feel Sam watching him. The grandfather clock in the hall chimed and he looked that way, thinking of the clock at the base of his parents' stairs.

"Chess has never been my favorite game," he said.

"Too easy?"

He turned his gaze to Sam now. Sam had a way of looking past his defenses, but Michael never felt threatened by the intrusion. In fact, he sensed he was in safe company.

Sam looked back to the chessboard and started replacing the pieces. "One more game then I'll let you go to your reading."

One game turned into a two-hour battle. They didn't talk, Sam didn't lecture, and Michael didn't run.

Neither the Parkers nor Red asked too many questions about his past. When Sam asked if he planned to stay around until spring, Michael told him, without hesitation, he would stay as long as they would let him because he knew, the way he knew he loved Beth Thomas, he was home.

Except for round-up time, when extra help came in, Red and Michael had the bunkhouse to themselves.

Despite the improvements in his life, the nightmare still visited. The first time his scream cut through the still night, Red jumped out of bed and turned on the light, automatically reaching for his rifle.

Michael was in the corner of his own bed with knees drawn tightly to his chest and his hands covered his head with his hands. His whole body trembled.

Red hurried across the room. "What's wrong?"

Michael forced himself to lower his hands and tried to focus on Red. "Bad dream," he managed.

"You been listening too close to the reverend again, haven't you?"

It took a moment for Michael to register the humor. Still, the best he could do was a nod.

Red turned and went to his closet, coming back to the middle of the room and the old table where he placed a bottle of amber spirits and two glasses. He poured two fingers into each glass, picked one up, swallowed all the contents then looked back to Michael who was still shaking.

"Have a drink with me."

Red told Sam about the incident the next morning after Michael and Nellie left for town.

"I have never seen anybody that scared in my life. Something bad is in that kid's head, Sam, something real bad." Red twisted the coffee mug in his hands and shuddered. "Sweet Jesus, I can still hear him screaming."

Sam studied him for a minute. Not much scared Red, but right now he looked as if he had seen a ghost. "Did he explain?"

"I didn't ask him to. We played poker instead."

Sam frowned at him, "Poker?"

Red smiled. "Even at three in the morning, the boy was sharp enough to take me for five bucks."

Michael wrote to Kevin and Beth and apologized for leaving without saying good-bye. He briefly explained about jail, Red, Nellie, Sam, and Wyoming.

Beth took her time responding but when she did, the simple words cut him to the quick.

I realize Silverpail is no teeming metropolis and the bar didn't have much to offer in the way of a future, but a ranch hand in Wyoming? Do you expect me to believe you have moved up in the world? Why won't you just tell the plain truth for once about why you had to run away from me?

Michael couldn't tell her the plain truth. He couldn't identify what that was yet. He only knew that someone like him didn't deserve her sweet love.

Kevin was much more forgiving than Beth. The next summer, he accepted a run that brought him north. His wife, Audrey, was nearly six months pregnant, but insisted on riding along. Kevin parked the rig in front of the Parker house and helped Audrey down before facing the red-haired woman on the porch.

"Good afternoon, Ma'am. My name's Kevin Thomas and this is my wife, Audrey. We're friends of Michael O'Mara. Does he still work here?"

At the mention of Michael, the woman's expression softened and she smiled. "You'll find him down in the barn, but I think your wife should wait here. We had a lot of rain last night and the path is pretty muddy. I don't think a pregnant woman should try it."

"Thank you."

Kevin started to open the door of the cab and started to help Audrey back inside when the woman called to them.

"Don't go back in there honey, come on inside the house. I just made a fresh pot of coffee."

Michael had been cleaning horse stalls for over an hour. He was hot and hungry with only one more to finish. He paused to wipe his forehead and saw the shadow of a man in the doorway.

"That you back there shoveling manure, Brooklyn?"

Michael walked toward the silhouette. "Kevin?"

"I took a run up to Jackson so I could drop by and harass you."

Michael smiled widely and pushed his hat back on his head. "It's good to see you."

"I tried to talk Bethie into coming. She said she'd rather spend her time watchin' grass grow then called you a whole string of bad words, I'd repeat them for you, but it would only guarantee my spot in hell."

"You don't have to tell me. I have it in writing."

Nellie prepared a garden salad, homemade bread, fried fish, and strawberry shortcake for lunch. Michael was the most silent member of the party. So far, he had told Nellie, Red and Sam little about himself and had no idea what the unpredictable Kevin might toss out for conversation. For once, Kevin didn't say much that made him uneasy.

After the meal, Michael saddled two horses and took Kevin for a tour. They paused on a high ridge and Kevin took a deep breath of the fresh air. "I tell you what, I love Texas, but this place is something special."

"I don't want to ever leave," Michael said.

Kevin gave him a long look. "If I can get my stubborn sister up here, she just might understand you a little better."

A storm brewed in the distance and lightning split the sky. Thunder rolled over the mountains and Michael's horse startled and swung to the right. After getting the strong animal under control, he addressed Kevin's statement.

"I'd appreciate it if you'd let it go, Kevin. She's better off thinking I'm a loser." He turned his horse and started toward the house. "Come on, let's get back before that rain gets here."

Michael glanced back over his shoulder to be sure Kevin followed. The big man was watching the approaching storm with fascination.

Michael reined his horse in sharply and turned in the saddle. "What are you doing?"

Kevin smiled benignly, "Looking at life from a loser's point of view."

Michael's horse jumped as lightning flashed again. "We don't have much time. That storm is moving in fast."

"Wait just a minute." Kevin pulled a camera from his coat pocket and aimed it at Michael. "Smile, cowboy, this one is for Bethie."

Beth was eating breakfast and thumbing through a magazine when Kevin tossed a packet of photographs on the table in front of her. She looked up at the packet then up at him.

"What's this?"

"Some pictures I took when Audrey and I went north."

Beth's mouth twisted in annoyance. "Michael?"

"Maybe one or two. And don't go sticking pins in them or anything. I'm gonna put them in my scrap book. I'll make you copies if you behave."

"I don't want to look at pictures of him."

Kevin grinned and opened the packet. He pulled out the best of Michael, tossed them on the table, and walked to the counter to pour a cup of coffee. Beth didn't pick any of the photos up, but allowed her gaze to drift over one in particular. Michael was on horseback, lightning flashing behind him. He looked so alive she expected him to speak.

Kevin looked over her shoulder and nudged her. "He makes a good looking cowboy, don't you think?"

"Why are you doing this to me?"

"Because you're the key to this whole thing. Mike has some stuff to work out and when he does, he's going to come looking for you. You'll just have to be patient."

Beth stared at the photograph, an old ache rising. "Is he dating anyone?"

Kevin rubbed his chin. "Does a sheep named Rosebud count?"

Beth grinned and picked up the next picture of Michael. He had draped an arm around Audrey's shoulders and his bright smile competed with those eyes for attention. Indeed, he looked healthy and peaceful, which both pleased and annoyed her.

"He looks happy, doesn't he?" She said.

"I don't know about happy, but he seemed more settled. Those people really seem to care about him."

Kevin watched the shift of emotions on her face and moved in for his best shot. "Maybe, you could ride along the next time," he said quietly, softening.

"I'll go when Michael invites me," she said, rising. She no longer had an appetite and threw away her breakfast.

Chapter 11

Sam placed brochures from the universities of Wyoming and Utah on the kitchen table in front of Michael. "We think it's time you thought about doing something with that fine mind of yours."

Michael couldn't look at either Nellie or Sam. He stared at the brochures until his vision blurred. His heart pounded in a full-blown panic attack. Without warning, these well-intentioned people had jerked him back in time. He didn't want to leave the security of the ranch.

Sam watched him carefully. "I know you're content for now, but you've got to think of your future."

"I don't want to leave," he said without looking up.

"This ranch is a business. I'm fifty-five years old and my way is outdated. Down the road, I'm going to need somebody who will be able to take care of the business properly, someone familiar with these new laws and all."

Michael finally lifted his head and looked at them. He had been with them for three years and knew they were fond of him, but this offer was more than he deserved.

Nellie laid a hand on his forearm. "First, we need to address the issue of high school."

Michael couldn't concentrate. The past was here in this cheerful kitchen, pulling at him. "High school?"

"Did you graduate from high school?" she said carefully.

He sat back in his chair and took a deep breath.

Sam patted his shoulder. "We only want what's best for you."

"That's right," Nellie agreed.

Michael looked from Nellie to Sam. They knew so little about him. He felt like a parasite. He took what he needed from these trusting, honest people and gave nothing in return.

He was unable to look them in the eye. "I've already completed a bachelor's degree."

He sensed, rather than saw, Nellie's quick glance at Sam.

"I guess you shouldn't have too much trouble with this little scheme of ours then." Sam said.

Michael nodded and closed his eyes, trying to slow the pounding of his heart. They meant well.

"What's wrong, honey?" Nellie asked quietly.

Sam immediately interceded. "Now, Nell, maybe he doesn't want to talk about that."

Michael shook his head and took a deep breath. "I owe you the truth."

"We never took you for a liar because you never say anything about your past," Sam shot back quickly.

Michael looked him in the eye now, as Nellie stood to get the coffee to refill their cups.

"I'm sure you tell us what's important," Sam said.

"There's so much…" Michael began, but the rest wouldn't come.

Sam's watchful gaze didn't falter. "We'll be here when you're ready to talk."

After listening to the ranching problems and listening to the business side for three years now, he understood Sam's plan was the best thing for them. He also understood he needed to go back to school just for himself.

Of course, there was the matter of his heart and Beth. Maybe, if he got a business degree he could have something to offer her after all. He weighed the issue for a week and finally told Sam and Nellie he would go.

After obtaining his transcripts from NYU, he applied to and was accepted into the joint law and business degree program at the University of Utah. For the first time in his life, he would be close in age to the other students in his classes.

Nellie's cousin, Ben, owned a small horse ranch northeast of Salt Lake City. The previous winter, Ben suffered a severe stroke that left him a prisoner in his own body. In addition to caring for Ben, his wife, Claire, managed the ranch alone. Nellie arranged for Michael to take care of their horses and help with Ben, in return for room and board.

Nellie made the trip with Michael in the old truck they gave him. They parked in front of an Easter-egg blue, white-trimmed, three-story Victorian mansion and Michael couldn't help staring. Nellie laughed at his expression.

"It's something isn't it? After Ben's first wife died, he nearly grieved himself to death. Then he met Claire and insisted on building this for her." She paused shaking her head. "I'm pretty sure Claire would have settled for something a little quieter, but she loves Ben and never said a word."

"It seems out of place."

"Oh, honey, that is putting it mildly. Oh, there's Claire." She waved at a woman approaching them in the distance and lowered her voice. "Now, don't be shocked, but Claire's a little younger than Ben."

Michael watched Claire approach from the stables. A cowboy hat shaded her face. She wore faded overalls with a loose work shirt. Still, nothing could hide the fact that this was a woman.

She hugged Nellie enthusiastically and they talked for a minute before Nellie introduced them. Claire looked up at Michael and the sunlight lit her face, revealing lively blue eyes that nearly matched her eccentric home. She pulled off her gloves and smiled at him, beautiful, confident, radiant even.

"Well, you're no runt," she said with a smile.

Michael didn't hear everything she said. His mind was spinning. Claire was beautiful.

"Excuse me?" He said.

"Aunt Nellie described you as a skinny kid," she explained.

"He is skinny. I feed him and feed him, but he doesn't gain an ounce," Nellie said.

During the three years in Wyoming, his body had stretched to a little over six-feet-two-inches and he weighed a lean one-eighty, hardly the criteria for a runt, but he didn't mind Nellie's description. Nellie was incapable of meanness. She fussed over him like he was her own and the mothering suited him just fine these days.

Claire glanced back to Nellie with a wry smile. "Time to get your eyes checked, Aunt Nell."

Though Nellie was only visiting for five days, she had packed three suitcases and an overnight bag. Claire and Nellie chatted while Michael removed the luggage from the truck.

The interior of the house was dark and cool. He took a minute, allowing his eyes to adjust to the dimness, before following Claire up the carpeted stairs. Michael wrestled Nellie's suitcases to the second floor, relieved when Claire directed him to put them in a room only a few more steps away. Claire showed him the stairs that led to his room on the third floor then rejoined Nellie, who was speaking to her cousin Ben on the first floor. Michael brought in his own bags and looked over his new living quarters on the top floor.

The entire third floor had been converted to an artist's studio for Claire. There were no dividing walls and the openness appealed to Michael's need for space. A bank of windows on the outer walls provided a panoramic view of the rolling pastures of the small ranch and the mountain valley beyond.

At one end of the long room was a large four-poster bed nestled halfway into a cozy alcove. Next to the bed were a table, lamp, and a vase with fresh flowers. Near a small side window, there was an oak table with one straight-backed wooden chair, a tall bookcase and another lamp. There was a small private bath with plenty of towels and more flowers. After hanging his clothes in a wardrobe, he walked to the big window at the far end of the room and smiled. The view was nearly as perfect as the one from the Parker ranch.

Michael found Nellie and Claire in what was once the living room. Claire's husband, Ben, lay on his back in a hospital bed and they stood on either side, looking at each other, talking over him.

Michael came to the end of the bed and connected immediately with the man's dark eyes. One thing was very clear to Michael, this man was angry. Michael looked away, around the room. There were photographs everywhere of Ben before the stroke. This frail invalid had once been a big, healthy man.

Claire introduced them and Michael met Ben's gaze again, letting empathy rise, understanding the purgatory of confinement.

"Hello, Ben," he said.

Ben's anger shifted to something easier. He kept the connection and grunted at Michael, blinking once.

Surprised, Claire looked from her husband to Michael and smiled. "He likes you."

Nellie patted Ben's hand. "He's a good boy, Ben."

Nellie kept talking to Ben, stroking his face soothingly, a touch that reminded Michael of Beth. He looked away from them and found Claire staring.

She cocked her head toward the door, "Want to help me with lunch?"

He nodded and followed her to the kitchen, which was oversized like every other room in this house. Claire went to the sink, turning her back to him. For the first time, Michael noticed the golden braid stretching down the length of her slender back. From there, his gaze wandered at will. Claire had some very inviting curves. He suddenly realized he was staring at her body and walked to the back door to have a look outside instead.

Claire began slicing tomatoes. "Aunt Nellie's very proud of you. Did you know that?"

Michael turned back, surprised to find her watching him.

"I hope it doesn't make her blind."

"Well," Claire laughed, "if she really thinks you're a skinny little boy, she's as blind as a bat."

"Why do you call her Aunt Nellie?"

"I've known her all my life. She was my mother's best friend. I always called her Aunt Nellie, even after I married Ben."

Michael watched her slicing haphazardly at a ham with a sharp knife and cringed. "Can I help with that?"

"Yes, please, before I slice off a finger. It's been so long since I had any company in this house, I'm nervous as a cat."

He went to the sink to wash his hands. "I imagine it gets pretty lonely out here."

"I used to love this place, the house, this property, and our horses. Ben was so alive. I was never lonely before." She sighed and a note of sorrow entered her voice, "Now, everything has changed."

Michael dried his hands and took the knife from her. "I noticed a lot of photographs around the house. Are you the photographer?"

"It's my newest passion. I'm an amateur of course. Ben built a studio and darkroom for me out behind the house. I'll show you later, if you'd like. I was just starting to make some money on weddings and portraits when Ben had the stroke. Since then I've been too busy just taking care of him and this place to do anything else."

"Well, now that I'm here to help, maybe you can start again."

"I hope so. Michael, I have to be honest. When Aunt Nellie told me she was bringing me some help in the form of a skinny little college kid I thought great, another responsibility." A little smile softened her features. "Now that I've met you, I think it might have been a blessing."

Michael settled into a tough routine. He rose before sunrise, fed the horses then drove in to Salt Lake and attended a full schedule. Afternoons, he worked with the horses and cleaned the barn. He helped with Ben's care before dinner to give Claire a break and studied long into the night.

One Saturday afternoon, three weeks after he arrived, a short, stocky block of a woman walked in the front door without knocking as Michael leaned over Ben. He straightened up as she tossed her coat in a chair.

She came closer, eyeing him, her face spreading into a humorless smile that did little to soften her tiny, mean mouth.

"I heard Claire hired some help," she said, offering a soft, fat hand. "I'm Ben's daughter, Naomi."

He couldn't extract his hand from her moist grip quickly enough. "Michael O'Mara," he mumbled.

"Where's Claire?"

"Picking up some prescriptions. She should be back soon."

Naomi turned her back and patted her father's hand, "Hi, Daddy. How are you feeling today?"

Michael excused himself and went to the kitchen where he was replacing the trap under the sink. He sat on the floor and stretched out on his back under the sink. Soon, he heard Naomi enter.

She pulled out a chair and sat at the table, watching him as she consumed a big bowl of Claire's blackberry cobbler. "I hear you're a college student."

Michael reached for a wrench and didn't bother to respond.

"How long have you and Claire known each other?"

"Three weeks."

"Did Claire tell you my father's a wealthy man?"

Michael pulled the wrench counterclockwise, forcing a stubborn ring to turn.

Naomi tapped his leg with the toe of her shoe. "Did she even bother to show you the house in the back where the help is supposed to live?"

The wrench slipped and Michael's hand collided with the sink. He slid out, rubbing the injured knuckles and biting back a nasty reply.

"I can't have this conversation with you now," he said.

Naomi dropped the spoon into the bowl with a noisy clatter. "You just understand one thing, my father's money is just that. When his body gives out and he leaves this world, that money is going to his children. So don't get your hopes up boy, the only thing you're getting around here is laid."

Michael got to his feet. "Lady you're way out of line."

Naomi's piggy-eyed gaze slid over his body in a slow appraisal that made his stomach turn. "I wasn't born yesterday," she said.

Michael grunted. "I can see that."

"You better watch your step. I can have you removed from these premises."

Michael tossed the wrench into the toolbox and headed for the door. "Go on and give it your best shot."

He walked back to Ben and paused before the makeshift sick room to take a deep breath before going inside. Ben's eyes found him immediately and looked toward the ceiling the signal to raise the bed. Michael pushed the button and kept his eyes on Ben, waiting for the cue to stop. Ben didn't give him one. Instead, Ben seemed to be examining him.

He released the button, "High enough?"

Ben grunted and Michael straightened the blankets.

"I'm here," Naomi said. "I'll take care of my father."

Michael turned toward the door, but she grabbed his sleeve.

"I want you out of here," she said. "My father's suffered enough. I won't have him put through the humiliation of what's going on between you and Claire."

Ben's mouth began to work, but he was unable to utter more than guttural noises. Michael knew Ben well enough to know his daughter's mean speech had upset him. Michael turned his back on the puffy-faced, bleach-blonde and leaned over, touching Ben's arm, looking him in the eye.

"It's all right, Ben. Claire's not here right now."

"He doesn't understand," Naomi said.

"Yes, he does. He just understood everything you said about his wife."

Naomi came over to the bedside and looked down at her father, "Daddy? Can you hear me?"

Ben's dark eyes flashed and he grunted at her. Naomi took a step backward, startled.

"Well…my goodness." She cleared her throat and pulled at the hem of her blouse, squaring her shoulders. "I'm sorry you had to hear that, Daddy, but someone has to look out for your best interests."

"Naomi, you're such an irrepressible bore," Claire said, entering behind them.

Naomi was speechless, for a minute or two anyway. Michael wanted to lend Claire his support, but knew his anger would get in the way, so he left them to their family squabble and went back to fix the sink drain.

Hours later, the wind howled outside the house, dragging what little concentration he had away from the work on his desk. He gave up and went downstairs.

Claire was in the living room, rooting through a stack of old records in the bookcase. Ben's dark eyes followed Michael from the door to his bedside.

Michael leaned over him. "Can you hear the wind out there? This is turning into a full-blown storm."

Claire swung around in surprise. "Do you know anything about classical music?"

He shrugged. "Some."

"Ben loves Chopin. I'm looking for this one record he used to play all the time, but I can't remember what it's called."

Michael knelt beside her and glanced at the records, finally pointing to one.

"How about the waltzes?"

Claire looked at him in surprise for the second time that day. He offered a little smile and stood again.

Claire tilted her head to the side, her eyes narrowing. "Do you play the piano?" she asked.

He glanced at Ben and the man's eyes seemed more alert than usual. "It's been a long time." Michael responded.

Claire hurried to the parlor grand in one corner of the room and lifted the cover from the keyboard. Michael looked from Ben, to the piano, to her.

Claire smiled. "Please? Ben just loves piano."

He sat in front of the keys and flexed his fingers. Claire hovered just to his right.

"Don't you need some sheet music?"

He stared at the keyboard and shook his head. He knew he didn't need to read the notes, he remembered more than he cared to. He warmed up by playing a few scales then let memory reign.

The vibration moved through the floors, through the walls, taking him to the place where the memory of heaven and hell converged. His fingers took over and the pedal rose and fell beneath his right foot in Utah while his spirit glided elsewhere.

He opened his eyes and watched Claire standing on the other side of Ben's bed, caressing his face. Michael remembered Beth's gentle hands and a sharp pain shot through him.

As the last note faded, Claire applauded softly. "You are an amazing creature."

Michael slowly lowered the cover over the keys and walked to the bed. Ben's dark eyes sparkled brightly.

He smiled at Ben. "I hope you forgive my rusty fingers."

Ben made a garbling sound and blinked once, his signal for pleasure.

Michael said goodnight and went back to studying. Tonight, he had crossed into old territory and made a discovery. No one was standing over his shoulder anymore waiting to criticize or punish if the piece wasn't perfect. No one owned this gift of music but him.

A soft rapping sound interrupted his work. Michael looked up from the books and papers spread over his desk.

Claire smiled at him from the head of the stairs. "I forgot to thank you for what you said to Naomi."

"Believe me, I didn't say half of what I wanted to."

Claire came all the way in and lifted one of the books on the desk, frowning at the title. "Law? I thought you were a business student."

He put down his pen and stretched his back. "It's a joint degree."

Claire smiled wistfully. "I wish I had more education."

"It's never too late."

"It is for me."

"Because of Ben?"

"I won't abandon him. I know it may be hard for you to see it, but Ben is a wonderful man and I love him."

Michael frowned at her. "I wasn't suggesting you should walk away from him."

"I'm sorry, I didn't mean to imply that you did. It's just that everybody seems to expect me to leave him. My love isn't for his money or things. Sick or well, I love him."

Once more, Beth crossed his mind. He looked away at the bank of windows, his voice barely audible. "Ben's a lucky man."

Michael had a long, sexually-charged date with a pretty graduate student and drove back to the ranch with sleep in mind. This hadn't been their first date and probably wouldn't be the last, but nothing would come from dating other women. His heart was still in Texas.

He entered the house a little after two and walked softly to Ben's bedside. Halfway into the room, he found Claire glaring at him from the sofa. He turned and went to the kitchen without speaking and she followed.

He didn't look at her while he poured a glass of orange juice. "Is Ben all right?"

"He's fine."

"Why are you still up?" He asked.

"You're later than usual."

Michael returned the juice pitcher to the refrigerator and faced her. "I didn't know you were keeping track."

"I'm not keeping track," she snapped.

"Claire, don't do this. I don't have the energy."

"Maybe you should stay home and sleep instead of catting around all night."

He swallowed the last of his orange juice, went to the sink, and rinsed out the glass. Claire turned and ran to her bedroom. Michael followed and knocked softly on her door.

"I think we should talk about this," he said.

"No."

He took a deep breath and stepped inside. She was sitting on the edge of her bed with a wad of tissues in her hand. Her eyes were red and puffy from crying.

"Get out of here!"

"Do you think it would be better to hire someone else to take care of the ranch?"

"No, of course not."

"Then what are we going to do?"

"I don't know." She slapped the mattress with her fist. "Damn it, I don't want all of those people to be right about me."

"They're not right about you and you know it," he snapped. He took a deep breath and softened his tone. "Claire, it's been almost two years since Ben's stroke. Two years of being alone, of being completely responsible for his care, isolated here in this house. This isn't a normal situation. Don't be so hard on yourself."

"What am I going to do? I sit here when you have a date and I get so jealous it makes me ill. I wonder if you're making love to the girl you're with. I lay down here at night thinking about you until I think I'll lose my mind. There are nights I wish I had the courage to get out of this empty bed, climb those stairs, and slip under the covers with you, just to feel a warm body next to mine."

"We can't do that," he said.

"Are you strong enough for the two of us?"

"I won't hurt Ben."

Claire crossed the room and peered up at his face. "I think Ben knows how I feel about you."

Standing before him, barefoot, her long hair flowing soft and golden, her warm body just inches from his caught him off guard. Vulnerable, her lips parted slightly, watching him.

"I can think of a thousand ways to justify wanting you," she said stepping close to his body.

The desire in her gaze poured liquid fire into his veins. The sensation made him weak and he nearly leaned over and kissed her mouth.

"When tomorrow comes you'd regret it," he said softly.

"No, I don't think I would."

He took a step back and she reached out, but before she could touch him he turned and started up the stairs, aware that she watched.

"Goodnight, Claire."

Chapter 12

In May, Michael took a bus to Silverpail where he caught a ride to Dallas with Kevin and Audrey. Beth was graduating from college and this seemed the perfect excuse to see her again.

Beth didn't say a word when he got out of the car. She stared up at him and tears filled her eyes.

Kevin wrapped an arm around her shoulder, "Surprise."

She didn't take her eyes from Michael's face. "I can't believe you came," she whispered.

They were only four feet apart and she was even more beautiful than he remembered. "Kevin wouldn't let me warn you," he managed.

Beth smiled and Michael couldn't keep his distance any longer. He wrapped his arms around her, lifting her off the ground.

She laughed and hugged him back. When he put her down again, she wiped her eyes and took a friendly swing at her brother. "I hate you, Kevin."

"Yeah, just like a kid hates Christmas."

That evening over dinner, Beth introduced Michael to her roommate, Andy. Michael knew she dated, but Beth hadn't mentioned sharing an apartment with the same guy for the past year in any of their letters.

After she introduced them, he stared down at Andy with a shock too significant to hide. Kevin had described Andy as "a long-haired, radical wanna-be." Michael wouldn't be so kind. Andy had stringy shoulder-length hair and a goofy smile. A pair of blue-tinted Ben Franklin glasses rested on the end of his pointy nose. He was a skinny, pale, runt of a guy, in baggy bell-bottoms and a tie-dyed shirt.

Stunned, Michael looked from Andy to Kevin, a little frown creasing his brow. Kevin couldn't stifle a laugh and Audrey nudged him with her elbow.

Andy extended a small hand. "It's a pleasure to meet you, Michael."

Michael accepted the hand, careful not to squeeze too tightly, the way he wanted to do.

After a long, uncomfortable evening with Beth and Andy, Michael climbed into the back seat behind Kevin and Audrey for the ride back to the motel and with a little prompting by Kevin launched into a lengthy, sarcastic assessment of Andy. When they pulled into the motel, he said goodnight and headed for the small bar on the corner.

Kevin found Michael sitting at the bar, a glass of dark liquid in front of him and eased onto the next stool. "Mind some company?"

"Suit yourself," Michael muttered.

"What are you drinking?"

"Bourbon."

Kevin shook his head. "Man, you're in one nasty mood."

Michael sighed. "I'm just tired."

Kevin laughed shortly. "You're just jealous."

Michael drew back, frowning at him. "Why would I be jealous of such a jerk?"

"Because he's sleeping with my sister and you're not."

Michael grunted and looked away at the late night news on the TV over the bar.

Kevin ordered a beer and slapped him on the back. "You know I'm right."

"Shut-up."

"Make me," Kevin laughed.

Michael's blue eyes flashed angrily, but the anger was with himself.

"You better be careful, Mikey," Kevin teased. "You've gotten much bigger, but you ain't big enough yet to admit you're wrong."

"I'm unsuitable for her, Kevin. It's that simple."

"You shouldn't fight nature. It will always drag you back to where you began until you get it right. Sort of like a dog chasing its tail."

Michael laughed shortly. "What the hell is that supposed to mean?"

"It means you're destined to suffer, because you deny the truth. You love Bethie and she loves you. It's one of those sweet, once-in-a-life time things. You're trying to run away from something predestined by nature."

Michael grinned at him. "Have you been reading fantasy books again?"

"Go right ahead and make fun of me. I'll just sit here, laughing at your misery, while you try to think up a real good reason for not going over there right now and kicking the ass of that little pinch-faced, tight-assed, troll-looking son-of-a-bitch and taking the princess to the castle where she belongs."

Michael groaned and picked up his glass, downing the contents in two gulps.

Kevin pointed his long-necked bottle of beer at his friend. "One of these days you'll see the light. I just hope I'm there to see you get down on your knees and beg my sister to forgive you."

"Broken record," Michael mumbled.

"Gets on your nerves, doesn't it?" Kevin elbowed him in the ribs. "Come on, old friend, let's get shit faced."

Kevin talked him into drinking boilermakers. Neither of them drank often and the price for such indulgence was the worst hangover of their lives.

Michael picked up a pair of cheap sunglasses in a gas station across from the motel before leaving for the ceremony. The sun had already increased his headache from the moderate to crushing level and he hoped the mirrored shades would save what was left of his brain. He took the chair next to Audrey and fought the sick feeling in the pit of his stomach.

"The weather is perfect." Audrey nudged him in the side. "Don't you think?"

Michael had no time to consider the weather. Perspiration covered his face and nausea was coming on strong. He groaned and closed his eyes.

Audrey laughed at him. "Are you going to make it?"

"She'll shoot me if I don't."

On the other side of Audrey, Kevin growled at them. "Must you people talk?"

Audrey shook her head. "You two are pathetic."

After the ceremony, Michael skipped the celebration with Beth and her boyfriend and took a cab back to his room where he turned the air conditioner up to maximum, stripped off his shoes and clothes and fell onto the bed.

Later that afternoon he was sleeping soundly when someone knocked on the door, each rap sounded like a sledgehammer hitting the door.

He rolled over and sat up as the knocking grew insistent, "Just a minute!"

He slipped on a pair of jeans and opened the door to a bright sunset. Tiny needles of light shot through his eyes, straight into his brain. He frowned in pain and shielded his eyes from the sun. Beth's silhouette backlit by the red light matched the fiery expression on her face.

"Well, may I come in?" Beth said.

He opened the door wider and stood back, waving her inside.

Beth picked her way through the clothes on the floor and rubbed her bare arms. "It's like an icebox in here. Will you turn that thing down?"

He turned the air conditioner off and left the door ajar then picked up his clothes and threw them in a chair while she talked.

"I can't believe you and Kevin showed up for my graduation with hangovers. Kevin says you were feeling down last night, so he went to a bar with you."

He walked past her and eased down on the edge of the bed. "Would you like to sit down?"

"I can't stay. I'll just say what I said…ugh, say what I came to say, and you can go back to sleeping it off."

Michael grimaced as new pain shot through his head. The meanest headache in the world was back.

Beth glanced around the room at his personal belongings. So much had happened in the last four years, then again nothing between them had really changed. A sudden wave of sadness filled her. She faced him again, “I feel exactly the same way about you as I did four years ago and I have no idea why.”

She took a deep breath and exhaled slowly before continuing, ticking off all the points of her dilemma on her finger tips. “You write at least once a month without fail. You always call on my birthday and Christmas, but beyond those measly efforts, nothing has really changed. I thought I was ready to move on then you show up for my graduation and turn me inside out again.”

He stared unblinking, not offering any kind of defense. Beth straightened her back and glared at him.

“So, when will you have your degree?”

“I will have my MBA next spring.”

She blinked a few times, digesting the obvious. “You already have your bachelor’s?”

He watched her warily. “Yes.”

She took a step toward him, speaking in a lower tone. “When did that happen?”

“1968.”

“The year we met?”

He nodded slowly, watching her, wary now.

Beth shook her head. “When did you graduate high school for crying out loud?”

“The year before Kennedy was shot.”

She peered closer at him, her eyes narrowing. “When you were twelve?”

He shrugged and sat forward putting his elbows on his knees.

She shook her head and threw up her hands. “I have no idea who you are.”

“Yes, you do, Beth.” He rubbed his face roughly. “Sometimes you know me better than I know myself.”

The statement was one of the most direct things he had ever said to her and it took her a moment to recover. He looked up at her and they stared across the four feet separating them, locked in understanding, lost for a moment. Beth, who always had more words than him, spoke first.

"After you finish school what are you going to do?"

He shrugged. "Go back to Wyoming."

"What's the point in getting all this education then?"

"I promised Sam and Nellie I would. They believe I can run the business better with a piece of paper to frame and an initial or two behind my name."

"Is there a girl in your life?"

"Girl?"

"Are you dating anyone?" She punctuated each word with mock sign language.

He stared and his face flushed in anger, but apparently a sharp comeback failed to spring to mind.

Beth allowed herself a quick assessment of his more mature body. He wasn't wearing a shirt and his jeans weren't buttoned at the waist where her gaze lingered on the brass button for a heartbeat too long. He was definitely growing up.

She had to look away, down, anywhere but at him. Spotting one of his shoes, she kicked it across the room. "I told you four years ago that I loved you." She kicked the other shoe which bounced off the wall. "I promised I'd wait until you resolved your problems. I always told myself you'd come back to me."

"Right," he snapped, "Tell that to Andy."

Beth could not repress a satisfied smile. "I hear you had quite a bit to say about Andy. Care to share your opinions with me?"

He laughed and shook his head, "No."

"Michael, I'm going to wait until you're finished with this college adventure of yours, but I won't wait beyond that. If you don't let me know what you want by that time, I intend to move on."

"Are you giving me an ultimatum?"

Beth pretended to think about it for a minute then smiled without any hint of humor. "Yes, I believe I am."

He leaned back on his elbows and smiled lazily, unknowingly giving her libido a tantalizing shock.

"You're so dangerous," she murmured taking a step back.

"What?"

Her eyes watered and she hurried to the door, but paused with her hand on the doorknob to look back at him. "Sometimes, when Andy makes love to me, I close my eyes and pretend he is this mythical blue-eyed hitchhiker I dreamed of when I was younger, but most of the time I'm just grateful that Andy isn't anything like that." She took a quick shaky breath. "You break my heart."

She turned and walked out, leaving the door wide open. It took a moment for Michael to move and when he did he ran, catching her only a few feet from the door.

"Beth, please don't give up on me. I'll be finished in a year."

"Then what?"

"Then...then I'll...if you want, we'll see where we go from there."

Against her best judgment, she softened a little, "One more year, Michael O'Mara."

Michael was outside talking to a buyer about several horses when a nurse called his name from the back porch. Near the end of summer Ben's condition had deteriorated and hospice had taken over.

He hurried to the house and the nurse held the screen door open. "He's gone," she said quietly.

Michael found Claire next to Ben's bed, gently stroking his forehead.

"It wasn't supposed to happen like this," she murmured. "He was better. I had so much hope."

One of her teardrops fell onto Ben's calm face and Michael touched her shoulder gently. "I'm sorry, Claire."

A few weeks after Ben's death, a thunderstorm rumbled down the plain. Thunder shook the house and rattled the windows, waking him. Michael opened his eyes, startled to find Claire standing a few feet away.

"What is it?" Michael asked.

She turned and ran from the room. Michael threw the covers back and started after her then on second thought turned and pulled the quilt from the foot of his bed. He found her sitting on the bottom step huddled close against the wall, her face in her hands. He sat next to her and wrapped the quilt around both of them. She snuggled next to him and he put an arm around her shoulders as she began to cry.

"I don't know how I'm going to go on with the rest of my life."

"One step at a time, just like always."

"Easy for you to say," she mumbled into his shoulder.

He could have told her he spoke from experience, but right now Claire's pain was too deep and feeling that pain was probably the very first step. So, he didn't argue. He held her and listened, eventually guiding her to bed like a child and tucking her in with a kiss on the cheek.

Michael nearly had his degree when he finally saved enough to purchase an engagement ring for Beth. Their letters and phone calls had increased over the past year and their relationship seemed finally on track.

The ring was a single stone, nearly a carat, the best he could afford. His plan was simple. Graduate, fly to Dallas and beg her to marry him. He planned to offer her a life together on a little plateau at one edge of Sam's ranch when he had enough money to build them a home. He showed Claire the ring that evening.

She examined the ring and smiled as she handed it back. "It's beautiful. When are you going to ask her?"

Michael snapped the box closed. "The minute I'm done with my classes."

"Do you plan to live in Texas then?"

He fingered the velvet box and shook his head. "When I've got enough money, I'll build a house on the ranch and tempt her with Wyoming."

"That could take years."

Michael nodded, "I've got it figured at three."

"Three years? This girl has already waited five. You're asking a lot, Michael."

"I know, but I can't ask her to live in the bunkhouse with Red."

"You don't have to live in Wyoming."

He looked at her directly. "Beth and Wyoming are the only two things I've ever been sure of."

Claire smiled at him. "Wow, you actually said it."

He blushed shyly. "I've never felt this good."

Claire rose halfway and kissed his forehead. "You deserve to feel good."

On his twenty-fifth birthday, Michael pulled into the entrance to Claire's ranch just as the mail carrier arrived. He leafed through the mail and found a letter addressed to him from Nathan B, Inc. He opened the letter and frowned as he read.

Five minutes later, he entered Claire's studio and stood near the table where she was marking photographs.

She glanced up curiously. "What's up?"

He held up the offensive piece of mail. "Did you enter photographs of me in a contest?"

"Oh, yeah, I forgot all about that. Did you hear from them?"

He sighed and leaned against the counter, throwing the letter on top of her photographs. "I'm a finalist."

She laughed. "Is this bad news?"

"Don't you think you should have at least asked me?"

"You need the money." She squeezed his face gently. "With this face, you were a sure thing."

He walked to the screen door and stared out. Claire picked up the letter and skimmed over the contents.

"They want me in New York by Friday," Michael said.

"Oh no, you'll miss your graduation."

He turned and leaned against the doorframe. "I'll miss a lot more than that."

"It's only for six weeks."

"Read the letter again. Six weeks is their option, not mine. I could be stuck in New York for over a year."

"So? Don't go."

"I have to. Unless I press charges against you for forging my signature, I'll be in breech of contract."

She winced at the news. "Oops."

"Yeah."

Claire folded her arms over her chest. "If you win, you'll get five thousand dollars. The money would give you a great start. I'm sure Beth will understand."

Michael shook his head and stepped outside. He knew Beth too well, she was through being generous.

Chapter 13

The plane banked left and descended through thick gray clouds bringing the New York skyline into view. Michael turned away from the window and took a deep breath. His heart was beating so loudly the guy next to him probably heard.

A flight attendant paused by his seat and smiled directly at him then turned to the man seated next to him. “Please, fasten your seatbelt, sir.”

The man buckled the belt and grinned at Michael, “You get her phone number yet?”

Michael managed a phony smile and looked away.

He might be an adult, there might be some semblance of control, but a wise man wouldn’t be on this plane. His false smile turned bitter. After eight years on the run, he had come full circle.

Michael finished a long session at the gym and took the elevator back to his hotel room. His photo shoot with Nathan B, Inc. was behind him. Now all he had to do was wait and pray they chose someone else. He had just opened the door to his room when the phone rang.

“Mr. O’Mara? This is Tanja Ehrlich with Nathan B. Mrs. Bartholmew would like to meet with you in her office.”

He glanced at his watch. It was nearly five in the afternoon, “When?”

“Now of course.”

At six, he walked into the plush office of the owner of Nathan B and approached Grace Bartholomew, the tiny, white-haired matriarch. She waved him to a chair opposite her desk.

"Would you care for a beverage, Mr. O'Mara?"

"Water, please."

She sat back a little, eyebrows lifting in surprise then turned to her assistant, "I'll have coffee," she said then looked back to the notepad on her desk.

Michael glanced around thinking the room more closely resembled a cozy, feminine den than a business office. Soft pastels and hidden lighting created a quiet ambiance. His assessment ended when a painting caught his eye.

"Are you a fan of Cassatt?" Grace asked.

He turned his attention to her and shrugged. "I've never seen a Cassatt before."

She glanced at the painting and smiled. "She expressed the mood of motherhood so well."

Michael didn't know much about the moods of motherhood. His mother had never shown much emotion for him either way. He sat back in the chair and hoped Mrs. Bartholomew would get to the point quickly.

She turned her attention back to her desk and slipped on a pair of half-glasses then pointed to a proof sheet. "You are exactly what I had in mind."

He exhaled and sat back in the chair. Grace looked at him over the top of the glasses. "I heard that" she said.

He offered her a little smile and shifted his weight.

Grace continued to stare. "I thought the news might make you happy."

"Staying in New York isn't my idea of a good time."

"Why? I should think it would feel like home to a Brooklyn boy."

The little hairs on the back of his neck rose and Michael sat straighter.

Grace didn't miss a thing. "I had you investigated."

His eyes narrowed and he sat forward a little. "Why?"

She shrugged and responded in French. "Now that I've found my golden goose, I must be careful. Tell me, why in the world did you walk away from MIT?"

Michael's restless feet made him stand. "I want out of this contract."

Grace looked up at him, nonplussed by his agitation. "Would you prefer to hear no in Latin?"

"I prefer to say good-bye," he said.

Her soft expression hardened. "Sit down."

He sat heavily in the chair as she continued.

"I'm not going to torture you with what I learned, Michael. In fact, I'm so pleased with you I'd like to add a bonus." She paused for a smile. "Of course, there's a catch. When you're not working on the ads, I want you to work with me. I'd like your input on some ideas I'm kicking around."

"Why?"

Grace looked him in the eye. "I never pass up a golden opportunity when it's laid at my feet."

Martin Edger knew he was late and should hurry. Yet he remained, frozen in place, staring at the fifty-foot billboard in Times Square. Just yesterday, a California beach beauty was up there, promoting a woman's right to smoke menthol cigarettes. Today, there was Michael O'Mara.

Over eight years had passed since Martin last saw him. Though the man in the ad exhibited a bright smile Martin had seldom witnessed, time hadn't diminished the unforgettable impact of the rare blue eyes.

A blast from a car horn jerked Martin out of his reverie. He glanced back to the billboard before hurrying away to catch up with his life. He didn't have time to consider the subject again until he went to bed and turned on the TV to catch the news. During a commercial break, he saw Michael for a second time that day.

A camera panned up the backside of a set of legs clad in a pair of neat-fitting blue jeans and stopped at a man's waist. Sexy music throbbed in the background. The camera zoomed in as a feminine hand slid into a snug back pocket of the man's jeans. On that pocket, stitched in bright silver letters with a blue background, was the company logo.

Martin nudged his wife, Gail. "Do you remember Michael O'Mara?"

Gail lowered a book and frowned. "Yeah, I was the social worker. Remember?"

"Watch this commercial. See if the guy looks familiar."

The camera moved up Michael's bare back and rested on his profile. Michael turned halfway and smiled at the woman. She looked over her shoulder at the camera and whispered, "Nathan B, always a perfect fit." Michael's arms went around her and he looked directly into the camera.

Gail raised her eyebrows. "Wow."

"I never thought I'd see him again. I've always been curious about how he turned out."

Gail sighed and went back to her book. "You can see how he turned out, Martin. He's tall, dark, and devastating."

"Well, I can see I'd better not invite him home to dinner."

Gail let the book drop to her lap. "Do you intend to contact him?"

"Do you see something wrong with that?" He already knew the answer, but didn't want to give in.

"He was your patient."

"He was much more. This kid..."

"Excuse, me, but I just saw him and he's definitely no kid."

Martin studied her for a minute. "Fine, this *man*, had a big impact on my life, Gail. I need to talk to him, that's all."

"You're playing with fire. Let it go."

Martin tried for weeks to get information from Nathan B with no success. Though she still didn't agree with his interest, Gail decided to help. She surprised Martin with tickets to a Nathan B fashion show.

Martin cringed at the thought of attending a fashion show, but wanted to end the mystery more. After spending forty-five restless minutes watching the women's parade, it was a relief when the lights dimmed and the familiar music used for the TV ads began.

"Ladies and gentlemen, our male collection."

Michael entered in a burst of music and light followed by other male models.

Martin studied the tall man walking down the runway and knew he was looking at Michael. His high cheekbones, strong masculine jaw, shoulder length hair, and sculpted body made him look like Adonis and Alexander the Great rolled into one. Given the history, most people would say he was lucky to be so handsome, but Martin knew the odds were high that underneath this perfect package was still a very injured soul.

When Michael reached the end of the runway, he scanned the crowd and offered a bright smile, until he saw Martin when the smile faltered for a heartbeat. He nodded to Martin before turning and walking back.

Gail nudged him, "It looks like he remembers you too."

Michael left the stage and the show went on with the parade of men's fashions. He was the last to emerge for the finale. He wore a black vest, jeans, cowboy hat, and boots. This time Martin noticed Michael's lithe, sexual grace.

"No wonder he has this job," Gail murmured.

An usher tapped Martin on the shoulder and smiled.

"Mr. O"Mara would like to know if you would join him backstage."

Gail rose and kissed Martin on the cheek. "I have some shopping to do. I'll see you at home."

"Don't you want to say hello?"

She shook her head quickly. "I think this situation is dangerous at any speed."

Martin stood in the doorway, overlooked in the backstage commotion. He watched as Michael finished buttoning the cuffs of a long-sleeved shirt and listened to the group of people around him. A small, silver-haired woman said something that drew his attention and he smiled genuinely at her, accepted a kiss on the cheek from a beautiful, slender model. Despite everything, Martin thought he still looked like he was ready to run.

In the center of the room, a middle-aged man was making a speech about his pride in their successful show. Martin stepped to the side thinking Gail was probably right, he shouldn't be here.

As others applauded the speech, Michael spotted Martin and hurried over, offering his hand. He towered above Martin's smaller frame.

"It's so good to see you again," Michael said.

"You too, I couldn't believe it when I saw you in those ads."

His smile grew thin, "A means to an end, Martin."

He turned to pick up a jacket from the back of a chair. "Lets get out of here and have some dinner, I'm starving."

He shrugged his shoulders into the jacket and Martin followed him to a waiting limousine. Michael gave the driver the address of a restaurant and opened the bar inside the car. "Would you like a drink?"

"I'll take a beer." Martin settled back in the soft leather comfort. "Is this your limousine?"

"It belongs to the company. Mrs. Bartholomew believes taxis are too tacky for a Fifth Avenue cowboy in designer jeans."

"I thought Nathan B was Nathan Bartholomew's company."

"She named the company after him. He's taken over as the designer, but believe me Mama's in charge."

Michael handed Martin a cold beer and poured bottled water over ice for himself.

Martin held up his bottle in a salute. "I'm happy you survived."

Michael smiled coolly. "Your medical attention wasn't that bad."

They settled into a soft leather booth and ordered drinks. After the waiter left, Michael sat back and looked across the table to Martin.

"Was that your wife sitting next to you?"

Martin nodded. "Her name is Gail. Actually, you're the reason we met. She was the social worker who helped me get you away from your parents."

Michael gazed around the restaurant. "Why didn't she come backstage with you?"

"She thinks this is wrong, that I'm crossing a line."

Michael nodded. "It's sort of a standard between us."

"You know, I've still got that airline ticket and the note you left on my table."

Michael laughed. "Why?"

"Well, at first, I hoped you'd change your mind and come back. Later, it became a symbol to me, a reminder, that no matter how much I wish it were so, some things are beyond my control."

The humor evaporated. For the first time that night Martin felt their old connection.

"No one is that powerful," Michael said soberly.

"So what have you been doing all this time? Did you ever go back to college?"

"I received an MBA from the University of Utah last year."

"Wow, you went in a totally different direction. Why business?"

He shrugged, "It seemed more practical."

"So why are you modeling?"

He sat back and sighed, "Again, practical reasons. It's only for a while, until I clear some debt."

"What about Utah? How did you wind up there?"

Martin listened and watched him across the table as he gave a breezy account of the last eight years of his life while only one moment of their history dominated his thoughts. He could still see Michael in that bloody bathtub, could hear that disheartened wail, a sound that had left an indelible imprint on him. Since that day, every time he looked at an injured child, he heard the lament of Michael's broken spirit.

The man sitting opposite him right now seemed confident, perhaps even happy on some levels. Yet, in bringing Martin up to date, he sidestepped the issue of the past and offered only a breezy account of the last eight years. Though Martin had hoped for the best, he understood Michael hadn't resolved the pain. His first impression was correct…Michael was still running.

The phone rang at a little after eleven on one of the few nights Michael managed to fall into a peaceful sleep. He rolled to the edge of the bed and grabbed the receiver, mumbling hello.

"Oh, my gosh, were you sleeping?"

Beth's voice snapped him back to the real world. He sat up in the bed and turned on a light as she continued.

"I guess modeling must be harder than it looks if it can put you to bed at eleven on a Friday night."

He grunted and rubbed the sleep out of his eyes. "What's up?"

"Can't I just call to talk?"

"You never call me, Beth."

She laughed softly. "Gee whiz, why do you think that is?"

"I don't know, but I'm certain it's all my fault."

"I had dinner and shared some excellent wine with a few friends tonight and on my way home I heard that song, "Crimson and Clover" and it reminded me of our last date. I guess the combination of wine and song made me feel sentimental."

The memory of that night made him smile. The knowledge that nothing had changed took the pleasure away.

"I wish things could be different," he said quietly.

There was a long pause from the other end. He could hear her soft breathing and closed his eyes, recalling every line of her face.

"Have you heard much from Kevin lately?" she said.

"Why?"

"He and Audrey are really struggling. He hasn't gotten much work in the past nine months. He tried to get a loan to start his own business, but he's already stretched to the limit. I wish I could help them."

"Everyone is having trouble with this recession. Nellie and Sam are thinking of selling off part of the ranch."

"Oh, no, how sad for them."

"They have been so good to me, Beth." He paused for a breath and debated on whether he should reveal the plan he had in mind. "How much does Kevin need?"

"He told me he tried to get a loan for twenty-five thousand."

"The land should be worth more than that."

"He won't put the land up for collateral because we own it together. I told him I'd sign over my share, but you know Kevin."

"I wonder if he'd take the money from me."

"Where in the world did you get that kind of money?"

"I didn't say I had it," he said, then added carefully, "but I could get it."

There was a moment before she responded in a very cautious and suspicious way, "How?"

"My contract with Nathan B is coming up for renewal."

On the other end she slammed something like a cabinet door. "Damn it!"

"Kevin saved my life, Beth. I owe him."

Beth was out of breath now and he realized she was moving around.

"He wouldn't want you to sell your soul to get it," she said.

"He doesn't have to know," he countered cautiously.

She sighed loudly. "So, this is my reward for being sentimental. I have to choose between my brother and you. I swear you are the most frustrating person I've ever met."

"Why don't you come here for a visit?"

"I haven't lost anything in New York."

He laughed softly, unable to keep the hurt out of his voice, "Thanks."

"Don't sign that contract, Michael."

There was a shift in her tone and he knew she wasn't making a request.

"I hate your ultimatums," he said.

"You better pay close attention to this one. I'm sick and tired of indulging unrealistic expectations when it comes to you."

Six weeks before his contract expired, Grace's lawyers offered a new one, which he rejected. Grace immediately demanded to see him in her office. Michael went into that meeting torn in two directions. He didn't want to ignore the needs of the others that had helped him so much, but staying meant losing Beth.

It might have been easier to stick to the plan of asking Beth to marry him if he hadn't spoken with Red that past weekend. Red told him Sam had seen a realtor and a piece of his property was now for sale, the same piece Michael always wanted to build a home on.

Grace eyed him from her side of the desk. "So, what will it take to convince you to stay?"

"You know I don't want to stay. I have a life to get back to."

Grace nodded and sat back in her chair, twiddling a pen in her hands. "Michael, you know Nathan has no interest in running this company. I'm 63 years old and frankly, I'm weary of the grind. I'm looking for capable hands to take the responsibility off my shoulders."

She rose and walked around her desk, sitting on the edge near him. "I'd like to offer you the opportunity."

"No."

Grace held out a legal document. "Have a look at this contract before you say that."

He gave it a cursory glance and handed it back. "I need to give this some thought."

"What will it take?"

He shifted his position and thought for a minute. He had worked closely with Grace over the past year, but didn't understand how that could possibly be enough to convince her.

"I don't have much experience, Grace. Why are you pushing this?"

"You're good, Michael. I like your approach and the fact that you do your homework. You're about as sharp as they come."

She picked up the contract and held it out to him. "I'm making a very generous offer. All I'm asking for is ten years."

His eyes widened in disbelief. "Ten years?"

Grace settled back in her chair. "All right, the length of time is negotiable. Let's talk money."

Beth's phone rang four times before she picked up. Her voice was never sexier than when she just woke. Michael smiled, savoring the moment of what might be their last conversation.

"Were you sleeping?" He asked.

"Well, yeah, since it's only eight in the morning here. Some people think that's normal on a weekend."

"I've been calling you all week."

"I went to New Orleans with some friends. Why didn't you leave a message?"

"I have some news that I should tell you directly."

Beth cleared her throat. "What?"

Her question was guarded. She always knew him so well. He swallowed hard. The next words were going to hurt.

"I signed the contract," he said. "I'll be staying in New York a while longer."

A long silence fell between them before she spoke. He wanted to rush in and beg her to forgive him, to explain his reasoning one more time, but he couldn't. She had a right to be angry.

"You consistently amaze me," she began.

Michael cringed, waiting for her to finish, but Beth knew her prey. She let him wait.

"You don't belong there and you know it."

She punctuated the sentence by slamming down the receiver.

Chapter 14

There were only two main offices on the twenty-third floor, Nathan Bartholomew's and Michael's. His was at the end of a long, carpeted hallway. There were windows on two sides of the room, a fully stocked bar, refrigerator, a small conference table, and an informal area with a sofa and a couple of chairs. Next door was his assistant's office and beyond that the office of their personal secretary. Nathan occupied the identical suite at the opposite end of the hall though he was seldom there.

Michael sat behind his desk in a roomy leather chair and swiveled around, looking west across the Hudson to the horizon. Staying here was playing with fire. Two thousand miles across that river was the only place he wanted to be.

The plan was to help Sam, Nellie, and Kevin then insure he was a rich man before he returned to Wyoming in five years.

All he had to do was stay focused on the goal and keep Beth off his mind. They hadn't talked since she slammed the phone down in his ear and he feared they were really finished this time.

Hearing voices in the hallway, he rose to investigate and left his regrets for a while. Amy, the receptionist, was trying a key in the door next to his office while a tall, leggy redhead in a business suit watched.

"I'm so sorry, Miss Walker," Amy told her. "The locks are all new."

"Maybe I should try," the redhead suggested impatiently.

Amy shrugged and handed over the key, then noticed Michael standing there.

"Mr. O'Mara, we were just trying to open Ms. Walker's door. Did you have a problem with your key?"

"No."

The redhead glanced at him, but quickly returned to the door, wiggling the knob in frustration.

"Amy," he said, "why don't you call security? They probably have a master key."

Amy nodded and hurried away. The redhead abandoned the key in the door and walked toward him. She offered her hand and smiled. "I'm Kelly Walker, your administrative aide."

Michael had chosen Kelly from a stack of resumes Grace sent his way. Because he had been tied up shooting commercials, Grace conducted the interviews for him. Kelly was nearly ten years older than he, with considerable experience in the garment industry. According to Grace, Kelly had worked for some successful men, but never received the recognition or promotions she deserved. Working as his assistant gave her salary a boost, but she was working with a novice and Michael expected some resentment since only Grace knew he intended to groom Kelly to move into his position in five years.

Michael shook her hand gently and stared openly at her emerald-green eyes.

"Is there a problem?" she asked sharply.

"Please, excuse me. I've never seen eyes like yours before."

Disarmed by his soft tone, she seemed to relax. "Well, what a coincidence. I was just thinking the same thing about yours. I hear that shade of blue is the natural color."

Michael smiled slowly. "Is that a problem?"

She laughed and seemed to relax a little, "Touché."

"Come with me, Kelly. I have a temporary solution."

She followed him inside his office where he opened a door that connected their offices.

She sighed, "Wonderful. Thank you."

"You're welcome. Go ahead and look around, I'm going to make a pot of coffee."

At first, most found Michael's manner disconcerting. He was a careful listener and chose his words carefully, often leaving little room for argument. The staff at Nathan B soon realized he made no rash or unplanned decisions. The new boss kept himself well acquainted with all phases of the business.

He cut his hair short, dressed in Nathan B jeans and long-sleeved, oxford button-downs. Except for work-related functions, he had no social life. He worked, six days a week. He left his apartment at six and walked four blocks to a gym for a rigorous workout. He arrived at the office promptly at eight forty-five every morning. He always stayed late into the evening and often took work home.

Within six months, he had expanded their base and tightened the reins and no one associated with Nathan B doubted that he was in charge.

One of the inducements Grace tempted him with was a penthouse in Manhattan. The apartment was within walking distance of the offices at Nathan B. She seldom used it anymore and signed it over to Michael for a nominal fee.

The elegant two-story apartment came with a private elevator. The foyer was bigger than his office. The entrance hall had a thirty-foot ceiling with a crystal chandelier. A polished black and white marble floor added to the depth. A curving staircase led upstairs to the master bedroom and two guest rooms.

To the right of the entrance hall was an all white living room and was once Grace's favorite room. Plush carpeting, overstuffed furniture, bar, lamps, even the throw pillows were white. French doors opened onto a balcony that provided a panoramic view of Central Park.

To the left of the entrance hall was a surprisingly masculine study with floor to ceiling bookcases and a wet bar. There was a dining room with seating for twenty, the kitchen, and servant's quarters. Michael used only the study and master bedroom and seldom ventured near the kitchen.

The bonus he received for signing the contract had been very generous. Getting Kevin and Sam to accept the money was difficult, but he finally persuaded each man to take the money, Kevin as a loan and Sam toward the purchase price of the land.

Michael turned an intense focus to the task of making this time in New York pay, pursuing money the way he had pursued the scholarship to MIT. He slept little and worked every day. Regret over Beth rode his shoulders every step of the way.

Occasionally, Martin talked him into spending an evening with him and his wife, but even these pleasant evenings seemed intrusive.

One Friday afternoon, Martin called to remind him about a dinner date just as he was about to attend a meeting in the boardroom.

"I didn't forget," Michael said. "I'll see you at seven. I'm sorry, I have to run, I'm late for a meeting..."

"Wait, don't rush off. I have another purpose for this call. Would you have any objections if we brought a friend along?"

"Of course not. Martin, I'm sorry, but I have to go. I have a roomful of people waiting for me."

"Gail thinks it's time we pried you out of your cocoon."

Michael laughed. "Oh, I get it, your friend is a she."

"Yes, and she's beautiful, if you go for that petite, exotic type."

"I don't have time for women."

"Damn it, Michael. You need this. You have no social life. You live like a man obsessed."

"I am a man obsessed."

Kelly appeared in the doorway with the proposal he needed for the meeting and he waved her inside as Martin continued.

"Are you telling me you don't want to come now?"

"No, Martin, I'll be there."

"Good. I'd hate to have to come over there and wrestle you into the car."

Michael flipped through the pages of the document and his mind drifted from the conversation.

"One more thing," Martin said, drawing him back, "Gail wanted me to remind you to wear a suit. The restaurant is fancy."

He frowned and circled a paragraph on the third page. "I'll see what I can do."

At five-thirty, he looked through the closet adjacent to his personal bathroom at the office and cursed his forgetfulness.

Kelly poked her head around the corner. "What in the world is the matter with you?"

"I'm meeting some people for dinner at seven. I promised to wear a stupid suit and I don't have one here."

"Nonsense. This is Nathan B remember? It's what we do and I believe they are well acquainted with your measurements."

He glanced at his watch and frowned. "It's already five-thirty. It will take forty-five minutes just to get to the restaurant."

She laughed at him, "My goodness."

He frowned at her. "What?"

"Do you have a date?"

He shook his head. "No."

"Let me call downstairs," she said hurrying away. "We'll have something ready in thirty minutes."

He arrived only fifteen minutes late. He occasionally frequented this restaurant for business occasions and the maitre d' recognized him immediately and showed him to Martin's table.

Martin tapped his watch and smiled, "Nearly on time, for once."

"I got lucky with traffic," he said, bending to kiss Gail's cheek.

"Thanks for wearing the suit," she whispered, then turned to the woman on her left. "Nicole Edmunds, this is Michael O'Mara."

Nicole smiled up at him and her dark eyes sparkled in the candlelight. She wore a simple black dress with a scooped neckline. Her dark hair fell around her shoulders in natural curls so smooth and shiny they resembled satin ribbons.

"It's a pleasure to meet you," she said, in a surprisingly husky voice. She offered a small hand and he grasped it carefully, as if she were fragile.

"The pleasure is mine."

He ordered a scotch on the rocks and took a seat opposite Nicole. Martin started to speak, but Gail touched Michael's hand, demanding his attention.

"Nicole's meeting with some broadcasting people on Monday about a nationwide television news show. We convinced her to come down early and spend the weekend with us."

Michael glanced at Nicole, who smiled uncomfortably and reached for a glass of ice water.

"Why don't you come out tomorrow, Michael?" Martin said on cue. "We plan to barbecue some steaks."

Michael took his drink from the waiter and swallowed half of it. This had been a long week and it looked as if Martin and Gail were going to make the evening tedious.

"You don't have to be there until four," Gail said.

"Maybe we could go to that new dance club out by the lake," Martin suggested with a smile, "Might as well make a night of it."

Michael faked a yawn then smiled at Nicole. "Aren't they cute when they're like this?"

Just after they ordered dinner, a business associate stopped by the table to speak to him. Michael stood and spoke briefly with the man about a recent Nathan B acquisition. The man apologized to the others for interrupting their meal and left.

"You know David Amburg, I'm very impressed," Martin said when Michael returned to his chair. "I didn't know you traveled in those circles."

Michael shrugged, "Just business, Martin."

"I can't tell you how many times I've tried to get an appointment with him."

Surprised, Michael focused on him, "What for?"

"I need some help with an idea of mine."

"Could you be a little more specific?"

"I want to start a home for abused and runaway kids. You know, like a safe house."

Michael took a swallow of his drink and glanced around the restaurant. "What do you want David to do?"

"I need financial backing and guidance. His commitment to helping children is incredible. With his help, I could pull all this together. Do you think you can get me in the door?"

"Martin," Gail interrupted, "I don't think your being fair to Michael."

Martin thought that over for a minute, then nodded and looked back to him. "She's right. I'm sorry."

"I'd be happy to see what I can do," Michael said then turned to Gail and stopped her protest. "It would be my pleasure."

Two other people stopped by to speak to Michael before they finished dinner. Though Michael was gracious, his patience was wearing thin.

"And people wonder why I stay home," he grumbled.

Martin laughed and patted him on the back. "Being famous and sexy is such a burden."

Michael looked across the table to Nicole. "I'm sure you know how it feels."

"Sorry," she said, with a smile. "I'm not famous and sexy either."

Martin interrupted impatiently. "So, Michael, are you free tomorrow?"

Michael shook his head. "I'm shooting a commercial. It's the only time I can work it in."

"You won't be doing that all day, will you?"

"We'll do it until the director is happy. I can't say how long that will be."

They finished dinner and Martin suggested they go to a nightclub. After a few drinks, Martin and Gail joined the crowd on the dance floor and Michael turned to Nicole.

"Would you like to dance?"

"I don't care for this song. Thanks anyway."

He nodded and took a sip of his third drink then glanced at his watch.

"What time do you have to get up in the morning?" she called over the music.

He held up four fingers.

"Wow, you probably need to go don't you?"

He shrugged and looked to the dance floor, watching Gail and Martin. Sleep still didn't come easy. He was lucky if he managed five hours a night. The next song was a slow ballad and Nicole tapped him on the shoulder.

"I'll take you up on that offer now if you're still interested."

On the dance floor, he took her hand and she moved close. Michael breathed in her spicy perfume and his much ignored libido stirred to life. He wanted to pull her closer, feel her body against his, lay his cheek on her soft hair and more. He caught Gail's watchful gaze from across the dance floor and smiled.

One week after discussing the safe house with Michael, Martin received a call from a man who introduced himself as Barry Meier, a financial consultant hired by Mr. O'Mara. He asked when it would be convenient to meet for a discussion regarding the safe house.

"I think I'd like to talk with Michael first," Martin said.

"Mr. O'Mara won't be directly involved in this Dr. Edger. He prefers to supervise the funding and leave the rest to you and me."

"Funding?"

"The project Mr. O'Mara has in mind won't rely on donations. The foundation will have a private income. Mr. O'Mara has placed substantial opportunities at our disposal. Dr. Edger, I've had a good measure of experience in this area..."

Martin found it difficult to concentrate on the rest of the conversation. After concluding the call, he leaned back in his chair, angry with his enigmatic friend. How typical of Michael not to call and explain. This habit of excessive restraint frustrated Martin. He lifted the receiver and took his anger out on the keypad as he punched in the private number to Michael's office. When he asked to speak to Michael, his call was transferred to Michael's assistant.

"I'm sorry, Dr. Edger, Mr. O'Mara is out of town."

"When will he be back?"

"Not until the twenty-second. Is there a message I can relay to him?"

Martin bit back his anger. "Please tell him to call me when he has time."

Late one evening, two months later, Michael finally returned his call.

"So," Martin began. "You're still alive. I hadn't heard from you in so long, I thought you'd vanished again."

The master of the avoidance kept his tone level. "I called you in June, but your secretary said you were on vacation. Where did you go?"

"Disney World."

Michael laughed at Martin's flat tone. "And did you have fun?"

"The girls are too young to appreciate something like that, but Gail insisted. It appears Megan is terrified of Mickey Mouse. So, where have you been? Why were you traveling all summer?"

"Promotional stuff. I've been to San Francisco, LA, Denver, Chicago, Boston, New Orleans, Dallas, and so on."

"Sounds hectic."

"Exhausting is more like it. I understand you've been trying to reach me."

"I wanted to thank you for the financial help and sending Barry Meier my way. He's fantastic. I think I just might realize this dream because of you, Michael."

"You're welcome."

"I don't understand why you don't want your name mentioned though. What you're doing is so incredible…"

"I appreciate your respect for my privacy," Michael broke in softly.

"Sorry, I forgot the golden rule. Never get personal with Michael O'Mara."

"It's not that."

"What are you afraid of?"

"Saddle sores, prostate cancer, male pattern baldness…"

"I'm trying to have a serious discussion here."

Michael groaned, "Why is this such an issue with you?"

"People will think you're doing a wonderful thing."

"Martin," he said the name slowly, as if summoning patience. "I refuse to find my life splashed across the entertainment section just to make you happy."

"You know that's not what I want."

"I don't like people prying into my past."

"That's because you still believe you were responsible. Michael, you were an innocent kid. What happened was not your fault."

There was silence from the other end for nearly a full minute and Martin knew he had crossed the line by bringing up the past.

When Michael spoke next, his tone had a definite edge. "I don't think I've ever said thank you for everything you did for me."

"Yes, you did. Don't change the subject."

"Well, I'd like to thank you again."

"Michael…"

"I mean it, Martin. Without you, I'd probably be dead instead of an adult with a mind of my own. You have noticed that, haven't you?"

"All right, already. I'll leave you alone. Can we move on?"

"Please."

"Do you remember Nicole, Gail's friend from Syracuse?"

"Tiny, long black hair, big brown eyes, incredibly sexy voice?"

Martin laughed. "Well, I guess you do. She's finally settled here."

"She's living with you in Jersey?"

"No, of course not, you know what I mean. Anyway, we're having a Labor Day barbecue and I thought you might enjoy coming out."

"And what does Nicole have to do with this?"

"She'll be here. This isn't a date, just a little nudge."

"I get it."

"Don't even think about telling me you're going to be busy. I don't want to hear it."

"As a matter of fact, I'm leaving the day after for vacation, but I don't have any plans Labor Day."

"Fantastic. You know, Gail is sure you two are perfect for each other."

"What time should I be there?"

"Why not come out Sunday night? We can hit the course early and shoot eighteen holes before the barbecue."

"I can't. I have to attend a fundraiser with Grace on Sunday night. Besides, you know I don't play golf."

"All right, party pooper, be here at one then."

Michael was the last to arrive at the barbecue and had just said hello to Nicole when Martin pulled him away for more introductions. After the meal, the men gravitated to a round table near the pool where Martin's brother-in-law launched a passionate discussion about a current scandal in local politics.

After a while, Michael went to the bar just inside the open doors of the house and poured himself the first drink of the day. He caught Nicole staring and started over, but Martin put a hand on his arm, demanding he lend an opinion to the argument at the men's table.

Bored with the topic and Martin's insufferable brother-in-law, Michael wasted no time. He swallowed part of his drink, took a deep breath then told them the mayoral candidate they were discussing was neck deep in financial mismanagement of several building contracts and an indictment was likely.

Martin looked at his brother-in-law, "See? I told you, Chuck."

Chuck ignored Martin and squinted at Michael suspiciously. "How do you know Deluca is involved? I haven't heard a thing about him."

Michael shrugged and took another swallow of his drink. He didn't want to discuss politics. He hated talking about politics. He said so from the onset of the debate, but they insisted on drawing him in anyway.

"You act as if this doesn't concern you." Chuck sneered at him, slurring his words. "I suppose you're too busy prostituting yourself in those jeans to worry about such petty issues."

Michael stood reflexively. "It is time for me to go, Martin. I'll talk to you when I get back from vacation."

He started to walk away, but Gail stopped him. "Would you mind giving Nicole a ride back? She doesn't know anyone here other than Martin and I and she'd probably jump at the opportunity to leave." Gail gripped his forearm and kept her voice low. "It will be good for both of you."

"Yes, Ma'am," Michael said and kissed her cheek. "I'll go ask her."

"You're amazing! All it took was a couple of shoves, a few blows to the head, some skywriting, telegrams, phone calls, and writing on the wall for you to get the hint and take some initiative." She grinned and pinched his cheek. "That's what I love about you, you're so quick."

Michael opened the car door for Nicole and offered to put up the top on his black convertible, but Nicole insisted she would enjoy the fresh air and quickly braided her long hair. He made polite, small talk as he wove through the side streets toward the interstate and merged with unusually light traffic. He was driving a conservative fifty-five when she tapped his shoulder and shouted at him over the wind.

"Do you always drive this slowly?"

Michael glanced her way and grinned. "Want to go faster?"

She laughed. "I'm sure you didn't buy a Porsche so you could drive like my grandmother."

Michael hit the gas, shifted, switched lanes, and passed a few cars before shifting again. Soon they were riding the outside lane, doing ninety. At ninety-five, she covered her face. Laughing, Michael slowed down to sixty.

Nicole lowered her hands and laughed. "Now, it feels like we're standing still."

He shrugged. "Do you want to drive?"

"Drive? This car? In New York? No way."

"Why not? I'm insured," he said, grinning. "Besides we're still in Jersey."

"Thanks for the offer, but no."

When he parked in front of her apartment, she invited him to join her for a cup of coffee at an Italian restaurant on the corner. The doors to the restaurant were open and the smell of pizza drifted down the block. There was a jukebox playing fifties hits and a sprinkling of customers scattered at the booths and tables.

Nicole gave her order to their teenage waitress and the girl turned her attention to Michael.

"Oh my gosh!" she gushed. "You're that blue jean guy, aren't you? I don't believe this."

She turned and ran to the back of the restaurant to tell her mother and older sister who stared at him through a pass window. Michael placed the menu between the garlic shaker and the napkin dispenser then sat back in the booth.

Nicole studied him with an amused expression. "You really hate being recognized, don't you?"

He nodded. "I wish I never did the ads."

"You didn't have to do them. They didn't threaten to break your legs or anything, did they?"

"Let's just say I owed a friend."

"So friendship was your motivation for prostituting your body," she said.

One eyebrow lifted and he stared hard. "Excuse me?"

"That's what Chuck said wasn't it?"

"Chuck's opinion doesn't count."

"It must have counted for something, you left the party."

"Ah, so you're a psychologist as well as an eavesdropper." He shifted his position and looked around the restaurant.

"Okay, so I eavesdropped. I was bored with the women's conversation about preschool and boob jobs. How did you know that about Deluca anyway?"

He looked back to her and didn't bother to veil his annoyance.

Nicole winced and sat back in the booth. She took a sip of her ice water and offered him a little smile. "I'm sorry, the question was from my journalist side."

Michael looked out the window to the street and watched some children play on the sidewalk. The neighborhood resembled the street in Brooklyn where his parents lived, suddenly reminding him of all that was irreversible.

Shrugging off his melancholy, he turned back to Nicole. "How do you like living here?"

"I'm getting used to it, but, to be honest, I think I'll always like a smaller city. Why don't you tell me about living out west? I've always wanted to visit that part of the country."

They talked for almost two hours, forgetting the time and then he walked her to her door.

"I'd invite you inside, but my place is a mess."

"That's all right. I'm leaving on vacation tomorrow and I need to go home and pack. Would you mind if I called you when I get back from my trip?"

Nicole smiled broadly. "Let me give you my number."

She opened her purse to search for pen and paper, but found neither. "Let me get a pen." She turned to go inside, but he stopped her with a light touch on her arm. Nicole turned, now two steps higher they were eye level.

He smiled, "I won't forget," he said.

Chapter 15

The moment Michael stepped off the plane in Wyoming he breathed easier. He needed the comfort of his real home to make the next stretch in New York tolerable. He rented a car at the airport in Jackson and used the drive to unwind and set the pressure of New York aside.

Sam still brought the cattle down from the summer pastures to the lowlands on horseback. Michael saddled a big bay and lent a hand for the first time in years. Though his body was sore after twenty miles in the saddle, the uncomplicated life under the wide-open sky was just what he needed.

After nearly two weeks with Nellie, Sam, and Red, he forced himself to leave and flew to Dallas. He rented a car at the airport and drove to Silverpail for a visit with Kevin, his wife, Audrey, and their three sons.

After dinner, Michael and Kevin sat on the front porch steps and Audrey settled on the porch swing to feed their three-month-old. Kevin rambled from one subject to another and Michael only half-listened. Being there reminded him of Beth and the nearly acute pain resurfaced. Surely, his heart would stop longing for her one of these days. Their last conversation still haunted him on many long, lonely nights, but being here was almost more than he could tolerate.

Kevin finally drew his attention by casually mentioning Beth's plan to marry the next spring. He felt Kevin's watchful gaze and didn't respond at first. Finally, he shifted his position and cleared his throat before he spoke.

"Have you met him?"

Kevin smiled, obviously enjoying Michael's discomfort. "She brought him up a few weeks ago. His name's Drake. What kind of name is Drake? I'll tell you what…it's a damned duck name."

"Is Drake his last name?"

"Hell no, that's his first name. The last name is Blake."

Michael grinned, "Drake Blake?"

"Isn't that stupid? I can't wait to meet this guy's parents. I bet they're brain surgeons or nuclear physicists."

Michael stretched his long legs in front of him and let a few minutes go by while he digested the news of Beth marrying someone else. "Do you like him, Kevin?"

"He seems all right, I guess. He's not right for her of course. The right one came along years ago. Unfortunately, he turned out to be slow in the head."

"Kevin," Audrey said. "Michael's our guest. You must be polite."

Kevin puckered up and aimed a kiss at her. Behind his back, he flipped Michael the bird.

"You know," Kevin began, after a few minutes of silence. "I think all those people in New York would be amazed if they knew the real you."

Michael expected another joke and waited for the punch line as Kevin continued.

"Until you stumbled near Wyoming and found a home, you were one lost kid. When I saw you on that ranch, I knew you found exactly where you belonged." Kevin sighed deeply. "Now, you've gone and made a mess out of everything by taking this job. I have to say you're not quite the genius everybody thinks you are. Then again, Beth could be right, maybe you're just short on common sense."

Audrey shook her head and stood with her sleeping baby. "You're like a broken record Kevin. Let it go, for heaven's sake."

Michael held the screen door open for her and noticed a car kicking up dust on the road leading to Kevin's house.

Kevin's face spread into a broad smile. "Well, speak of the devil."

Beth jumped out of the car and hugged her two older nephews with enthusiasm.

"Hey, Bethie!" Kevin picked her up and swung her around.

She wasn't prepared to see Michael standing there watching her. Damn the man, he looked more appealing than ever. This relentless attraction angered her.

"I wouldn't have come, if I'd known you were visiting," she said.

Kevin's oldest son tugged on her arm. "Are you and Uncle Michael getting married?"

Beth and Michael gasped in unison then looked to Kevin who just shrugged. She looked from her brother to Michael for a long moment then knelt in front of her nephew.

"No, honey, Michael and I are never going to be more than friends."

Kevin patted Michael's chest, right over his heart. "That one hurt, didn't it?"

Beth kept her attention on her nephews. "Why don't you boys carry my bag in the house? I brought you each a present."

While Kevin's boys fought over her bag, Beth turned to Michael. "Don't I even get a hug?"

Michael flinched, as if her sharp tone had wounded him, but stepped forward and wrapped his arms around her. The quick, warm crush of his body against hers twisted her insides into knots.

Beth pulled away and squinted up at him. "How's New York?"

"The same."

"The same as what? The same as Texas, the same as Wyoming, or the same as what you ran away from when you were seventeen?"

Michael stepped back and there was a snap of anger in his eyes.

"It's good to see you too," he said.

She took a step closer and looked up at him, "Liar."

She pushed passed him and went inside.

Beth found it difficult to sleep. Knowing Michael was just down the hall on the old sofa bed was more than she could tolerate. He might be the basis of a lot of her misery, but she wanted to be near him, look at him and hear his voice one more time.

She dressed and opened the door. Light filtered down the hall from the living room and she realized she wasn't the only one who couldn't sleep. She paused at the edge of living room, watching him study the loose papers in his lap.

He didn't hear or see her approach. She sat nearby on the sofa bed and watched him for a few minutes before speaking. "I see you still don't sleep very much."

Slowly, Michael raised his head and looked at her, propelling Beth back to the moment she started to fall so hopelessly in love with him.

Her arms ached from resisting the need to reach for him, to wrap around him. She wanted to kiss his soft mouth one more time. She needed a little honesty at this point. Life was suddenly out of focus. She had said yes to another man and here she was pining over the unobtainable, again.

She had no idea what he found so fascinating, but he just stared at her, seemingly speechless. She had undone the braid and her hair hung loose over her shoulders to her waist. She wore a man's large Dallas Cowboys T-shirt, white shorts and thick socks, comfortable, but hardly alluring attire. Still there was something deeply sensual about his appraisal and she lashed out at him again.

"Cat got your tongue?" she snapped.

He turned his attention back to the proposal, but this time his gaze didn't move over the page and she understood he stared at the pages to keep from looking at her.

"Did Kevin tell you I'm getting married?"

"Yes," he said finally.

She sighed loudly, "Would you rather be alone?"

He put the papers aside and rubbed his eyes roughly. "I hope you're enjoying making this so difficult."

She frowned, "I'm making this difficult? How dare you."

"I didn't know..." he began, then lost his voice and stopped to clear his throat. "Oh, God, never mind."

He got to his feet and she laughed outright. "What's the matter with you?"

Michael didn't reply. He didn't need to say a word. His expression said it all. Nothing had changed. Beth stood on the bed and walked to the edge closest to him, without breaking eye contact.

"Tell me," she said quietly.

He looked away, but Beth cupped his chin in her hand and turned his head back, forcing him to face her. He took in a deep breath and surprised her by turning his cheek into her hand, stealing a caress.

Tears stung her eyes. "I need to get on with my life," she said.

She had meant that as a statement, yet the words sounded like a plea. He blinked a few times, opened his mouth, but the words she needed to hear failed to make the journey from his brain to his mouth.

"Michael, I can't go through the torture anymore. Even now, you refuse to tell me how you really feel and what you want. It's not fair."

He nodded quickly. "I know."

Beth punched the solid muscle of his upper chest with her fist. "Don't stand there and tell me I know, like this is beyond your control. For God's sake, I can see how you feel, it's written all over your face."

She drew closer and though their bodies didn't touch, she felt his warmth. Every time he allowed her to get this close, her senses were magnified. Again, her mind registered the clean, masculine scent of him. His soft, irregular breathing kicked her heart into overdrive.

"Is it really worth all this effort?" she said. Her tone dropped to no more than an entreating whisper. "Are you satisfied? Do you believe I'm happier because of your sacrifice?"

She put her hands on either side of his face and looked deep into his eyes. "Why are you convinced you're not worthy of love?"

A small, wounded sound escaped his lips and for an instant, the resistance in him faltered. His eyes filled with tears and he closed them tightly, muttering a curse. Beth tried to wrap her arms around him, but he turned and walked out the front door.

Michael tried to resist the responsibility for Beth's pain by making her to blame. After all, she was the one who was engaged. She probably never really loved him anyway. She clung stubbornly to the ideals of first-love syndrome like they were still teenagers. Besides this particular stubborn streak, she always slapped him with questions he could never answer or she examined the dark corners of his life with that acute insight of hers. Beth Thomas had turned into a restless, demanding woman.

In the end, no counterfeit logic or righteous indignation saved him. He loved the owner of his heart; he would always love her.

One week after returning to work, Michael called Nicole for a date in an effort to get Beth off his mind. Nicole suggested they meet for dinner near her office. Michael arrived ten minutes early and waited another ten minutes before she appeared. The moment she walked in he felt like someone had turned on a bright light. He hadn't noticed how much Nicole resembled Beth until that moment. This relationship was over before it had a chance.

Over the course of dinner, Nicole unintentionally changed his mind about their chances together. She informed Michael that she didn't intend to let her heart rule her life. She believed most women compromised their needs for the men in their lives. For now, her career would remain foremost in significance. She seemed perfect for the short-term future he had in mind. When the time came for him to return to Wyoming, there wouldn't be any heartache.

Restlessness and dissatisfaction had been his constant companions for most of the holiday season and he couldn't wait to put these days behind him. Each day he woke up longing for specific changes and every day he shut those needs down. This was the only approach he knew that would help him survive the intolerable. By the time New Years Eve rolled around, he was walking on an even thinner edge.

He spent the first half of New Years Eve attending a dinner party at Grace Bartholomew's mansion on Long Island. Later, he headed back to Manhattan for a party hosted by Barry Meier, the business consultant he hired to assist Martin. He immediately spotted Martin and Gail and joined them.

Martin grinned crookedly and slapped him on the back. Obviously, he had indulged in a little champagne.

"Hey, old friend, where have you been all night?" Martin said.

Michael kissed Gail's cheek and gave her a quick hug.

"A dinner at Grace's," he said.

"Where's Nicole?"

"London."

Someone tapped his shoulder. Turning, Michael found himself nearly eye-to-eye with a tall woman in a short red dress that clung to her tanned, voluptuous body and showcased her long, shapely legs. Natural curly blonde hair fell about her shoulders. She flipped her hair over one shoulder and smiled.

"Baby you look good enough to eat," she drawled. "Aren't you that blue jean guy?"

Michael couldn't help smiling. She leaned forward and kissed his mouth quickly, pulled back only inches and stared up at him seemingly surprised.

"Sugar," she whispered, then kissed him again on the mouth. This time Michael responded in kind. She pulled back slowly, playfully batting her eyelashes, and fanning the air with her hand.

"My goodness, it's suddenly so warm." She offered her hand. "I don't believe we had a proper introduction. I'm Melissa Cole."

He took her elegant hand and smiled. "Michael O'Mara, blue jean guy."

"I can't tell you how absolutely charmed I am. Are you accompanied this evening?"

He shook his head, "No. What about you, Melissa?"

"Well, to tell you the truth, I was hoping I just got lucky."

A waiter drifted by with a tray of champagne and Michael lifted two glasses, offering one to her.

"Why, thank you, Sweetheart. I'd love some champagne."

Melissa turned her charming smile on Martin and Gail.

"Melissa Cole," Michael said, "these are my friends Martin and Gail Edger."

Martin seemed completely thunderstruck. "Yes," he managed nodding his head quickly. "I can't believe I'm standing here talking with you. You're so incredible. I have every record you've made. Your voice never fails to send shivers through me, especially when you stretch a high note."

Melissa pinched his cheek. "Why thank you cutie."

Martin giggled like a little kid. Gail glanced at him with amusement and took Melissa's outstretched hand. "It is a pleasure to meet you."

Melissa made small talk for a moment then turned her attention back to Michael. "I've been dying to meet you since I saw that very first ad. My God, you have such extraordinarily beautiful eyes. They're yours aren't they?" She laughed heartily. "Listen to me I sound like a teenager. Of course, I know they're yours. What I meant is you don't wear contacts, do you? Please, tell me they're real."

"They're real," Gail said tightly.

Melissa lost most of her smile and turned, studying the smaller woman for a moment. "It seems I've offended you," she said quietly. "Please accept my apology."

"I'm not offended, Ms. Cole. I'm stunned."

"Me too! Man what a kiss!" Melissa laughed, her mood changing again. She looked back to Michael. "I am expected at another party, care to join me?"

They never made it to the other party. Michael and Melissa ushered in the new year at her hotel room then continued to drink and have sex well into the next day, slept for a few hours then started all over again.

When Nicole returned from Europe, she was well aware of his dating Melissa. On their first date over dinner she broached the subject first.

"So, are the rumors true about you and Melissa Cole?"

He sat back from his dinner, watching her for a moment. She was using a detached approach, but he knew her better.

"You didn't want an exclusive relationship," he said.

"Don't jump the gun, Cowboy. Just tell me the truth."

He couldn't help but grin, "Cowboy?"

"Michael, please."

"Yes, I spent some time with Melissa while you were gone."

She appeared to take the news in stride. She took a bite of her dinner, sipped her wine, dabbed at her mouth with her napkin then rose and picked up her purse.

He started to rise, but she held up a hand. "Don't bother." She leaned forward and placed a hand on his shoulder. She smiled coldly, "I hope she consumes your heart while it's still beating."

Chapter 16

Michael stepped off the elevator and turned toward Nathan's office. His focus remained on Nathan's production assistant who was selling him on an idea with a rapid-fire pitch. Michael didn't see the man in the waiting area jump to his feet.

"Mike?"

He looked up and spotted the name O'Mara stenciled over the pocket of a worn army jacket, and cringed.

The man smiled apprehensively. "Don't you know me?"

Michael stared hard while his mind ran the gamut of emotions. If this were any other member of his family, he would have kept walking.

He faked a smile, "Of course, Bobby."

His brother's nervous smile faded fast and he turned toward the elevator. "I'm sorry. I shouldn't have come."

Michael took a deep breath and stepped into the minefield, "No, wait."

Bobby stopped in front of the elevator and Michael turned to Nathan's assistant, "Tell Nathan I'll be a few minutes late."

He guided Bobby to his office and closed the door. He tossed a stack of papers on his desk and went to the wet bar. "Would you like something to drink?"

"Isn't it a little early for that?" Bobby joked weakly.

Michael glanced at him. "I'm offering you coffee or juice, but there's tap water if you feel like living on the edge."

Bobby smiled sheepishly. "Coffee would be great."

Michael poured one cup and placed it on the coffee table. They remained standing, examining the changes in each other. Bobby's haggard appearance shocked Michael more than anything. His shaggy hair was oily and he probably hadn't shaved in at least three days and there were dark circles beneath his eyes. He smelled of stale cigarettes and booze.

Bobby offered another weak smile. "I can't believe how much you've changed."

His tone seemed light, but Michael could see his brother was on the edge. This conversation would take much longer than he had to give right now.

"I'm sorry, Bob, but I have to go to a meeting. Can you wait here until I finish?"

Bobby's mood immediately soured. "Maybe I shouldn't have come at all. I wouldn't want to interrupt your busy life."

"Be fair," he snapped.

He tried to keep the edge out of his voice, but couldn't. He felt cornered. Right in front of him stood the thing he dreaded most about being back in New York.

Bobby looked to the floor and ran a hand through his dirty hair. "How long will you be?"

"It should take about an hour. I'll have my secretary bring you some lunch. What would you like?"

Bobby looked up at Michael, his eyes teary and bloodshot. "Jesus, Mike, I'm at the end of my rope and you want to know what I want to eat?"

"Yeah, I left my magic wand in my other life."

"I'm sorry."

"Stop saying that," he said sharply. He drew in a breath and went to his desk for the notes he needed for his meeting. "Stay here and wait for me. When this meeting is finished, we'll go to my place. It's not far. I'll help if I can, I promise."

Michael watched as Bobby slowly took in the grandeur of the entrance hall. Bobby looked back to him and offered the first genuine smile. "Apparently life has been kind to you after all."

"And how has it been for you?"

"Well, you know what they say..." he began, then his eyes filled with tears and he shrugged. "Life's what you make it."

Michael gently guided him to the couch in the library and sat nearby. "What can I do?"

"Shit, Mike, I promised myself I would never bother you. I mean when I saw those ads it was a real kick just to know you were still alive. I knew if you wanted to see me you'd call or make some kind of contact, but of course you never did. I thought you'd earned the right to be left alone." He paused, sighing loudly. "Unfortunately, no matter what I try, life seems to go in circles and keeps coming back to you. Everything I do, every dead-end street I travel, takes me back to one place. You're the key and without your help I'll never find the answer to a way out of this hell."

"I don't understand."

Bobby looked at him hard. "Yes, you do."

Michael studied him for a minute. "Let's talk about you."

"Okay, where did we leave off? Oh yeah, you remember, it was 1967. Well, I did two tours in Nam. I was actually grateful to be there the first time. The place seemed a lot saner than that last summer at home. After the Army, I moved back to Brooklyn, got a job, a wife, and had three kids before I knew what hit me. Lately, I've been taking speed so I have enough energy to work my day job and drive a cab four hours a night to support my family." He paused for a deep breath. "I'm a typical O'Mara, I confess my sins, beg forgiveness then do the whole thing all over again. Any spare time is devoted to drinking myself stupid."

Bobby paused and closed his eyes, took a deep breath before looking back at Michael. "There's one more little detail, last Sunday I punched my six-year-old son in the face."

Michael inhaled reflexively and Bobby's gaze bore into him, his voice soft, apologetic and accusatory. "You see, it always comes back to you," he said.

Michael felt an old anger rise out of the past like a surge of wildfire. "Nonsense," he managed tensely.

"No, Mike, the nonsense is you and Dad, you and Uncle Frank, you and Mom, and some big, ugly secret. Did you think the rest of us weren't affected by it?"

Michael couldn't believe the responsibility Bobby just shoved his way. "Why are you asking me?"

"Because I can't get a straight answer from anybody else! I know you are at the root of the problem and I want you to explain it to me."

Michael stood quickly and walked to the fireplace, turning his back. Deep inside, the sealed place had cracked and the fresh air breathed life into the most despicable memories. Helping Bobby meant opening that door wider.

He turned and met Bobby's direct gaze, speaking tightly, the only way he could manage. If he opened his mouth further, he might start screaming.

"If you want my help, you have to make this about you."

Later that night, Michael checked Bobby into a center for alcohol and drug abusers. While Bobby was in the hospital and struggling to get back on his feet, Michael planned to provide an income for his wife and three children, but he would stay far away from Bobby's therapy.

After that night in Texas when Beth sucker punched him and became privy to the core of his shame, Michael placed his need for her on the highest shelf of the vault he reserved for unresolved pain and sealed the door.

A few days ago, he received an invitation to her wedding. That small rectangle of paper sliced through the steel vault like a sharp laser and set the pain free.

Melissa flew in on Saturday for his birthday and he hoped being with her would remove the renewed heartache for Beth, but from their first touch, he understood Beth was back to stay.

For his thirtieth birthday, Melissa threw a surprise party for him in the ballroom of the Ritz, telling him it was a party to kick off her new album and tour. When they arrived, a waiter seated them with members of her band, and Melissa's business manager.

After dinner, Melissa took the stage with her band. Once the lights dimmed, they launched into a campy version of The Boy from New York City. Behind the band, stills from the blue jean ads ran on a large screen and the deception became clear. Darkness hid the hot anger creeping into his face.

The show ended with an outtake from one of the earliest commercials, back when he had no control over the content and they shot the same commercial repeatedly for hours. After the blonde model blew the line about the perfect fit one more time, Michael looked over his shoulder at the camera for the close-up and crossed his eyes.

With that frame frozen on the screen, Melissa launched into Happy Birthday. Waiters pushed a cake with five tiers of blazing candles into the darkened room and everyone stood and sang.

Michael did his best to appear appreciative. Reading his mood, Melissa wrapped her arms around him, and kissed his lips quickly, holding him a moment longer.

"I'll make it worth your while if you behave," she whispered in his ear. Pulling back, she smiled broadly. "I love you baby, happy birthday."

Michael's phony smile had frosty edges. "Thanks from the bottom of my heart."

"Thank me later, Sugar. Right now, there are some people waiting for you."

She showed him to a table where Bobby, Kevin and Audrey, Gail and Martin, and Kelly waited. His smile became genuine when he saw Kevin and Audrey. He accepted Kevin's hug and kissed Audrey, before greeting the rest.

Kelly smiled up at her boss. "Were you surprised?"

"Melissa says you helped with this. I thought you were happy at Nathan B," he shrugged. "Go figure."

Melissa pinched his ear and twisted it hard, "Stop being so ungracious."

"Ow! Damn it, Melissa." He rubbed the spot and looked around for the bar. "I need a drink."

"Wait here, your highness. I'll bring one to you."

Michael pulled out a chair and looked around the table, stopping abruptly when he came to his brother's curious stare.

He frowned. "What?"

"I can't tell you had a broken nose."

Michael immediately looked to Kevin, who grinned and shrugged.

"We all want to meet Bethie," Bobby said. Everyone except Michael laughed just as Melissa returned.

"Here's your drink," Melissa said coolly. "I think you'd better scoot on over to Grace's table and make nice before the boss lady gets her knickers in a twist."

Michael stood again, taking the drink. He raised the glass to his lips and drank half of the scotch.

"Oh, man," Melissa said, then sighed. "I see we're in for a bumpy ride tonight."

He leaned over and kissed her on the mouth before moving on to Grace and Nathan's table.

Melissa asked Grace to excuse Michael when the band started a slow song.

On the dance floor, Melissa looked up at him. "I heard your brother and Kevin talking about Kevin's sister. Tell me about you and Beth, all of it."

"We're friends."

"Somehow, I get the impression Beth Thomas is much, much more. When was the last time you saw her?"

"It's been a while. Why?"

"Because, Sweetness, I don't take it well when people lie to me."

He stared at her for a long moment then shook his head. "I can't understand why you walk around armed for war."

"I find unfaithfulness maddening."

Michael tensed. "I haven't been unfaithful, Melissa."

"Good. Keep it that way when you go to the wedding."

"I have no intention of going to her wedding."

She cocked her head to side, thinking. "Let's go together."

He laughed at the thought, "Absolutely not."

"You have been different with me all day. She's on your mind now that she's marrying someone else, isn't she?"

Michael stopped dancing and stepped back. "Don't do this."

"Don't ever lie to me."

"When did I lie to you?" He didn't bother to hide his anger this time. The question was loud and those around them stared.

"We're just friends," Melissa said, mocking him.

He turned toward the door, "The hell with this."

"Don't you dare walk away!" She grabbed his arm. "I want to finish this."

"Too bad."

"Michael, this is your birthday party. I worked very hard on this. So did a lot of your friends."

He stopped abruptly and turned around to her, trying to control his anger. Melissa stepped close and switched tactics.

"Come back inside. We'll talk about Beth later."

"There's nothing to talk about, damn it! She's a friend, that's all."

"That's the biggest bunch of garbage you've ever tried to feed me, Michael O'Mara. Whether you realize it or not, I know."

He rolled his eyes. "You know."

She squeezed his arm and her voice dropped to a whisper. "I can feel it when you touch me."

Kevin watched Michael drink himself into a stupor then helped Melissa get him into a limousine to take him home. He didn't take the time to notice much about Michael's apartment while helping him up the curving staircase.

"You're a whole lot heavier than you were at seventeen," Kevin said.

"I can make it on my own," Michael said with a wave of his hand.

In the bedroom, Kevin pulled down the covers, sat him on the edge of the bed, and helped him undress. "Go on, lay down."

Michael fell over and stretched out with a moan. "I'm going to pay for this tomorrow."

"Yep."

"Will you and Audrey stay here tonight?"

"We've got a hotel room."

"No, there's lots of room right here. I want to spend some time with you. Please?"

"We'll be here tomorrow. Go on to sleep, Mike."

Michael closed his eyes and sighed, "I hate my birthdays."

"I know."

"Why did she have to get married now?"

"Well, June is a bride's month."

"I'm such a fool."

Kevin smiled, "Yep."

"It hurts, Kevin. It really hurts."

Kevin flipped the covers over him and stood there for a few minutes listening as Michael's breathing deepened.

Kevin opened the doors to the balcony off the living room and stepped out to the edge, taking in the view of Manhattan. Audrey was already back at the hotel, but he was far from sleep. Melissa handed him a cold beer and sat on the ledge of the balcony looking toward Central Park.

"This place is something," he said.

"You must be very proud of Michael," Melissa said.

Kevin shrugged and looked away. "I might be I guess, if I believed all this made him happy."

"So, tell me about the Michael you know," Melissa said.

Kevin looked out at the night for a moment and came to a decision. "There's something I think you should listen to. I believe it will explain the Michael I know better than I ever could. I think someone like you will really appreciate it."

Kevin put a cassette in the library stereo and sat next to Melissa on the sofa. The live recording had a lot of background noise and the quality was poor, still the beauty and heartache of the song came through clearly.

She sat forward, listening intently. "When was this made Kevin?"

"In 1968 on his eighteenth birthday. He worked in a roadhouse bar when he lived in Texas. The leader of the band cornered him into performing and recorded this. I brought this copy for Michael. I was going to surprise him, but that will have to wait until tomorrow."

"Who wrote this song?"

"I'm pretty sure Michael did. I wanted you to hear this tape to prove a point. When I first met him, I thought he was just another injured soul afraid of trusting people. When he cracked that first line, I knew I had underestimated him. Michael knows a lot more about pain than I do."

Kevin took a deep breath and a swig of his beer. "What amazes me is his dedication to keeping the world at arm's length. He thinks he has to protect us from where he's been."

Kevin fell silent as Michael's voice rose and held a note, dragging him back to the doorway of Kelsey's bar. He shivered all over again as Michael hit the last note and squeezed his heart all over again

"The secrets are slowly killing him," Kevin concluded quietly.

He looked over to Melissa and saw a tear had slipped down her cheek.

"He loves Beth," she said.

Surprised, Kevin didn't know how to respond to the truthful statement without hurting her. He watched as she tilted her martini glass and drained the contents. He could think of nothing to say to soothe her feelings.

When he didn't argue, she smiled sadly. "Just my luck, I finally fall head-over-heels in love and the son-of-a-bitch turns out to be taken."

Melissa kicked off a new tour in Denver and Michael called her hotel to wish her good luck.

"You sound strange, Michael. Are you all right?"

"I'm just tired," he told her.

"Well, I don't think I've heard you say that before. Why are you so tired?"

"I just need some time in the mountains where I can simply exist and not make it all work for everyone else for a few days."

"I thought you thrived on pressure."

"Another myth dispelled," he said then sighed. "Well, I called to wish you good luck tonight not to whine."

"I'm glad you called. I needed to hear your voice. Can you join me in New Orleans next weekend?"

"Let me look at my schedule." He opened his appointment book and flipped a few pages. "I can fly in Saturday."

"I want you to come up Friday."

"I'll be in Houston on Friday."

"Houston? Where Beth Thomas lives?"

Michael sighed audibly. "Yes."

"Where are you today Michael? Where's your heart?"

"Please don't start this again. I don't want to argue."

"What's in Houston?"

He tossed the appointment book across the desk and got to his feet. "I work for a living. Remember?"

"Oh, shut-up."

He sighed loudly. "Melissa, you have to get beyond this. I've never given you a reason to feel this insecure."

"You're such a liar! I swear you're an emotional black hole."

"You're giving me a headache. I'm going."

"Don't you dare hang up on me, damn it!"

"Stop playing games."

"Me? Could it be possible you don't realize how you feel about her?"

"It doesn't matter how I *feel* about her," he snapped.

"It matters to me."

He groaned loudly and walked to the bar for a drink.

"You should get on a plane to Texas right now. Take that woman in your arms and make love to her. At least give it your best shot because you'll never be over her until you do."

"How magnanimous of you."

"Hardly. I simply demand all of you or nothing."

She threw the phone at the wall, disconnecting his call. Michael stared at the receiver for a minute then dropped it into its cradle.

Melissa was on the phone when he walked in her hotel room in New Orleans early on Saturday afternoon. She offered her cheek for him to kiss, but Michael ignored the gesture and made a drink instead. He sat and made small talk with her personal assistant.

Melissa concluded the call and smiled coolly. "I wasn't sure you were coming."

"Why's that?" His even tone had such a discernible level of acid that the assistant stood reflexively and excused herself.

Melissa hardly noticed the assistant's departure. Her undivided attention was on him. "I suppose the fact that you haven't answered my calls in over a week might have something to do with it. Where were you?"

His temper flared. "Are you going to start this again?"

"You've changed since you got that wedding invitation."

"I have not."

"Michael, honey, you are so delusional."

He got to his feet. "I didn't come here for this."

"Why did you come?"

He shrugged. "We used to have fun together."

"Until you let another woman come between us."

He laughed shortly. "I believe that was you."

Melissa crushed her cigarette in an ashtray and picked up her second drink of the day. "Get out of here."

Melissa called repeatedly, leaving long messages on his machine, usually after consuming a fair quantity of alcohol. She cried, ranted, raved, pleaded, and threatened him to no avail.

A few weeks into the tour, she collapsed on stage and was taken to the hospital. When he heard the news, Michael relented and called her. After spending a few minutes tolerating the terse attitude of her assistant, he demanded to speak with Melissa.

"What do you want Michael?" Melissa shouted from an extension where she had obviously been listening all along.

"I heard you collapsed."

"I had a spontaneous abortion. What's it to you?"

"You lost a baby?"

"Don't worry, it wasn't yours."

He closed his eyes and took a deep, audible breath. She had evidently been at the bottle and it wasn't even ten in the morning out in LA.

Melissa laughed. "Gee-whiz, did that surprise you?"

"I'm sorry."

"Sorry for what, for breaking my heart?"

"No, you managed that by yourself."

"You are such a jerk."

"I have to go. I'm glad you're all right."

When the alcohol wore off, Melissa resumed calling. Michael talked to her, but made it clear they were finished. One week after the spontaneous abortion, Melissa's assistant woke Michael at two in the morning.

"I'm sorry to wake you, Mr. O'Mara, but I thought you would want to know. Melissa overdosed on her pain meds this evening."

"How bad is it?"

"Critical, they admitted her to the ICU." Carol sighed loudly, "Do you think you could come see her? I think it might help."

Michael flew to Los Angeles and went directly to the hospital. Melissa was no longer in the ICU and had a private room and private nurse. Melissa's staff scattered when he walked in the door.

Melissa refused to look at him. He sat next to her and took one of her hands in his.

"Why did you do this, Melissa?"

"Someone as strong as you would never understand how it feels to hit bottom."

"Let's talk about you."

"I don't want to live without you," she said, her voice weak. "It hurts too much."

"Melissa, it would never work."

"We can fix what's wrong."

He met her eyes directly and shook his head.

"I hate you," she said.

He wiped a tear away and brushed a strand of hair back away from her face. "And I hate the abuse you put yourself through."

"Believe me, I don't want to live like this anymore, but my heart is breaking. I was so afraid of losing you, I messed everything up."

"I can't let you take all of the credit." He pulled her into his arms and she cried against his shoulder.

"I'm always going to love you. You can't take that away from me," she said.

He stroked her hair, wishing he could recapture the freedom he used to feel with her. Unfortunately, those feelings were built on quicksand. He knew the truth all along. They had many things in common, but love was never on the list.

Martin came to collect him for a charity engagement. After receiving no response from Michael, the doorman admitted Martin to the building. Martin found Michael sitting in the dark living room and turned on a light near him.

Michael's appearance shocked Martin. He still wore the same clothes he threw on at three the day before and hadn't shaved for two days. He looked as if he hadn't slept in a while and held a half-empty bottle of scotch in his left hand.

He squinted up at Martin with bloodshot, red-rimmed eyes. "Why are you here?"

"Tonight's the open house. Remember?"

Michael shook his head. "I'm not going."

"I can see that. Want to tell me what's going on?"

"No."

"The thing with Melissa is all over the news. Is that what's wrong?"

Michael set the bottle on the table next to him. "What thing with Melissa?"

"Somehow I get the impression you know exactly what I'm talking about."

"Go away, doctor." Michael sighed and rubbed his face roughly.

"I'd like to think I'm your friend."

"Okay, go away, friend."

"I'm coming back after the party's over. We'll talk about this."

"I don't need a baby-sitter, Martin. I'm Irish and this is a wake. I'm honoring the dead."

Michael rested his head on the back of the chair and looked at Martin then closed his eyes. His voice was hoarse when he spoke.

"Please go."

"I'll swing back by on my way home, okay?"

"No. I'll be passed out by that time."

"You're a very strange drunk, Michael O'Mara."

After Martin left, Michael called the doorman and predicted the future of his employment status should he ever admit another person without prior approval. He switched on the answering machine and finished the scotch. He was still awake at eleven that evening when Martin returned, but he refused to answer the buzzer and this time the doorman obeyed the rules.

He felt the nightmare skirting the periphery of his thoughts, pressing in like an unwelcome guest, waiting for his guard to weaken. He'd been awake for nearly twenty-four hours when he finally succumbed to sleep on the couch in the den.

Late that morning, he sat straight up on the couch with the image of Uncle Frank's lifeless body still in front of him. While his scream still echoed in the room, he threw the empty bottle of scotch at the fireplace and cursed his life.

He went back to his routine and allowed work to consume his days. He ate most of his meals alone or with people he didn't care about. Finally, he returned to the silence of his apartment where he worked in the study late into the night.

The events with Melissa made him admit to his need to love and be loved. No matter how he tried to ignore the facts, this carefully constructed life was superficial and meaningless. He couldn't shake this new emptiness. He wanted to take time off and get away. He needed the comfort of Wyoming, but Grace was in Europe and Kelly wasn't ready to take over, so he shut down and just worked.

Chapter 17

Michael ran into Nicole at Martin and Gail's tenth wedding anniversary party. They started dating again and both remained devoted to their work. She was pretty and intelligent and Michael enjoyed her dry sense of humor. A relationship with Nicole was less intense than with Melissa, but it was easy and one he could hold on to, if he overlooked his lack of true passion for her.

One evening Michael allowed Bobby to persuade him to come to the old neighborhood for dinner. The last time he walked these streets was the morning after he cut his wrists. He had been weak and the Valium Martin had given him had dulled his senses. Still, he managed to run nine blocks to the subway.

Tonight, he sat in the back of a cab and watched the still familiar streets roll by, and a slow, steady chill spread through his body. There were too many ghosts here.

He paid the driver and hurried inside the restaurant without looking right or left. He found Bobby at a table near the back. Sitting across from Bobby was his old childhood antagonist, Danny D'Angelo.

When they were kids, Danny accused him of being a snob and labeled him a "fag." Michael was used to the sentiments, most of the kids in the neighborhood felt the same way. For six years, he managed to ignore their contempt, but Danny went out of his way to demean him. Michael hadn't seen him since Danny managed to goad him into a fight on the street in front of his parents' house the night before his sister's wedding when they were both sixteen.

Bobby smiled and waved him over to the table and Danny D'Angelo stood, offering his hand.

"Wow, you got big, just like your old man," Danny said.

Michael was taller than his father, but in no way as burly, in fact he more closely resembled his Uncle Frank if anyone, but he would never admit that to anyone.

Danny grinned. "Do you remember me?"

"Of course I do."

"I got my own carpet cleaning business now. Here, take one of my cards."

Michael accepted the card as a woman walked up behind Danny and placed a hand on his shoulder. Danny swung around quickly.

"We're waiting for you," the woman said stiffly.

"Sorry, honey. I ran into some old friends. This is Bobby O'Mara. Bobby and I went to school together. We used to live on the same block."

Diane said hello to Bobby then looked at Michael as Danny introduced them.

"And this is Bob's younger brother, Michael, the only guy who ever kicked my ass. Michael, this is my wife, Diane."

Diane frowned at Michael. "Have we met before?"

Danny laughed a little too loudly. "Baby put on your glasses. Michael's the stud that models those over-priced blue jeans everybody thinks they need."

Bobby pulled out the chair next to him and waved Michael into it. "Where's Nicole?"

"She's working in Italy for a few weeks."

Diane stared at Michael for a minute then nodded. "I haven't seen you in any of those commercials for a while. Have you stopped making them?"

"I don't have time anymore."

She smiled. "Gee, that's too bad."

"Hey now," Danny exclaimed. "I might get my feelings hurt if you sit here and flirt with him all night."

Danny's tone was light, but Michael got the impression Danny was a jealous man.

Diane's smile slipped away and she turned to Danny. "For heavens sake, I was kidding around."

"Of course you were," he said, offering a chilly smile. "So was I."

Michael stood abruptly. "Bobby, if the waiter comes would you order a burger for me?"

"Sure. Where are you going?"

"I need a drink."

By the time Michael returned, a young woman had joined the table. Her fair skin and almost white hair seemed to lighten the dimness of the bar.

Diane made the introductions. "Christine, this is Bobby's brother, Michael." Diane looked to Michael. "This is my cousin, Christine Hatcher."

While she introduced them, he looked down into Christine's wide eyes. She had an open, sweet face and he immediately wanted to move her far away from Danny.

"Christine is a music major at Julliard," Diane said in general. "She's a genius on the piano."

Michael picked up his drink, took a swallow, and felt Bobby watching him.

"I guess you and Chris got something in common, don't you, Mike?" Danny said. Without waiting for Michael's response, he turned to Christine. "Mike graduated high school when he was like ten or something and got a scholarship to…" he looked at Michael, "what school was it?"

Michael shrugged. "That was a long time ago."

"MIT," Bobby put in.

"My God," Diane said. "How high is your IQ?"

Christine looked at Michael. "I hate being talked about like this, don't you?"

"You guys have my sympathy," Danny said. "It is such a burden having everything handed to you while the rest of us have to work our asses off."

Michael opened his mouth to speak, but Christine said it for both of them.

"No one ever handed me anything, Danny. You don't know what you're talking about."

Michael saluted her with his drink. Everyone else stared in surprise at Christine.

Surprised at her bold statement, Danny sat back in his chair. "You have to look at it from my point of view."

A small furrow creased Christine's forehead. "No, I don't, what ever gave you that idea?"

"All right, you two, let's move on," Diane sighed.

While Bobby's wife and Diane were busy changing the subject, Michael downed all of his drink and caught Christine's studied gaze. He looked at her directly and smiled. Her pretty face held an expression so warm and kind it reached inside and found a foothold.

Grace had convinced him to do an interview about his impact on Nathan B and his image now graced the cover of a national newsmagazine. He gave in because he believed it helped Nathan B, but hated every minute of the intrusion. He insisted they stick to the issues related to business and stay out of his personal background. While he didn't talk about his life, they still did their homework and printed some of what they found.

On the Saturday after the article came out, he rose early, worked out at the gym in his apartment building and took a shower then settled into his study to review the details of Nathan's upcoming Paris show when Melissa called. She had been sober for nearly a year now and he was used to her occasional phone calls. They had actually become good friends despite their history.

As usual, she plunged right into the conversation without preamble. "Hey, I didn't know you were such an accomplished scholar, Mr. Wizard of Fifth Avenue."

"Hello to you to."

"Michael is all that stuff true? Are you like a billionaire now?"

"That was last week. This week I'm a trillionaire."

"I can't believe we had all that hot sex and you never muttered a single word of French."

He rose and crossed to the bar, "Melissa stop."

"All right. I have a more important purpose for this call anyway. I'm sending you a demo tape. I wanted you to be the first to hear it and I want only your most honest opinion."

He dropped ice in a glass, only half listening. "Why? You never asked my opinion about your music before."

"Good grief, are you drinking? It's only eleven in the morning, Michael."

"Answer my question."

"I want it to be a surprise."

He sighed loudly, "You know I hate surprises."

"I sent it out today. You should get it in a day or so. Call as soon as you listen to it."

Two days later, a courier dropped the tape off at his office. Michael tossed it in his briefcase and took it home that night. He stopped for dinner, collected his dry cleaning, and finally arrived at his apartment a little after nine. The phone was ringing as he unlocked the door.

"Well? Did you listen to the tape?" Melissa said.

"I just walked in. Let me call you back."

"Oh, for heaven's sake, will you hurry up? I can't stand the suspense."

Michael went into the library and popped the tape in the machine then made a drink at the bar. He pushed the play button and familiar notes floated over the speakers. Melissa began to sing the lyrics and he sat down hard on the couch in shock. When the phone rang ten minutes later, he hadn't moved.

"Well," Melissa asked, "what do you think? Do you like it?"

He put a glass of scotch to his lips and swallowed three times before he responded. "Where did you get that song?"

"Your friend Kevin gave it to me when he was there for your birthday. Can I use it, Michael? It's incredibly beautiful. What made you write it? Where did your inspiration come from?"

"I was a very serious kid."

"Kid? How old were you?"

"Fourteen."

"Sweet Jesus, you wrote something that magnificent at fourteen and quit?"

"You don't understand, Melissa. I never meant for anyone to hear it."

"You aren't making any sense. What are you telling me?"

He relaxed against the back of the couch and took a deep breath. "Look, I have to think about this."

"You'll make a bundle. I'll give you credit."

"If I let you use it, I don't want my name connected with it, ever."

"I will never understand you even if I outlive Methuselah," she said. "Will you at least tell me the title?"

"I never gave it a title."

"Want to hear the title I was thinking of?"

He sighed again louder this time, truly not interested, "No."

"Angel's Blues, it reminds me of your eyes."

"How poetic," he said under his breath, rubbing his forehead with the cold glass.

"Why are you so cranky?"

"I'm tired."

"Tell me the truth."

"I already did."

"Then go home to Wyoming and visit your real family. They always work some kind of magic on you up there."

"I can't."

"Nonsense, you can do anything you want. Just read that article, you're superhuman."

He stretched out on the couch surprised by how good the soft leather felt. "I've missed your nagging."

"Ah, but I hear you've replaced my nagging with that of the petite Ms. Edmund's."

"She doesn't nag."

"Oh, that's right. She's a working girl. Oops, pardon me. I suppose that makes her sound like a hooker, doesn't it? I meant, she's a career woman, your equal, she would never nag. I have one question though. I hear her natural body temperature is around eighty-four degrees, is that true?"

"Melissa..."

"I still love you, Michael." She hung up quickly as usual without bothering with so much as a good-bye.

Eventually, he accepted her word that his name would never be connected to the song and let her have all rights. Angel's Blues was released three months later and shot to the top ten on the charts, where it remained for seven months and Michael never chose to listen to the song other than that one time on the demo tape.

Michael received an invitation to a recital from Christine Hatcher, the girl he met in the bar with Bobby a few months back. Something about her was so far removed from every other thing in his life that he found himself drawn to her. He rescheduled a business dinner with Grace and Nathan to attend. If anyone had asked him why, he wouldn't have had a direct answer. Other than the memory of her sweet face and warm smile, he couldn't admit why he felt compelled to go.

He arrived after the program started and sat in the back. Christine was the third person to perform and played her piece flawlessly. She wore an ankle-length black dress. Her long, almost white hair radiated brightly under the stage lights. She looked even more delicate and vulnerable than he remembered. She was young, probably not even old enough to drink yet. He felt like an old man in comparison.

At the reception immediately following the program, Michael found her in the crowd. She stood next to her cousin, Diane. Fortunately, Danny D'Angelo was nowhere in sight.

Michael smiled as he walked the last few feet that separated them and Christine spotted him.

"I didn't really think you'd come," she said, her face brightened with a smile. Her light blue eyes met his and the beauty of her astounded him.

For a moment, he was tongue-tied. He cleared his throat and shrugged off the awkward, boyish feeling. "I almost missed your performance. I didn't get here until seven-thirty."

Christine smiled and nodded, her pale skin blushed crimson.

Diane saved them both. "We're going out for dinner, Michael. Would you like to join us?"

"I'd love to. I haven't eaten since early this morning."

Diane did most of the talking and he was grateful someone had something to say since Christine didn't seem to have much to say tonight either. Michael listened to Diane and responded graciously. Finally, he looked across the table to Christine.

"I liked your choice for the program this evening. Is Bach a favorite of yours?"

"No, not really, the piece was chosen for me. I thought I sounded mechanical, but then I always do when I play in front of an audience."

"Pretend you're playing for yourself. Lose the world."

She considered his statement for a moment then leaned closer. "Do you play an instrument?"

He smiled and shook his head. "Not anymore."

"What did you play?"

"Piano, a long, long time ago."

"I'd like it if you'd play for me sometime."

He laughed softly. "No, you wouldn't."

The waiter approached with the bill and Michael reached for it.

"I can't let you pay for this..." Diane began.

Michael scanned the bill and placed a credit card inside the leather folder. "It was my pleasure."

Michael walked them to Diane's car. Diane unlocked the doors and went around to the driver's side. Michael opened passenger door and stood back for Christine.

"Thanks again for inviting me," he said.

She smiled softly. "Thank you for coming."

Lately, Nicole had acquired some contradictory habits. Work was still foremost in her life, yet she had started surprising him with weekend getaways, special romantic dinners, and brought him expensive gifts from every country she visited. Once or twice when they were making love or concluding a phone call, she even said she loved him.

Previous to these sporadic efforts and sentiments, Michael had no illusions about their future. As far as he was concerned, they would eventually go their separate ways. Now she was changing the rules of their relationship and seemed to be considering something more meaningful. One Saturday night over dinner, the inevitable finally descended.

"I have a job offer in LA," she said between bites of salad. "It's a morning show. No more traveling around."

He glanced up from his own salad. "Are you interested?"

"I'm not sure. I thought I'd run it by you."

Confused, he frowned at her. "Why?"

"I want your opinion."

"I don't have an opinion when it comes to your career."

She stared at him hard. "I want your opinion," she repeated.

"Tell me more about the job then."

After a brief description of the positive aspects of the job, he told her the opportunity sounded perfect for her then tried to change the subject, but she grew stone cold quiet. After dinner they went back to his apartment where she forced the truth.

"I'm serious about taking the job on the West Coast," she said.

Michael knew she was fishing, but didn't want to go down that path. "If that's what you want, I'm happy for you."

"Is that all you have to say?"

"I told you, this isn't my decision."

"I thought we were a couple."

He sighed heavily and rose from the couch. They had been arguing for over an hour now and he was weary of the topic.

She turned around on the couch, glaring at him. "I'm sorry, is this tiring you?"

"I don't know what you expect."

"I thought you might at least pretend you wanted me to stay."

He leaned against the doorframe and folded his arms over his chest. "Where did you think we were headed? Did you think we'd get married?"

Suddenly her eyes were filled with big, fat tears. "Damn you, Michael," she said and turned to reach for a tissue.

"I didn't mean to hurt you. I'm sorry."

She threw up her hands. "You drive me crazy. This is the most frustrating relationship I've ever had. I know you're all locked up emotionally, but I can't stay away from you. I feel like an addict. One look at you and I'm sucked in."

"Sucked in?"

Nicole nodded slowly. He stared for a minute then went to the bar to make a drink.

She wiped the tears from her cheeks and straightened her back. "I'm going to accept the offer."

He dropped ice into a glass and reached for the scotch. "Fine."

"You really are an asshole."

Michael slammed the glass down on the marble countertop and took two quick steps toward her. Reflexively, Nicole stepped back.

"I'm an asshole?" He was angry now, too angry to try to avoid anything. "What about you? For you, I'm a sacrifice of valuable time. It makes me feel really romantic to know you'll pop in between trips to Europe and the Middle East."

"All right let's get married, Tarzan. Keep me barefoot and pregnant."

He cocked an eyebrow, "Now I'm an ape man?"

"Yeah, your Brooklyn roots are showing, time for a touch up."

He went back to the bar and found he'd cracked the glass. He tossed the glass in the trash and reached for another as she continued.

"All this time, I thought I was receiving devotion from someone who's incapable of even the slightest commitment. I guess that makes me an idiot."

"Is that the way you see me? Like an ego-toting Neanderthal?"

She shrugged and reached for her purse. "Actually, I think being brilliant never allowed you the chance to be a person like the rest of the human race. A big piece of your personality is seriously arrested."

Nicole walked to the door where she turned and continued in a softer tone. "And sometimes I think somebody hurt you so deeply that you're going to be forever walking wounded."

She slammed the entry door and he stared at it for a long while. Nicole not only resembled Beth, sometimes she had Beth's insight.

Michael celebrated Christmas in Wyoming with Sam, Nellie, Red and Red's new wife. On the plane back to New York, he vowed silently that this would be his last year of the grind. On the afternoon of New Year's Eve, he was back in his apartment.

He ignored the messages on the recorder and leafed through the mail quickly before unpacking and showering. His phone was ringing when he stepped out of the shower, but his recorder was full and didn't pick up. He didn't feel like talking to anyone yet, but the caller was persistent and kept calling back, until Michael finally conceded.

"Hey, you're home!" Bobby said. "What are you doing tonight?"

"I didn't make any plans."

"This will ruin your image little brother. Want some company?"

"What's up, Bob?"

"Angela took the kids down to Miami to visit her mother and I'm bored. I'll bring a pizza and a movie."

"Sure, come on."

Michael rewound the tape in his answering machine and made a drink while he listened to the messages. The first message he answered was from Kevin.

The hall door stood wide open and he didn't acknowledge Bobby's arrival. Kevin's news had him pacing with the phone in his hand.

"Beth's pregnant?" he said into the receiver.

"The baby's due in late May," Kevin said. "I'm trying to talk her into naming it Michael if it's a boy."

"Gee thanks."

"How was your vacation?"

"I had a great time. Hold on." He turned to Bobby and pointed toward the kitchen. "The kitchen is back there. I'll be off the phone in a minute. "

Bobby nodded and headed for the kitchen.

"Okay, I'm back," Michael said into the phone. "You may resume torture."

Kevin didn't hesitate. "What about women? Are you still doing the celibate two-step?"

"I was seeing Nicole again, but she moved out to the West Coast and we called it quits."

"Ah, Mikey, when will you wake up? You need a good woman like my Audrey."

"You are still a broken record."

"Not really. I keep finding new ways to torture your foolish self. Haven't you noticed?"

Michael laughed softly, "Yeah. Are we finished with that for today?"

"Well, since you finally admitted it, I think I can walk away with a little satisfaction. Good night and happy New Year."

Michael joined Bobby in the kitchen. The pizza was warming in the oven, filling the room with a wonderful aroma.

"That smells great," Michael said.

"I know. I'm starving. I almost ate a piece on the way here. You look good, but then you always do when you get back from out there. Maybe I can tag along some time."

Michael shrugged. "Sure."

"So, Beth's pregnant. How does that feel?"

Michael frowned at him. "How does what feel?"

"Well," Bobby said, "I got the impression she used to be pretty special."

"She's still special."

"To you?"

Michael glanced at Bobby then turned away to get some plates. He didn't want to answer. Bobby could be as relentless and Kevin.

Bobby stared at him for a minute then shrugged and opened the oven door to check the pizza. "Remember that girl, Christine, Danny's wife's cousin?"

"Sure."

"I keep running into her all the time. I'm starting to think she's following me." He pulled the pizza from the oven and inhaled the scent. "She always makes polite conversation like, 'hi, it's so great to run into you again and how is Michael,' all in one breath. I think she's got a crush on you."

Michael separated a slice of pizza and popped it onto a plate, thinking about Christine.

"What were you telling Kevin about Nicole?" Bobby asked, "Is it over?"

"We finally called it quits," Michael said.

"You don't have very good luck with women do you?"

Michael took a bite of pizza and shook his head.

"I remember that blonde you were seeing back in sixty-seven. Man, what a body. I couldn't believe it when I found out Max married her. Did you know they had a kid?"

Michael nearly choked. "She came back?"

Bobby laughed at his expression. "What's the matter with you?"

"Jean married Max?"

"Yep."

Michael swallowed a big bite, "Are they still together?"

Bobby shook his head. "She left him quite a while back."

"Did she take the child with her?"

"She left him with Max for a while, but came back for him eventually." Bobby squinted at him. "Why?"

"Him?"

"Will you please tell me why this is important to you?"

"He's my son."

Bobby sat back and studied him for a few moments. "Are you sure?"

Michael nodded quickly and glanced at the clock on the wall, but it was too late to call Max.

"Sweet Jesus, Mike, I wish I'd known. Jean had a bad reputation for the way she treated that kid."

"I wonder if Max knows where I can find him."

Max still lived in the same brownstone. Michael knocked three times before Max answered the door. Max had aged significantly. He had lost most of the brawn and his hair was completely gray.

He stared for so long Michael thought he needed to explain. "I'm Mike O'Mara. Do you remember me?"

"Of course I remember you, Mike. What can I do for you?"

"I wanted to talk to you about Jean and the boy."

Max stared hard. "They're not here."

"I know that. I..."

Down the hall, a tenant stepped out of their apartment and Max opened his door wider. "I guess you might as well come in."

The sound of a football game blared from the television and Max reduced the volume before waving him to a chair. "Want a beer?"

"No thanks."

Max sat nearby in a recliner and examined him. "You've really changed Mike."

"I think we both have."

"So what do you want?" Max's tone was bitter, mean even.

"I want to know if you can tell me where Jean is."

Max sat forward his face reddening. "Why?"

"I'd like to see my son."

"Your son? Excuse me, but I believe my name is on the child support checks."

"Then you know where she is."

"Not exactly. I mail the checks to some attorney in Connecticut. Jean makes sure I don't know where she is. She knows I'll come for Brian."

"Brian?"

Max sighed and stared at the television for a minute. "Brian Michael. He looks exactly like you. I think that's what makes Jean so mean to him."

Michael considered that statement a minute, remembering what Jean had threatened. Guilt rose in his gut, making him nauseous.

"Don't you pursue your rights as his father?" he asked softly.

"I don't have the money to find her, Mike," Max snapped.

"What if I gave you the money?"

"Then what? We find him and I hand him over like a lost puppy?" Max shifted his weight and sighed. "Look, I realize I don't look like I'm in good shape to be raising a kid, but he lived with me for three years with Jean then she took off and we got along great for two years without her. When she waltzed back in one day with a handful of apologies to me, I still thought we could work things out, but about six months later she took off with him, my car and every dime I had in the bank. The money and car I eventually replaced, but taking Brian ripped the life right out of me. I guess you figured because he's not mine I'm incapable of loving him."

Michael took a moment to digest the layers of Max's speech. When it came to Jean, Max still had the same anger and jealousy even after all these years. In some ways Max hadn't changed at all.

"I'm just interested in…" he paused before saying the name for the first time, "I'm interested in Brian's well being."

"I knew how you felt about the baby." Max said. "Jean told me you tried to convince her to let you have him."

"I was afraid she wouldn't be a good mother."

"Well, you always had more foresight when it came to her than I did. Wherever Brian is, I'm afraid he's suffering."

A heavy silence fell between them. Michael looked around the room, thinking of the last time he was here, the bloody bathroom and his wish to end his life. He fought the urge to leave as Max rose from his chair and walked toward his bedroom.

"I'll be back in a minute," Max said.

Michael forced his eyes to the television and drummed his fingers against his thigh. The football game was at half time and a marching band had taken over the field, banners flying, people cheering. There were only three short blocks to his parents' home, twenty steps to the bathroom, and four feet to the front door.

Max returned and shoved a picture frame at him. "That's the last picture I got of Brian. He was in kindergarten."

The little boy in the picture did indeed look like an O'Mara, though Michael couldn't see his own characteristics. Wide innocent blue eyes stared back at him and he felt like a failure.

"He's such a sweet kid," Max said. "I miss him."

Max's voice was husky with emotion and Michael reluctantly handed back the picture. "I'm sorry, Max."

Max shrugged and put the picture on top of the television. "Do you ever see any of your family?"

"Just Bob," Michael said quietly.

"I'm glad he cleaned up his act. Bobby always had a lot of heart."

Michael didn't want to talk about Bobby. "Will you help me find Brian?"

Max fixed him with a cold stare. "If we can agree that he is my son and you will stay out of the picture once we find him."

Michael sucked in a deep breath, anger flushing his face red. "That is hardly fair."

Max pointed a finger at him. "I mean it, damn it, or no deal."

"Until he's eighteen then I'll tell him myself."

Max watched him carefully, "I guess there's not much I can do when he's an adult."

Michael set the wheels in motion that week through his personal attorney in Manhattan. It didn't take long to discover Jean had used a lot of aliases, including O'Mara. A private detective tracked her to a suburb of Cleveland, but before they could act, she disappeared into the fabric of America again.

The private detective found a brother in New Bedford, Connecticut, but the brother insisted they hadn't spoken in years.

No matter what they did, Jean managed to elude their grasp. Eventually, Michael had to accept the fact that he might not succeed. He continued paying the attorney and investigators, but put hope of seeing his son on the shelf next to his love for Beth.

On his thirty-first birthday, the phone woke him at four in the morning. He rolled to the edge of the bed and grabbed the receiver.

"Congratulate me," Kevin said loudly.

"For what?"

"I'm an uncle. Bethie just had a baby girl."

"Congratulations," Michael said flatly.

"It's kind of ironic what with this being your birthday and all, ain't it?" Kevin laughed.

Chapter 18

Over the July Fourth weekend, all attempts to concentrate on the work piled high on his desk had failed. On Friday afternoon he and Grace had discussed his departure from the company. He had six months left to ease Kelly into the transition and that knowledge made him restless.

Michael moved from his desk to the stereo and tuned in a favorite classical station then stared at the rows of books on the shelves that bordered the fireplace. He hadn't read for pleasure in a long time. In fact, in the past eight years he had seldom taken the time for any form of leisure. If he dared, seasoned guilt bolted out of the past to remind him that the lack of productivity was the affliction of worthless, idle men. Apparently, some of Uncle Frank's programming could not be undone.

The only freedom he ever knew came in Wyoming and he wanted that back. Six months sounded like an eternity.

The buzz of the intercom interrupted this train of thought. He immediately crossed to the speaker.

"Excuse me, sir. Miss Christine Hatcher is here."

Taken aback, he took a minute to digest the news that Christine would show up at his door. "Send her up."

He opened the door and waited for the elevator to arrive, thinking it odd that she would come here, especially on July Fourth when everyone but him seemed to have plans. Odder yet, he realized he looked forward to seeing her, beyond the distraction her sudden appearance provided. Unlike him, she was untarnished and completely devoid of shadows. She reminded him of sunshine.

The quiet elevator doors slid open and she stepped off. A thin, summer dress flowed around her long legs and her frank smile immediately dispatched his gloom.

Michael smiled. "This is quite a surprise. What brings you into Manhattan?"

Her smile wavered, "You."

Michael waved her through the door, "Please, come in."

"I hope I'm not interrupting anything."

She paused in the entrance, looking down at her reflection in the polished marble. Michael watched her silky blond hair slip forward over her shoulders as she lowered her head. She looked up suddenly and caught him watching. She offered a tiny smile and Michael's breath caught in his throat. This girl had a way of tapping the hunger in him.

He started to take a step back and caught himself. "Would you like a soda or something?"

She straightened her back and the smile disappeared. "I'm old enough to drink, you know."

One eyebrow lifted slightly and he fought a smile. "Okay," he said, turning toward his study. "Come on in."

She followed him to the doorway and her gaze took in the neat stack of papers on his desk.

"I don't want to interrupt your work."

"I wasn't working. Want do you want to drink?"

"Whatever you're having."

He smiled, relaxing a little. He intended to have scotch, but wouldn't offer this innocent girl a glass of his favorite poison. "Iced tea?"

Christine smiled back. "Sure."

While he poured her tea, she examined some of the same books he had been staring at not three minutes before. Michael placed her glass on the table and sat on the couch watching her. Christine joined him, sitting only one cushion away.

"I'm sorry I didn't make your graduation," he said. "I had a business trip."

She shrugged and picked up her glass. "I understand. I came to thank you for your gift. It was very generous."

"What are your plans now?"

"I've accepted a teaching position here in New York."

"Teaching? I thought you might perform."

"It makes me sick," she said, then laughed softly. "Every time I play I get hives and nausea. Besides, I enjoy teaching." She looked into his eyes again and sat up straighter, her demeanor changed the pulse of this conversation. "I'm twenty-three and I know what I want."

He leaned back on the sofa and eyed her, understanding fully before he asked what she was driving at, "And what might that be?"

"If they plugged all of our personal information into a computer I think we would be a very good match."

Michael grinned at her. "How logical, Mr. Spock."

Her smile slipped and she blushed. "Don't make fun of me."

"Have you had dinner yet?"

"No."

"Good, let's get something to eat." He was anxious to get out of there, to be somewhere public, this girl was entirely too tempting.

Michael stood at the head of the conference table, frowning at a layout while members of their advertising team waiting expectantly.

"Is this the best you've come up with?"

"We've got a few other ideas."

His secretary's voice interrupted, "Mr. Bartholomew on line five, Mr. O'Mara."

He put the receiver to his ear and hit the key. "Hello Nathan."

"Michael, mother had a stroke."

Michael picked up Grace's hand and rubbed it gently, thinking of the time he spent with Ben back in Utah. Hopefully, she wouldn't suffer that much. The doctors were guessing she would recover about seventy-five percent of her speech and could learn to walk again. This recuperation would take time, of course. In the meantime, Kelly wasn't ready to take on his load and Grace's as well. The six-month deadline was of course out the window. For now, he would set aside his own disappointment.

Grace slowly opened her eyes and looked at him directly. Looking at Ben had been one thing. This was much more personal.

"I'm sorry, Grace" he said.

While in Boston on business, the flu came on strong, but he muscled his way through the day and went on to Atlanta and then Chicago where the symptoms lingered. On the flight home nearly six days later, the pressure and pain in his head brought him to tears. He went from the airport to home and crawled into bed with a fever.

He was still in bed, propped up on pillows and staring at the television with puffy eyes when his housekeeper let Christine in the next day. He had forgotten they had a date for a play that she had talked him into seeing.

She paused at the foot of his bed and he held up a hand.

"Don't come any closer. I might be contagious."

"You don't even sound like yourself. How do you feel?"

"Awful."

She sat next to him and placed a hand on his hot forehead. "Wow, that's some fever. Maybe you should see a doctor."

"It's just the flu."

She kicked off her shoes and crawled onto the bed beside him to watch an old black and white movie. Soon, they both drifted off to sleep.

A cool hand stroked his forehead and he smiled. Fully expecting those cool fingers to belong to Beth, he opened his eyes, Beth's name on the tip of his tongue, but it was Christine who smiled down at him.

"I think we need to take your temperature," she said.

Recovering from his near slip, he reached for a bottle next to the bed. "I'll just take a couple of aspirin."

"I talked to your brother Bobby a little while ago, he says you have a close friend who is a doctor. Can I call him?"

He sneezed three times and lay back with a groan. "It's just the flu."

"Are you hungry?"

"No." He popped the pills in his mouth and swallowed a few gulps of water.

"I think I'll go down and make myself something to eat. I'll be back in a little while."

"Go home before you get this."

"Go back to sleep, Michael. You're much too crabby."

Michael woke the next morning when someone turned on the lamp beside the bed. He squinted in the light and recognized Martin.

"I hear you're sick," Martin said."

Martin examined him briefly and gave Christine a prescription that she immediately ran to have filled.

"That's a good looking nurse," Martin said.

"She thinks I'm dying."

"You might have pneumonia, Mike. If you don't feel better on Monday, I want you to go to the ER. For now, make sure you take the medication, all of it. Now, roll onto your side so I can give you a shot."

Michael complied without comment. He was too weak to argue.

By the next afternoon, he felt a little better. He ate the chicken noodle soup and orange sherbet Christine gave him. Though he hated both, he was starving. While he showered, Christine changed the sheets and set up a Scrabble game.

They played two games and she won both times. After putting the game away, she climbed on the bed. They watched another movie as the sun slipped away and the bedroom grew dark except for the flickering light of the television.

Michael was dozing when she reached over and touched his forehead. "I think your fever's back."

Christine let her fingers glide down, across his cheek, producing a pleasant tingling up his spine. Michael drifted with the soothing feeling. When her fingertips drifted toward his neck and chest, he opened his sleepy eyes, looking at her, into her. She moved closer and kissed his mouth, making her desire clear and he pulled her to him.

If he had stopped to think first, he wouldn't have touched her. After the passion ebbed, he felt better and miserable all at once.

She rose to one elbow and looked down at him, tracing his lips with a fingertip. She smiled sweetly. "I'm in love with you, Michael. I'm glad I waited for you."

He pulled back suddenly thinking clearer. She laughed at the surprise on his face.

"What?" She asked then added with a wave of her hand, "Don't worry. I won't get pregnant."

He threw the covers back and sat on the edge of the bed. The room spun violently and he fell back on the bed. Christine reached out and stroked his chest. The combination of cold air hitting his fevered skin and her touch rocked him and he shivered involuntarily.

She smiled and moved closer, pressing her velvety skin against his side. "I'll go to the doctor Monday and get the pill."

Michael couldn't believe the way his body reacted to her touch and pushed at her hand. "Stop that."

"Don't talk," she whispered.

Christine moved around in front of him and straddled his lap. She kissed his mouth with hunger. Feeling his cool reaction, she stopped.

"Too soon?" She asked.

His breathing was coming faster and he shook his head. "This is playing Russian roulette."

She stared at him with her wide innocent eyes and he was arrogant enough to meet her gaze. He was helplessly drawn to her, all the while knowing he shouldn't take one more step forward. He brushed the top of her cheek with the tip of a finger and she started to cry.

He sucked in a deep breath and pulled her into his arms. "I'm sorry, Chris. Please, don't cry."

"I couldn't help myself."

Michael sighed loudly, “That I can relate to.”

The workday was almost finished. He sat back in his chair and flexed his back. He was driving out to visit Grace that evening. She was doing better, but the recovery was slower than the doctors anticipated.

His secretary buzzed him over the intercom. “Mr. O’Mara, there’s a Diane D’Angelo here to see you.”

He met her at the door and Diane stepped inside. She didn’t wait for him to close the door before confronting him.

“I’d like to know what you intend to do about Christine.”

He frowned at her. “What are you talking about?”

Diane stepped close. “She’s pregnant.”

Michael took a quick breath as if she’d punched him. Diane ignored his reaction and continued.

“How could you do this to her? She’s so innocent. Damn you.”

He had seen Chris just last week and she hadn’t mentioned anything about a baby. He started to explain to Diane, but decided it wasn’t Diane he needed to talk to.

He turned and walked to his desk, picked up the receiver, and punched in Christine’ number. “Hi Chris, this is Michael. Mind if I come by? I think we need to talk.”

“What about?” She asked. “Is something wrong?”

“Diane just told me about the baby.”

Christine moaned. “She told you?”

“Why didn’t you tell me?”

She didn’t respond right away and he was pretty sure she was crying. “I’ve been waiting for the right time,” she said.

“There’s no such thing in this situation.”

“I knew you’d hate me.”

"Calm down," he said, stronger than he intended. "I'll be there in a little while."

An hour later, he was still trying to figure out what to do when he knocked on her door. Christine opened the door slowly and didn't cry until he hugged her.

"I'm sorry," she said. "This is all my fault."

"That's funny, I remember being there." He pulled back and wiped a tear from her cheek. "What do you want to do?"

"What do you mean?"

"Do you intend to keep the baby?"

"Where I come from, we don't believe there's any other choice. I have some money saved and my health insurance covers the hospital and doctor bills. We'll be fine."

He released her and stepped back with a thousand things on his mind. Christine examined his expression and her eyes filled with tears again.

"Hey, I don't expect you to do anything. Okay? I know you don't love me."

Though he had never acted on his feelings, he had known the truth for a while now. He had in fact fallen in love with her. This wasn't the absolutely certain, mind-numbing, blood-pumping, roller-coaster kind of love he had for Beth. Loving Christine was gentler, much kinder on his heart. She presented a different kind of challenge, but it was love after all, and he was weary of being alone.

He lifted her chin, looked into her eyes, and said every word with conviction. "Would you marry me?"

Grace frowned at him over the top of her glasses for a long time before speaking.

"Would you like a honeymoon?" Her words were still mushy, but after spending hours with her over the last few months, he understood her perfectly.

"I can't right now," he said. "There's too much going on."

She chuckled. "My God, you're romantic."

Michael twitched in his chair and sighed. "She's pregnant, Grace."

"Is that why you married her?"

"No. She is really a wonderful person."

"And you feel guilty."

Her observance struck bone and he winced. Grace smiled and patted his hand.

"Are you at least fond of her, Romeo?"

"I love her. She makes me feel grounded."

Grace studied him again. "Well, good, then maybe you can make it work."

Beth read the gossip column every morning over breakfast. On Sunday morning, she glanced at the headlines and flipped open the first page, ready to scan the entertainment section. There to greet her was a photograph of Michael and his new bride. She stared at the photograph and tears clouded her eyes. So, he had finally slammed the door.

She looked across the table and watched her baby trying to pick up a Cheerio with tiny pink fingertips while her husband stared at the sports section. At that moment, she understood two things clearly, she was a fake and she still loved Michael O'Mara.

When she was six months pregnant, Christine resigned her teaching position and started searching for a house outside the city.

Michael didn't want to sink money into a house, but the time wasn't right to quit Nathan B. Besides, Christine had been through enough changes for one year. Moving her to Wyoming to have this baby was more than he wanted to put her through.

Christine found a sprawling mansion, three stories tall with high ceilings and sixteen rooms in Connecticut. Christine was nearly as awed by the house as she was by the balance in the checkbook and credit line at her disposal. She planned every detail of the remodeling of their home carefully. Most of the third floor was Michael's. Half of the space was converted into a study. One quarter of the roof was a sloping, tinted glass ceiling meeting a smoked glass wall behind his desk. There was a large fireplace and wet bar. Floor-to-ceiling bookcases lined either side of the fireplace and the inside wall. An over-sized soft leather couch and two chairs created an intimate sitting area. Next to the study were a gym, sauna, and bathroom.

On the second floor were the master bedroom, nursery, family room, and guestrooms. The main entrance on the first floor was circular with a wide sweeping staircase and hall. The room immediately to the right of the entry hall was where Christine placed the single item she bought for herself. A grand piano rested on the polished parquet floor just waiting for her touch. Once the baby was born, this would be their new home.

In late August, Christine went into labor while he was at work. He immediately took a cab to the hospital where they shoved him into a gown and hurried into her room.

Her face glistened with perspiration from the strain. He bent over and kissed her gently.

"This really hurts," Christine said.

"The doctor says you're progressing very well."

She arched her back, moaning as another contraction began.

"Come on, breathe, Chris. You're holding your breath."

"I can't do this." She squeezed his hand hard and Michael was sure several of the bones cracked.

He pulled his bruised hand from her grip and pushed the hair away from her face. "Yes, you can."

"How dare you stand there and sound so damned calm. All of this is your fault. I promise, if I live through this, we're never having sex ever again."

"Whatever you say."

"Don't patronize me!"

"I'm sorry. What can I do to help?"

"Rub my back the way they showed you in class."

He massaged her lower back and she started crying.

"I'm sorry. I didn't mean it," Christine said.

Michael leaned over her and kissed her cheek as another contraction began.

Katherine Colleen O'Mara graced the world with her presence at seven that evening. The first time Michael held her, he handed over his heart without reservations. There had never been another moment in his life of such unconditional happiness.

Christine had chosen the name Katherine and Michael didn't mention it was his mother's name. They were going to call the baby Katie and he could live with that.

While Michael bathed Katie one evening, Christine announced it was time they discussed his side of the family.

"The only O'Mara I claim is Bobby," he said.

"Why?"

"Would you hand me a towel, please?"

He lifted Katie out of the bath and wrapped her gently, pressing her to his chest. Turning, he found Christine glaring at him and he frowned. "What?"

"I'm entitled to know why you have nothing to do with your family."

He stared and for the first time, he didn't shield her from the tougher side of his nature.

"No." The word came out softly, but the message was irrefutable.

Later that evening, after Katie was in bed, Christine sat in the chair opposite his desk and leaned on her elbows, staring.

Michael looked up from a report and waited.

"I want to talk about your family," she said.

He studied her face for a minute then sat back, pretending to have patience.

"I don't get along with my family. I realize you find that difficult to understand, but I have my reasons."

"What about Katie? Doesn't she have the right to know her grandparents, aunts, and uncles?"

He turned back to the work before him. "I think we can choose what's best for her."

"I don't know anything about your family. I wish you'd talk to me. I feel like I'm being lied to."

He tossed his pen on the desk and ran a hand through his hair. "Please, drop this subject."

"Katie is going to ask questions. How do you think she'll feel when she sees that Bobby's children, her cousins, know their grandparents, but she can't?"

He sat forward with a snap. "I'm not about to let you use emotional blackmail."

Christine jumped to her feet and leaned across the desk. "I want to know why!"

"I already told you why," he said tightly.

"You tell me nothing. I don't know anymore about you now than the day we got married. You treat me like a child. I'm tired of you slamming the door in my face."

"So, there's more to this than Katie knowing her roots," he said.

She shrugged. "Well, yes, I want you to talk to me. Tell me about your life, share yourself with me."

He closed his eyes, releasing a breath, fighting desperately for patience.

"Michael, I'm your wife. I'm supposed to be your most intimate friend. I love you with all of my heart, you know I do, but you act as if I'm prying when I try to get close. I don't understand why you don't trust me."

"I don't want anything to do with my family and that includes discussing them. Why can't you accept my word that I have very good reasons for that and leave it alone?"

"Maybe I could if I knew the reasons."

He groaned and headed toward the bar. "No."

"You're so stubborn!" She threw a stack of papers at him and stomped from the room.

Michael entered through the rear of the house and paused to talk with their housekeeper for a moment before climbing the stairs to the second floor. This had been a long, difficult week and he was worn out. Getting out of the office before five had been a major feat. All he wanted to do this weekend was relax.

Christine met him in the hallway, just outside the family room. He smiled at her as he topped the stairs.

"We have company," she said.

"Who?"

"I invited your sister Debbie to dinner."

His smile faltered. "Debbie?"

"Hello, Michael."

Michael turned and his youngest sister wrapped her arms around him. He returned the embrace weakly and saw Christine watching. Years ago, he doted on this little sister. He read to her, babysat her while his mother played bingo, and took her to the park. He had loved her unreservedly. All of that ended when the harshness of his life intensified and the right to fully enjoy the kinder, gentler side of life was stripped away.

Christine didn't understand that she had married a man estranged from his life, an observer who was disconnected from the living, and that the gift of a long lost relative was not welcome. Debbie held him, crying, telling him how much the family missed him, wanted to be part of his life. All he wanted to do was run.

He maintained a cool, but gracious front until Debbie left, then followed Christine to the family room and closed the double doors so Katie wouldn't hear the argument he was about to start.

"I can't believe you did that," he said.

"Did what? Reunited you with a sister you obviously adore? I'm so cruel."

"Have you forgotten that I asked you to stay away from my family?"

"I remember, but Michael I simply don't get it. I think I understand about your father, but not Debbie..."

He moved closer, tensing and anger rising. "You understand what about my father?"

Chris eyed him assessing his mood and a little more cautious now. "Debbie told me he used to hit you. You're mother said..."

"Damn it!"

He wheeled around and pulled the doors open with such force they smacked into the wall. He went upstairs to his study and slammed that door too. He stayed there pacing, staring out at the night, thinking and rethinking the possible repercussions of the evening.

Maybe he was overreacting. Debbie's presence hadn't been threatening. Maybe it would stop here. Even as that thought crossed his mind, he knew it was hopeless. Christine seemed determined to force the issue of family down his throat. She had opened the door and thrown out the welcome mat to all he dreaded. She could never understand his reasoning without the truth and he didn't trust anyone that much. For the first time, he considered leaving her and might have, if not for Katie.

At three-thirty, Christine entered and approached him warily.

"Go away," he said.

"I want to tell you how sorry I am."

"It's too late. You insisted on opening Pandora's Box, now we'll have to live with the consequences."

From that moment on Christine went to great lengths to hide her meddling, but he knew. He also understood that their marriage was a flimsy alliance at best and the tide was turning against them.

He began to spend most weeknights at the apartment in Manhattan, using the commute as an excuse. The truth was much more pointed. The nightmare was back in full force.

Martin watched Michael finish his drink and couldn't keep silent. They had only been in the restaurant for thirty minutes and Michael had already consumed two glasses of scotch.

"Why are you drinking like that?"

Michael held up a hand. "Don't start."

"What's wrong?"

Michael slid him a cold look. "I'd appreciate it if you'd mind your own business."

Martin studied him for a minute then sat back a little. "I talked to Bobby the other day." Martin said lightly then took a sip of his wine.

Michael folded his arms over his chest and eyed him, waiting.

"He told me you stay in town all week," Martin said. "He said you only go home on the weekends. Is that so?"

"It's too far with the hours I put in. I just get home and have to turn around and come back."

"Oh, Michael, come on. Even on your knees, that sweet baby is worth the trip."

He stared at Martin coldly, not interested in anyone else's opinion on how he should live his life.

Martin came right back at him. "Bobby says Christine has been to see your parents, is he right?"

Michael stood and threw two twenties on the table. "Enjoy your dinner, Martin."

A few days later, Martin made a trip to Connecticut. Christine took him to the family room and offered him coffee.

"I had dinner with Michael the other night," Martin said. "I'm very concerned about him."

She nodded and looked directly at him, "Me too."

"Christine, I realize you don't know me very well, but I'd like to be completely honest."

"Please, be my guest."

"Digging into Michael's past will only alienate him from you. Is that what you want?"

Christine's calm expression didn't change. "He needs to face his demons."

Anger swelled in Martin. Her calm, sensible approach was unfair. Of course, if she knew more, maybe she would have more empathy for her husband.

"Let me tell you about the first time I met Michael. Back in 1967, I did my residency in Brooklyn and was doing my ER rotation when one sunny afternoon the EMTs brought him in with a partially collapsed lung, a concussion, a broken arm, broken fingers, broken jaw and broken ribs and other assorted injuries that I can't remember, all this courtesy of his father. Except for Bobby, no one in that family, including his mother, even acknowledged the beating had occurred then or any of the other times."

Martin paused to catch his breath. His heart pounded and a thin layer of sweat broke out on his forehead. In the back of his mind, he could hear Michael wailing in that tub. Every measure of sorrow his friend had endured was in that lament.

He looked down at the cup of coffee in his hand and continued in a voice less strident. "Michael was a prisoner of war in his parents' house, Christine. If he doesn't want anything to do with them anymore, he's earned that right. If you love Michael, let go of this quest. You're playing with fire."

She was visibly shaken and rubbed her arms as if she were suddenly cold. "Why did his father do that?"

"I can't answer that for you."

"Do you believe there's a reason?"

Martin nodded, "Absolutely."

Christine stared at her hands for a minute. "There's this picture of him on his parents mantel. He's dressed like an altar boy and holding a candle and…." She paused, placing a hand at her throat, her voice shifting, nearly inaudible now. "Sometimes, when he's tired or his guard is down, I see that sad little boy staring back at me."

She shook her head and looked directly at Martin. "I can't help him if I don't know what went wrong."

"He doesn't want your help, Chris."

"That may be, but I can't live the rest of my life with him the way he is now."

Chapter 19

Michael left on a ten-day business trip to Chicago, LA, Houston, Boston and Miami. On his first night in Houston, he checked into his hotel and had time to spare before meeting a group of sales executives for dinner. He went into the lounge and sat at the bar.

This was Friday, the end of the workweek for most people. He had a meeting in the morning, a tour of a factory in the afternoon and a flight to Boston tomorrow night. The room hummed with the voices of people unwinding. Michael took his first sip of scotch and someone tapped him on the shoulder. He turned on the stool and faced a handsome, Nordic-looking man in a three-piece suit. The man smiled widely.

"Please, pardon the interruption, but some of the ladies in our group thought they recognized you as the guy who used to do those jean ads. Are you Michael O'Mara?"

He smiled politely, still hating to admit the truth. "Yes."

The man's smile spread even wider and he offered a big hand. "I'm Beth's husband, Drake."

Shocked, Michael forced himself to touch the extended hand and Drake pumped his arm eagerly. "This is a pleasure. I've heard so much about you from Kevin, I feel like I know you. I'm here with a group from work. Beth's supposed to meet me here. Would you like to join us?"

"No," Michael said quickly. "I can't."

Drake didn't hear the reply. He looked past Michael to the door and waved. "She'll be so glad to see you."

Turning, Michael found Beth's direct gaze focused on him. Her dark eyes drilled him to the chair and he froze. Drake met her with a brief hug and kiss, but Beth didn't shift her focus from Michael's face.

"What are you doing here?"

"I'm here on business."

Her eyes narrowed considerably. "I knew it had to be something really important to get you back to Texas."

"Honey," Drake said, seemingly oblivious to Beth's lack of attention. "I need to get back to my group."

Again, Drake offered Michael a big, white smile. "It was a real pleasure to meet you. Next time you're coming down this way, give us a call ahead of time and we'll get together."

Michael forced one more smile and Beth accepted Drake's kiss on the lips.

"I'll join you in a minute," she said.

Michael turned back to the bar and picked up his drink. He didn't want anyone to see his face when Beth slapped him with the anger he saw in her eyes. She took the stool next to his and ordered a drink.

"I hear you got married." She laughed shortly, "Not from you, of course, I had to read it in the paper, like some stranger."

"Sorry, we didn't send out engraved invitations like some people."

"You should have called, Michael. You owed me that much."

The bartender placed her drink on a napkin and Beth picked a piece of lint the cuff of Michael's jacket. One finger brushed his skin and tiny place she touched tingled, compounding his misery.

She took a sip of her drink and glanced at her husband's reflection in the mirror behind the bar then shifted her gaze back to Michael. "So, are you happy?"

"Not all the time, how about you?"

Beth glanced at Drake again and shrugged. "I'm considering divorce."

"Why? Drake seems like a decent guy. In fact, he sort of reminds me of Ken."

Beth frowned. "Ken who?"

Michael knew what he was about to say would be pushing her, but being this close hurt too much and that made him feel mean. He grinned and took aim. "You know Ken, Barbie's boyfriend?"

Beth's frown deepened then her face reddened. Finally, she smiled. There was no real humor or joy in her expression. She was ice cold.

"That's a very interesting observation, but, as usual, you're wrong. You see, Barbie's boyfriend married her and they set up house in Connecticut with their love child." She patted his hand gingerly, "Goodness, why am I telling you all this? You, more than anyone, would know all about that."

Michael grunted and picked up his drink. Beth slid off the stool and pressed against him, leaning close to his ear so that only he would hear. "I'm not happy Michael and I hate you for it. "

She walked away and Michael tossed a twenty on the counter to cover his drink. He left the bar feeling as if she had lifted him off his feet and shook him until every bone in his body rattled.

The confrontation with Beth made him determined to mend the gap with Christine. She was a good, kind-hearted person who loved him despite his shortcomings. Maybe if he tried harder, she wouldn't meddle. Maybe he could make this work, for Katie's sake if nothing else.

"Hope I didn't wake you," he said.

Christine took a long minute to respond. This was his first call during the course of the ten-day trip.

"Where are you?" she asked softly.

"At the airport in Boston. Unfortunately, it looks like I won't get out of here until tomorrow. Everything is on standby."

"You sound tired."

Just like her to say something about his well being. He really was a jerk.

"I was in a meeting most of the day. I've been sitting at the airport for about five hours."

"Can't you get a room and try again tomorrow?"

"I really need to get to Miami tonight. How's Katie?"

"Fine. She misses you."

"Did Barry Meier call?"

"Oh yes, I almost forgot. He left a message, something about Harbor House, hold on while I get it."

When she returned, she laughed softly into the phone. "This is like reading a foreign language."

She read the notes to Michael, but he really wasn't interested in Martin's project right now.

He took a deep breath and plunged in, hoping he could make his heart follow his plan. "Christine, I'm sorry for the way I've been the past few months."

"We can talk about that when you get home."

He heard the relief in her voice and felt a little better. If only they had ended the call there.

"Michael, I was just watching Melissa Cole on the Tonight Show. She said she dedicated that song, Angel's Blues, to you. Did you know that?"

He sat down in the phone booth, suddenly winded. "No."

"I didn't know it was that serious between the two of you," she said. "Yet another example of the man I don't know."

"I have no control over what Melissa says or does."

"I'm talking about your habits," she snapped. "Would it kill you to talk to me about anything with any depth to it?"

"I'm sorry…."

"Stop!" She sighed loudly. "Michael, you have to teach me how to live with you. I can't go on like this."

"I know. I promise I'll try harder."

He replaced the receiver and despite the line of people waiting to use the phone, he didn't rise immediately. A new kind of weariness had settled over him. He fingered the organizer in his lap, thinking of Beth. She was only a phone call away. He lifted the receiver and punched in the number he knew by heart, but the line was busy. He closed his eyes and leaned against the wall. Outside, someone tapped on the glass and he moved on.

He got an early flight out of Boston the next morning. He had been unable to get a room and stayed at the airport. He slept for most of the trip to Miami.

After checking into his hotel, he rescheduled his meeting for that afternoon and ordered coffee from room service, then took a long, hot shower and shaved the two-day stubble from his face.

He took a swallow of coffee and dialed his home number. Christine was more alert and surprised to hear from him twice within twenty-four hours.

"Is everything all right?"

"How would you feel about flying down to Palm Beach for a week or two?"

"Palm Beach? Are you talking about a vacation?"

"Grace has an estate there. I could really use some sunshine."

"That sounds wonderful."

"Can you get ready by tomorrow?"

"You bet. Are you going to work today?"

"I rescheduled for this afternoon."

"I love you. I can't wait to see you."

He closed his eyes and took a deep breath. "I love you too."

Christine invited Diane and Danny to join them in Florida. Christine, Diane, and Katie flew to Florida together. Danny couldn't get away from his business until the weekend and grudgingly said he wouldn't mind if Diane went before him.

The house by the sea was elegant and spacious with a private beach. Michael immediately took Katie down to the shore. He removed her little shoes and rolled the legs of her jumper up then set his barefoot baby on the wet sand. She lowered her head and studied her feet for a moment then looked up at him and started to cry.

He tucked the shoes in his pocket and lifted her to his shoulder. A soothing breeze and sunshine warmed them as they walked along the quiet beach. Michael started singing her favorite song. Katie bent forward until she could see his face and giggled. He laughed and some of the heartache lifted.

"Thanks Katie. Daddy loves you too."

Danny flew down for the weekend and on Saturday night they went to a nearby restaurant for dinner. Back at the house, Diane, Danny, and Christine sat on the balcony, enjoying the moonlight and warm breeze while Michael gave Katie a bath and tucked her into bed.

Instead of joining the others, he sat at the piano in the sunroom and began to play softly. He never seemed to have time to play and missed the relaxation. Making the decision to try harder with Christine had been the right thing to do. For once in his life, nearly everything was on track. He let his thoughts drift and didn't see Christine standing in the doorway.

"Why don't you ever play at home?"

He shrugged. "I never seem to have time."

She walked closer and watched his fingers on the keys. "I'm glad I didn't have to compete with you in school."

Michael took a deep breath and looked up at her, surprised to see a look of anger on her face.

"Is that Angel's Blues?" she asked.

He realized what he was playing and stopped immediately.

Her eyes teared. "I can't believe I've been so stupid."

He turned around to face her. "It's not what you think."

She folded her arms over her chest and sniffed.

"It's my song," he said.

"Your song?"

"I wrote it," he admitted softly.

"Is it about Melissa?"

He felt the wall rising between them. "I was fourteen when I wrote it."

"Fourteen? What did you know about love at fourteen?"

He looked out at the ocean. "The song is about the pretense of love."

She walked up behind him and put her hands on his shoulders. "Are you talking about your father?"

"No."

Christine frowned and moved around to face him, "Who then?"

Michael rose and walked to the open windows searching for a place to begin, painfully aware that she waited behind him as he wrestled with a decision.

"Damn it, Michael."

She turned and left him standing there staring out at the dark water, unaware how close she came to being the first person in over twenty years to hear the truth. Michael heard her footsteps retreating down the hall and put his forehead against the cool glass, fighting back old demons.

After they went to bed, he couldn't bring himself to apologize one more time. Instead, he made love to her with a craving he couldn't control. He reached out from the darkness and grasped blindly for rescue as if every point of contact was on fire and her body held the relief he needed.

Their lovemaking drained the last of his energy and he fell into a deep sleep and the nightmare, only this time the cold white hands had Katie, smothering her the way they had him. He struck the hands, tried to pull them from her, but his hands were small, like Katie's. He had no power, no strength.

"Please, let her go," he pleaded. "Take me. I won't fight anymore."

The thing in the dark laughed and released his daughter. Michael jumped to catch her, but she fell away from him. The hands gripped him now, tearing his flesh with fingernails sharp as razors. Just as the suffocation began, he watched Christine hand Katie to his father. His mother and siblings smiled as they stood in a semicircle around his father and Katie. No one noticed the beast drag him into the darkness.

He opened his eyes looking around the bedroom in shock. Chris sat beside him on the bed, a look of horror on her face and he knew he had woken her, probably with a scream.

"I'm sorry," he offered weakly.

She pushed the hair away from his forehead gently. "What in the world were you dreaming about?"

"Promise me you won't take Katie to my parents' house anymore."

She eyed him as if he had lost his mind.

"Do it, Chris!"

"I promise," she whispered.

Later that night, Christine was sleeping soundly in his arms when the nightmare made a second visit. Michael groaned then jumped violently, waking them both.

She squinted at him. "What is it?"

"Charlie horse," he managed, slipping away from her.

"Don't go."

He leaned down and kissed her forehead. "I'm going to walk it off. Go back to sleep."

Michael went out to the balcony and sat on the stone ledge taking the fresh night air deep into his lungs.

"I guess you couldn't sleep either," Diane said, from the shadows.

He jumped then fought for balance on the narrow ledge.

"Careful," Diane said, then laughed.

"I didn't see you sitting there."

She stood and held out a lit joint, "Care for a hit? It's good stuff."

He accepted the joint and drew deeply before handing it back.

Diane held up an open bottle of wine. "Would you like a sip?"

"No, I think I'll have scotch."

"Wow," she said with a shake of her head, "much too strong for me."

"Wine gives me a headache."

"Oh, all right, you talked me into it. I'll try one drink."

He walked inside to the bar and glanced at her over his shoulder. "Want me to add water?"

"Is it better that way?"

"I think it would be easier for you to swallow."

He added some water to her drink and turned to find her standing right behind him. She looked up at him and stared at him for a moment. He had seen the look before. She was seeing his shell, the façade he never truly connected to. He handed her the glass and walked away. He didn't want to deal with the curiosity he saw in her eyes.

After a moment, she followed him back to the terrace, "How about a walk on the beach?"

They walked along the water's edge, letting soft waves lap against their feet. Diane lit a second joint and passed it to him.

"I'm glad Chris invited me along," she said.

"I'm surprised you came."

"I have to admit I needed persuasion."

"Because of me?"

She laughed. "Wow, you really are bright."

"Why do you hate me, Diane?"

"I don't hate you. Originally, I just went along with Danny's point of view. When Chris got pregnant I thought you were taking advantage of her, because I saw her like a child who needed my protection." She smiled up at him. "Now that I know all three of you better, you're definitely growing on me."

He laughed softly and a shiver ran up his spine. The damned dream was right there, one step behind.

She looked out at the ocean and sighed. "I wish Danny had stayed in New York."

He figured she was making another joke. "That's no way to talk about your husband."

She took a long drag on the joint and handed it to him. "He's not going to be my husband much longer. He's messing around with someone else."

"I'm sorry," he said and inhaled deeply.

"It's okay, I've known for some time that I want something better than basic anyway."

Cool waves lapped at his feet and Michael looked down watching the wave recede, drifting with the high the marijuana brought. "Basic?"

"Yeah, you know, someone who settles for the essentials. Never breaks out either in thought or life. Danny never takes a risk. He's a missionary man, never deviates. I had better sexual partners in high school."

Michael laughed and handed the joint to her. "I think that's more information than I wanted."

Diane nudged him. "So how old were you the first time you had sex?"

She drew on the joint, coughed a little, and handed it back. It was too short and he shook his head. She threw the piece into the water and lit another.

Michael put his head back and took a deep breath of fresh air. "Sixteen, but I've never been sure I had the right to call it sex."

"Why not?"

"It was over in about thirty seconds. I was humiliated."

"What would the hordes of adoring women around the world think if they heard you're a thirty-second man?" she teased.

Michael stared out at the moonlit water and shrugged. "Maybe they'd realize I'm human."

They walked and talked, laughing at each other's stories for almost an hour. When they returned to the house, they found Danny pacing on the balcony.

He grabbed Diane's arm. "Having a good time?"

"Yes, as a matter-of-fact," Diane said, pulling her arm from his grip.

Danny leaned toward her, sniffing. "Are you drunk?"

"I'm a little high, but…"

Danny looked past her to Michael. "Forget you have a wife, asshole?"

Michael eyed him levelly. "Not for a second."

Diane shoved Danny. "Stop it."

Danny wheeled on her. "What's going on here? Are you charmed? Do you want him?"

"I don't have to listen to this." She pushed past him into the house.

"That's right. Go to bed where you belong." Danny called after her.

Diane turned back quickly, looking to Michael.

"Will you take me to the airport in the morning?"

"If that's what you want."

She turned and went inside again, and Danny turned on Michael. "Thanks you son-of-a-bitch."

"Apologize to her, Danny, you're wrong."

"No. I'm not. I've been watching the two of you flirt since I got here this morning."

Christine came to the doorway, holding Katie in her arms. Hearing Danny's last statement, she frowned. "What's going on?"

"Ask God's gift to women," Danny said, pushing past her.

Christine looked to Michael for an explanation.

"Diane and I went for a walk on the beach," he said. He nodded in Danny's direction. "To him, this means we're having an affair."

"Where's Diane?"

"Packing. She asked me to take her to the airport."

"No. I won't have it."

Christine handed Katie to Michael and took charge. After a lengthy and somewhat heated conversation with Danny in the kitchen, she called a cab to take him to the airport.

Michael rocked Katie back to sleep and went to bed as Christine and Diane talked. Finally, Christine closed the bedroom door, slipped under the cool sheets and cuddled against his warm body.

"Are you sleeping?"

"I was."

Her hand slipped over his chest and rubbed his abdomen. "Well, if you're not too tired, I was hoping you'd help me unwind. I really enjoyed making love earlier. It's been a long time since you've touched me that way."

Near the end of summer, Michael decided it was time to take Christine and Katie to Wyoming. Nellie met Christine and hugged Michael quickly before taking charge of Katie.

Sam was polite, but more distant than usual. Many times, Michael caught him watching, as if looking for some clue to a perplexing mystery. When he tried to meet Sam's gaze directly, he found he couldn't. As always, Sam had discerned the truth.

One afternoon, Michael saddled two horses and took Christine to the plateau where he always dreamed of building a home. He planned to tell her of his dreams, to finally reveal what he really wanted. They dismounted and walked to the edge. Looking down at the valley, he couldn't force himself to speak.

"This would be a beautiful place to build a house." Chris turned, smiling at him. "Don't you think?"

Michael walked away, picked up a rock, and threw it into the distance. She followed, her voice rising high and excited.

"This is home, isn't it? That's your real mother and father back there and this land is where you belong. The person you are back East is a fake, isn't he?"

He knew the penalty for locking her out was more questions, but he was lost in a landslide of truth. She was right. This was the place he wanted to build a home, but with Beth. Christine was the wrong woman and he was a fool for trying to make it work. Her voice penetrated his thoughts as she came closer, touching his shoulder.

"You have no need to talk about the family you left so long ago because they no longer exist, do they? Nellie, Sam and Red are your family, aren't they?" She grabbed his arm, squeezing the muscle. "Am I right?"

He finally looked at her and found his voice. "Yes, on all counts."

She threw up her hands. "Then why do you stay in New York?"

"The time isn't right," he answered tightly.

Chris let it go on that day, but on the plane home, she resumed the interrogation. "Explain why you've never talked about leaving New York."

"I'm not ready."

"What are you waiting for?"

He thought about his answer for a minute, then shrugged.

"Money," he said, turning his attention back to the newspaper in his hands.

"Come on, Michael, if you were to liquidate all of your assets what would you have?"

"I wouldn't do that."

"What if you did?"

He dropped the paper again, sighing loudly.

"Just give me a round number," she said.

He thought about it for a minute then rubbed his forehead. The subject was giving him a headache, so he tossed out a figure, hoping she would be satisfied.

"I'd put it at about eighty."

"Thousand?"

He stared, surprised she had no real idea, "Million Chris."

She gasped. "Are you talking about Nathan B or your personal worth?"

"Mine," he said, then shook his head and corrected himself, "ours."

"I had no idea," she murmured.

She didn't know the half of it. Eighty million was an old figure.

He laughed quietly. "I'm sorry it's such a shock."

"No wonder people treat you like you're gold. They all knew something I didn't. I hate that about you."

He looked away from her as she fussed around with a magazine in her lap, trying to shove it into her bag near her feet.

"All these damned secrets," she said loudly, talking to herself. "I have to pull everything out of you or I wouldn't know anything. Everyone knows more about you than I do."

He sighed loudly and shifted in his seat. "Please don't start this again."

"It's like the thing with Martin. I wouldn't have known about that if Diane hadn't told me."

"What thing with Martin?"

"The safe house. You never mentioned it."

"I don't mention that to anyone, Christine."

"Why? It's a wonderful thing. People will know that you care about kids."

"They'll want to know why I do it."

"I figure it has a lot to do with that picture of you as an altar boy."

He sat back again, closing his eyes, and his face flushed a deep crimson. Christine kissed his cheek and it took a lot of self-control not to turn away.

"You look so sad in that picture," she said. "When was it taken?"

"I was twelve."

"Were you an altar boy?"

He shook his head.

"Then what was the purpose of the photograph?"

"Christmas cards."

"So, why…."

He couldn't take any more. He unbuckled his seat belt and threw it aside, hurried to the bathroom and locked himself in for as long as he could take the confinement.

Chapter 20

The light on the telephone console flickered impatiently. He swiveled in his chair, looking west, across the Hudson before lifting the receiver. Christine seldom called him at work anymore. Since their trip to Wyoming, their marriage continued to spiral downward at a rapid pace.

"I thought you might want to know your father had a heart attack early this morning," Christine said.

He closed his eyes and willed himself to keep listening.

"They don't expect him to survive." She added, softening her tone. "I think your mother could use some emotional support. I'm going to help her."

He sighed heavily. "I don't see the purpose of this call."

"Of course you don't, you would have to give a damn about someone other than yourself first."

The line went dead. He dropped the receiver in its cradle and looked back at the view.

He drifted out into the hot August night and didn't feel the heat radiating from the concrete. He stopped by a favorite restaurant and ordered a light dinner, but had no appetite for food. After several drinks he stepped back into the night.

He hadn't known what he would feel when the time came to face the actual death of his parents. To his relief, he found great emotional distance from this one thing. He didn't care if his father died. Christine simply could not understand that he had no desire to commiserate with the dead.

Whether the prodigal son returned home or kept the status quo, his father would write the final act and have things his way as always. There would be no heartfelt apologies, no sentimental finale.

After four days of dodging phone calls and hermitage in Manhattan, he went home on Friday night. Christine was asleep in their bedroom and after checking on Katie he went upstairs to his study to stare at the television and drifted off to sleep.

"Michael!"

He swung at the figure in front of him and almost connected.

"What are you doing?" Christine jumped back.

The dark image receded and he saw Christine standing before him. He blinked a few times and swung his legs over the edge of the couch.

"I was dreaming," Michael said.

"You were doing a lot more than dreaming. I think your scream probably woke the neighbors."

He glanced up at her, past her, his heart still racing.

"The stress of distancing yourself from what's going on with your father is getting to you," she said.

Michael laughed bitterly. "Yeah, that must be it."

He could tell her and tell her, but she would never begin to understand without the whole story. Even then, she would probably never truly understand.

"I'm sorry I woke you," he said.

She knelt in front of him, peering up at his face. "Come to bed."

He didn't have the energy to fight anymore and followed her to their bed. Christine moved close to him, laying a slender leg over his, pressing close. One hand rubbed his chest, slipped to his abdomen.

"Maybe I could help you relax."

The consumption was total. His body took over and his mind went numb. Christine responded, but they weren't on the same plane. Swimming alone in this place of easy waves was far too comfortable.

The pitch gave way to smoother rhythm. Christine's nails dug into his back, but he didn't feel pain. All that mattered was sustaining this level. Then her body tensed, pulling at him, tightening around him. His breath caught in his throat and he slowed.

Christine applied a more urgent rhythm, compelling him to join her, took them forward, higher. Michael could no longer be separate. He held her tighter and tensed as they finished together.

For the first time that week, he slept peacefully.

Christine spent most of Saturday at the hospital with his family in Brooklyn while he stayed home with Katie. By that evening, Michael was so angry he wasn't speaking to Christine again. He intended to spend Sunday with Katie before taking the train back to Manhattan.

Early Sunday afternoon, he was in his study, reading a book to Katie when Christine returned from the hospital. Her grim expression said all he needed to know. His father was dead.

"We need to talk," she said.

He returned to the book, but the words were a blur. Katie grew impatient when he didn't speak.

"Read, Daddy."

"It's time for your nap, Katie." He lifted her and paused by Christine. "Give Mommy a kiss."

Katie offered a loud smack on her cheek, but Christine didn't take her eyes off him. The look should have dropped him where he stood.

Christine was still in his study when he returned. She stopped pacing when he appeared and swung around, greeting him with righteous anger.

"For God's sake, Michael, no matter what he did, he was still your father."

Michael met her gaze directly. "He was nothing."

He knew his coldness shocked her and didn't care. The phone rang and though he was closest, he didn't reach for it. She reached to answer it and he knocked it to the floor.

Christine bent and picked up the receiver. Michael headed for the bar.

"Sure, Bob, wait a minute," she said, then turned to him. "Will you talk to Bobby?"

He walked back from the bar and snatched the receiver from her hand. "What?"

"I need to talk to you about Dad," Bobby said.

"Sure, by all means, Bobby. Everyone else seems determined to drag me into this. Why shouldn't you?"

"Hey, I've never done that," Bobby snapped.

"Tell me then, what could you possibly have to say about him that I need to hear?"

"He wanted me to give you a letter from Uncle Frank."

Michael closed his eyes and gripped the receiver tighter.

"Well, shut my mouth," Bobby said.

Michael slumped in one of the leather chairs, a third glass of scotch in his hand. He heard Bobby talking with Christine downstairs and knew the moment was finally upon him.

Maybe Uncle Frank finally had something to say that could erase some of the damage. Maybe the letter contained an apology. He laughed bitterly.

"Maybe hell," he said.

Bobby came in waving an envelope. "Sorry, it took longer than I expected," "I had to go to the house to get this. It took me a while to find the thing. I wouldn't have gone to all of the trouble, but I promised Dad."

Michael stared silent and still, inside he felt like a hurricane simmering off shore.

"Mike," Bobby said, "yesterday afternoon, for the first time since you left home, Dad mentioned your name to me. If it means anything, I believe he finally regretted what happened between the two of you." Bobby held up the letter and smiled. "I think this letter proves that."

Michael quickly swallowed all of the scotch and went to the bar as Bobby continued.

"Dad said Susan found this letter addressed to you in Uncle Frank's things. He said he took it away from her because only you deserved to have it."

Michael walked back with a fresh drink and looked at the envelope in Bobby's hand. "Did you read it?"

Bobby shook his head and held the envelope out to him. Michael took the envelope gingerly as if it was coated in poison.

Bobby headed for the door. "I'll go downstairs and give you some privacy."

Michael placed the drink on the coffee table and took out the single-page letter written on Frank's pretentious personal stationery.

Michael,

Your actions today have left me no choice. All I worked for in this life means nothing. I cannot face the condemnation of my church and family. I know that when presented with the outrageous accusations of such an apparently innocent boy they would never choose to believe me.

I loved you deeply. I gave my best to you and you repaid me with contempt and treachery. I hope my death brings you great satisfaction.

Frank

As expected, Frank's last words held no mercy, no unselfish thought. Michael folded the letter neatly, returned it to the envelope, tossed it into the middle desk drawer and locked the drawer. He picked up his glass and downed all of the scotch. His heart pounded so fiercely in his ears he couldn't hear. The need to flee wrapped around his body like a boa, constricting his chest.

He got to his feet and descended the stairs slowly, each step taking him deeper into a dark abyss until at last he was submerged. He paused in the doorway of the family room where Christine stood talking with Bobby. They stopped and turned to look at him. He saw them, but was disconnected from this time and these people. He turned toward the stairs again.

Christine ran after him. "Are you all right?" She grabbed his arm. "Damn it, why are you always running away from me? Stay here and let me help you with this."

He shook off her hand and hurried down the stairs as Katie toddled down the hall.

"Daddy!" Katie wailed holding out her arms to him.

Though he heard Katie calling, Michael couldn't respond.

The sound of someone hammering pulled him from sleep. There was music, water running, and a child crying. He opened his eyes and looked around at pink tiled walls, the white tub he lay in, and his naked, bloody body. Fearing a repeat performance of his suicide attempt, he immediately looked to his wrists and found only his left hand to be the source of the blood. He had a couple of broken fingers and cut across his palm. He eased himself from the tub and turned on the water at the sink to wash the blood away for damage assessment. The mirror over the sink appeared to be the beneficiary of the blow that broke his hand. He didn't need to see his reflection anyway. He knew exactly what he would find.

He tore up a shirt and wrapped his hand as he followed a trail of clothes to the bed. There weren't any empty alcohol bottles and he understood he hadn't brought any booze into this room. When he entered, he had already consumed enough to keep him intoxicated for a while.

He didn't know what day this was or where he had stopped. The clock said eleven and a peek out the window revealed a dark night. The Porsche was parked in front of the room. Across the road a neon sign lit the foggy night and gave him a location. Somehow, he had made it to Chattanooga.

Suddenly, his legs began to tremble. He tossed the clothes on the bed and dropped on the edge. He considered calling New York then Wyoming and finally Texas, but didn't pick up the phone. Instead, he slept off his weakness and moved on.

Two weeks after disappearing, he returned to his home in Connecticut wearing black jeans, a black T-shirt, black boots, and a black cowboy hat and dark sunglasses. The sunglasses were to hide his eyes. The black clothing had been a drunken whim.

Christine waited on the first landing. Michael glanced up at her through the dark glasses as he ascended the stairs, but said nothing. He wasn't in the mood for war.

She followed him into their bedroom. "Where have you been?"

He tossed his keys and the glasses on the dresser, then pulled the T-shirt over his head and sat on the bed to remove his boots.

"Talk to me, Michael."

"I have nothing to say."

"Well, you'd better think of something. I'm tired of chasing you around in circles."

He knew his eyes would shock her, but looked up at her anyway, he needed the edge.

Christine gasped and stepped back.

He stood and moved around her, heading for the shower.

"Michael your eyes are bloody."

She grabbed his hand and he jerked away in pain. Christine stared at him in disbelief.

"Have you been in a fight?"

Michael slammed the bathroom door and leaned against it. He didn't want to come back here, but was past the point of disappearing into the horizon.

After a long shower, he went to his study, and poured three fingers of scotch into a glass then sat behind his desk and sipped poison while life kept rolling on around him.

Maybe they had a place in the Guinness records for least evolved human. They could put him in a wax museum somewhere. Tour guides could say he fooled everyone for years. Tourists could marvel at his life-like quality. They would whisper that he almost looked alive.

Running had always been a foolish notion, but he was only a boy when that all started. He knew better now. He couldn't run away from a ton of weight lashed to his back. He could pretend he wasn't carrying the thing, pretend he didn't feel the weight, but the burden grew, bending him, pushing him to his knees.

After all these years, nothing had really changed. There was still no light shining at the bottom of this empty well. He was still down here alone, still running in the dark.

He didn't blame Christine. In the end, her meddling hadn't produced the turning point. His father simply saved the best hand for last and the double-trump had him on his knees.

He slipped into Katie's room and lifted her from the bed. She woke, blinked a few times then smiled at him. He eased into the rocking chair and she snuggled close to his chest as he hummed her favorite song. Soon, she slept peacefully, unaware of the tears streaming down his face.

He didn't know Christine was there until she took Katie from him and placed her back in the bed. He wiped the tears away with his good hand. Christine took that hand in hers and pulled, trying to get him to come with her. He looked up at her slowly and shook his head.

"Come to bed," she said, as if he were addle-minded. He followed her out into the hallway and stopped.

"Wait," he began, but stopped, lowering his head. After a moment, he cleared his throat and continued. "I have to tell you something."

"Then let's talk."

He followed her into the family room and closed the double doors. She sat on the sofa and Michael walked directly to the bar to pour a drink. He took a deep swallow before joining her on the couch and couldn't bring himself to look at her.

"I think you should know I wouldn't have come back if it weren't for Katie." He paused, hearing her gasp, but then pushed forward. "I can't go on living life up to my neck in lies any more."

He took a long pull from the glass, looked her in the eye, and finally spoke the truth. "I want a divorce."

Christine slapped his face so hard his ears rang. Michael closed his eyes and lowered his head. He expected her to hit him again, but she stood, moving away to a safer distance. When she faced him again, she was in tears.

"What lies are you talking about? Did you ever love me?"

"I never lied about that," he said. "I just never loved you the way I should."

"Damn you to hell." She flung the doors open and turned to him. "I want you out of here, right now. Get out!"

At work, Michael found it difficult to concentrate and hid behind the assumption that the change was due to his father's death. He seldom spoke to anyone and drove Kelly to take nearly all the responsibility.

His behavior finally drew Grace's personal attention. Just before Christmas, Grace summoned him to her home for a chat over lunch.

Michael sat next to her on a blue silk divan and Grace didn't bother to hide her alarm. He had lost nearly thirty pounds and knew his appearance was shocking. He did his best not to look at her directly. Something, some demon, had taken residence in his body.

"What is it, Michael?" She leaned closer and took his chin in her hand, forcing him to look her in the eye. Her expression changed to sympathy. "Are you aware that you bare your soul to the world with these magnificent beasts?"

Michael closed his eyes and laughed miserably. Grace patted his hand.

"Is this because of the death of your father?"

"I wasn't close to my father."

"Sometimes that's worse."

He looked up slowly then away again. "I need some time off."

"Kelly is certainly competent. Take as much time as you need."

Before taking a leave of absence, Michael forced himself to address the situation with Christine. Phone calls always led to an argument, so he drove to Connecticut late one evening, hoping Katie would be asleep. He couldn't see her right now.

He parked in the drive and entered through the side door of the kitchen. Entering the main hallway, he heard voices. His footsteps on the thick carpet outside the piano room were inaudible. He stepped into the doorway and found Christine locked in a heated embrace with Danny D'Angelo.

"Tell me I'm jumping to conclusions," he said.

Christine and Danny separated quickly as Michael advanced. Anger boiled in him.

"I don't have to tell you anything," Christine said.

Danny kept his eyes on Michael. "That's right."

"Shut up and get out of my house," Michael snapped.

"Excuse me, but this is no longer your house," Christine said.

Those words finally stopped Michael's progression. He looked from Danny to her, controlling the fury with great effort.

"I need to talk to you," he said.

"Why now, Michael? You never talked to me before."

"I'm leaving New York and I want to make sure we're clear on a few things before I go."

"Leaving? Where are you going?"

"Call it a vacation."

She stepped closer to him, "For how long?"

Danny stepped beside Christine. "Since he's leaving, I guess you'd better tell him."

Christine tore her attention away from Michael and looked to Danny. "Not now."

Michael turned to Danny. "Tell me what?"

"You're gonna love it." Danny smiled widely at him and Michael barely suppressed the urge to punch him in the face.

Christine stepped between them and focused on Danny. "You should go. I'll call you later."

"I'll wait upstairs."

Michael stepped around Christine. "She said she'd call."

"Shut up, Mikey," Danny said. He stepped closer and poked Michael in the chest. "You're not calling the shots around here anymore."

Michael struck with such force the smaller man fell and slid fifteen feet across the parquet floor. He started toward Danny and Christine grabbed his arm.

"Michael stop!"

Danny struggled to his feet and backed away as Michael approached, dragging Christine with him.

"Get out!" Michael roared.

Christine moved in front of Michael, blocking his path. "Don't do this. You'll go to jail."

"Never mind, Christine," Danny said, wiping the blood from his nose. "I'll call it a night."

While she walked Danny to the door, Michael went to the kitchen for ice. Striking Danny had re-injured the freshly healed bones and his hand throbbed.

Christine opened the door and watched as he wrapped ice in a towel. "Do you think you can talk to me calmly or should we put this off?"

"Let's get it over with."

Christine insisted they talk in the formal living room, far away from Katie's ears. Michael went to the bar, poured a glass of scotch, and stayed on his feet. The rage had receded to a corner of his soul, ever ready, but his body felt like it was ready to explode into a million pieces.

He eyed Christine. "So, how long have you been seeing him?"

"Danny's just a friend."

"Right," he snapped.

Christine glared at him. "I'm not going to discuss him with you."

"Why not?" He shot back. "Why don't we get to discuss your mistakes?"

"And how many women have you slept with since you married me, Michael?"

Michael's eyebrows shot up in surprise. "You're sleeping with him?"

"Yes, Michael, I am. He's good to me."

"He is an asshole."

"Then I guess an asshole is a step up from what I had. Unlike you, he makes me feel important to him."

He stared at her in disbelief. Surely, she didn't believe Danny was good for her. He didn't have the energy to explore her poor choices right now.

"Can we talk about a divorce settlement and custody?" He knew his tone was cold. He couldn't help it.

"We can talk about alimony and child support, but I won't discuss custody. Katie stays with me."

He dropped his glass on the table and walked toward the hall. She ran ahead of him, blocking the doorway.

"Don't go up there. I told you Katie stays with me."

He frowned. "I was just leaving, Chris."

She released his arm and took a step backward, starting to cry. "I just don't know what to expect from you anymore."

Michael watched her, hating himself more with every breath. "For a while, you brightened all of the darkness in me and I loved you for that. I was selfish and I was wrong, but please don't take Katie from me. I'll do anything you want. You can have everything I own."

Something, deep in his core crumbled and he swayed on his feet. He turned again. He had to get out of there.

She grabbed his arm. "Michael, wait. I really hate what you've done, but," she paused and took a breath as though she too were exhausted. "I want custody, but I won't keep you and Katie apart."

He wanted to thank her, but couldn't speak. He looked away quickly, but not fast enough to hide sudden tears.

Christine released her grip on his arm, her voice softer now. "How long will you be gone?"

He shrugged and blinked back the burning tears.

"We'll meet about the divorce when you get back," she said. "Okay?"

He nodded and started away, but her voice stopped him again. "Want to look in on Katie before you go?"

Michael stepped into Katie's room and stood beside the bed looking down at her sweet face. The weight of guilt pressed down again. She deserved so much more than him for a father.

"She looks like an angel," he whispered.

Christine rubbed his shoulder. "She looks like you."

Michael turned and walked out of the room. He ached all the way to his marrow. He started to walk toward the stairs, but turned halfway down the hall. Christine was still near Katie's door.

"I know I don't have the right to give you advice, but please step back and take an objective look at Danny. He won't make you happy for long. He's beneath you, Chris."

He slipped his house key off the ring and placed it on top of the stair rail.

"Michael, don't. You can keep the key until we get everything settled."

He shook his head. "I don't want you to think I'll come walking back in whenever I feel like it. I know this isn't my home anymore."

"Wait." Christine walked closer, lowering her voice. "There's something I'd better tell you."

She lifted the key, fingering the metal before she spoke. "I showed the letter from your Uncle Frank to Danny."

The humiliation never ended. He started down the stairs with Christine on his heels.

"Michael, I was angry. I had the right to some answers." She grabbed a handful of his jacket stopping him. "Danny said the letter was your uncle's suicide note."

He shook off her hand. "Let me go."

"Danny suggested I go public about your relationship with your uncle unless you give me full custody of Katie. At the time, it sounded like the perfect revenge."

Michael gripped the rail so tightly pain from his injured hand shot up his arm to his shoulder. He wanted to scream.

"Katie worships you. I won't use her to even the score."

He had to move. He managed a curt thank you and walked down the stairs for the last time.

Chapter 21

Martin was in the middle of a call with Barry Meier about the safe house when his secretary interrupted.

"Please, excuse me, Dr. Edger, Mrs. Edger is on line three. She says it's urgent."

Gail didn't bother to say hello. "Can you get away for lunch?"

"My schedule's full…" he began.

"This is important. Juggle the damned schedule."

"What's up?"

"It's about Michael, but I can't talk about it now."

"All right. I'll see what I can do and call you back."

He found her waiting in a small restaurant near his office, out of patience and agitated. In all their years together, Martin had never seen her like this.

"What in the world's wrong?"

"Here," Gail handed him an open newspaper.

Before Martin read a word, he inspected the picture of a beautiful, sad-eyed altar boy and immediately knew he didn't want to read the piece. He skimmed the first two paragraphs of the column before tossing the paper down in disgust.

"No one pays attention to what these people have to say, Gail. They're always being sued because they fabricate the stories."

"I think you should talk to Michael anyway. Do you know where he is?"

Martin shook his head. He and Michael hadn't spoken in months.

Gail folded her arms over her chest, clearly appalled. "Who could be behind this?"

"My guess is Christine. She's very bitter about the divorce."

Gail shook her head. "I called her on the outside chance she could give me a phone number where we could reach him or something. She couldn't have been nicer."

"Well, I guess what really matters right now is that we've got to get to Michael."

Gail tapped the paper angrily. "That article says this uncle was the one who actually oversaw Michael's education as a kid and that Michael started telling terrible lies about him because he didn't want his uncle telling him what to do anymore."

She took a breath and sat back staring at the abomination lying between them. "He was a priest and he took his own life, Martin. The article says Michael was the reason."

Martin thought back to the conversation years ago in his old Brooklyn apartment when Michael told him, "You don't know what I did." Suddenly, Martin knew the truth and felt sick to his stomach.

"Did Christine give you a number where he could be reached?" Martin asked quietly.

Gail shook her head, concern clouding her face. "Are you okay?"

He took a big swallow of water and a deep breath. For now, he would keep his suspicions to himself.

"I'd better go. I'll call his office at Nathan B. If anybody knows where he is, it will be Kelly."

Martin expected resistance from Kelly, but she had seen the article just that morning, courtesy of a livid Grace Bartholomew. They were eager to find him as well.

"I wish I could tell you where he is, Dr. Edger, but I don't have a number. He calls every Friday afternoon to throw me a lifeline. To be perfectly honest with you, it doesn't even sound like Michael on the telephone anymore. He hasn't been himself for ages. I'm afraid this newest thing is going to take a nasty toll on him."

"I'd like to be there when he calls this Friday."

"He always calls around two."

Martin arrived at one-thirty on Friday and waited with Kelly in Michael's office for the phone call. At ten after two, a secretary informed them Michael was on the phone. Kelly punched the button, handed the receiver to Martin, and left the room.

"Michael?" When there was absolute quiet on the other end, he thought maybe Michael didn't recognize his voice. "It's Martin."

"I know."

"Talk to me."

There was a deep sigh from the other end. "What do you want?"

"Where are you?"

"Europe."

If Michael was in Europe, he probably hadn't seen the article. Relieved, Martin relaxed a little. "Why are you in Europe?"

"I've already been to Chattanooga."

"What's that supposed to mean?" Martin asked.

"What are you doing in my office?"

Martin took a deep breath and plunged in. "I'm afraid I have some bad news."

"Is it Katie?"

There was a pained urgency in Michael's voice that forced Martin to back pedal a little.

"Katie's fine."

"Good. Christine knows where I am in case of an emergency."

Surprised at the fact that Christine had lied to his wife, Martin frowned. "Christine has your number?"

"Yeah," he said then cautiously added, "why are you surprised?"

"Gail couldn't get your number from her."

There was a short pause before Michael spoke. "Why did Gail need it?"

"Well, we wanted to talk to you," he hesitated, took a deep breath then forged ahead. "There is a pretty nasty piece about you and your uncle in one of the rags."

After a long silence, Martin decided to push. "I think you should come home," he said.

"No, what I should do is put a bullet through my brain."

There was a soft click and the line went dead. Kelly hurried back into Michael's office, waving a paper at Martin.

"He was at a hotel in Cannes. His American Express bill came in today."

"You opened his mail?"

"No, not me," she grinned innocently. "Barry Meier called and told me the name of the hotel."

"Let's call that hotel."

The secretary opened the outer door. "Please, excuse me, but Mr. O'Mara would like to speak to you again, Dr. Edger."

Relieved, Martin picked up the receiver. Kelly hurried to her own office to call the hotel.

"I'm sorry for hanging up," Michael's said.

Martin was tired of dancing around the truth. "Tell me about Uncle Frank."

"No." Michael's voice was barely audible.

Martin gambled and pushed again. "Then tell me the story of the priest and the brilliant little boy."

"I can't."

Martin heard the pain in Michael's hoarse voice and cringed. He tried again, his voice full of urgency. "Michael, you're my friend and I love you. I promise, I only want to help."

"I'm sorry, Martin."

Again, the line went dead.

"Damn it!" Martin shouted.

Martin immediately called Gail to get her opinion about a trip to France. Gail's first concern was the probability that Michael would attempt a second suicide before they could reach him. She wanted to alert the police. Unfortunately, Kelly learned Michael checked out of the hotel three days earlier.

Later that day, when he should have been on his way home, Martin remained in his office at a complete loss. He needed to find Michael. Gail insisted he had done everything possible and should let go. Still, Martin knew she was just as afraid of the unthinkable as he was.

The private line rang, splitting the silence like a crack of thunder. Martin jumped for the receiver before it could ring again.

"I just spoke to Christine," Gail said, "Michael called her. She said he was furious about that article. It seems her boyfriend took information she shared with him to that paper and made a bundle on the sale."

Gail sighed and her voice dropped to a cautious level. "She said to tell you he's been at his apartment since last night. I figured if you showed the doorman your credentials..."

"I'm on my way."

"Want me to meet you there?" Gail asked carefully.

"No, I'll have to lie my way in there and I don't want you to be part of that. I'll call you when I can. Thanks honey."

Martin explained to the doorman that Mr. O'Mara had called in need of his assistance. He presented his license as proof and was allowed to enter one more time without approval. He found the door to the penthouse unlocked when he stepped off the private elevator. A sense of dread rocked him as he stepped inside the dark hall.

"Persistent, as always," Michael said from the shadows.

Martin hadn't heard him move. Michael's slim body was no more than a silhouette in the doorway leading to the formal living room. He turned back to the living room and slumped on a white sofa. Martin followed, stepping carefully into the shadowy room and bent to turn on a lamp.

"I prefer the dark," Michael said.

Martin took the nearest chair across from him. The smell of booze was certain and he figured the source to be the much-favored scotch. His vision adjusted quickly to the darkness and he spotted a half-empty glass in Michael's hand.

"Have you been drinking a lot?"

Michael's shoulders rose and fell in idle concern. "I guess Christine told you I was here."

"We're all worried about you."

He sighed loudly and shifted his weight on the sofa. "I talked to my lawyer today. He says Christine wants the house, all of my current and future assets, not to mention custody of Katie."

"Let's not forget your gonads on a platter."

Michael laughed bitterly. "Nah, she's going to let me keep those. She's hoping I'll be stupid enough to make more children with other women who won't let me see them."

"Michael..." Martin began, but Michael jumped ahead.

"I deserve it for being such a liar."

"Are you saying you didn't love her?"

He laughed harshly. "I tried to make it work because of Katie, but I ran out of energy."

"Does this weariness have anything to do with the letter from your uncle?"

"Ah, we're back to that."

"Michael, please." Martin stopped, drawing in a deep breath. "You're never going to be free until you let go."

Michael stared at the drink in his hand. Despite the prolonged binge, his thoughts were oddly lucid. The last three days had been the worst in his life. The bottom had been coming for a long time, but each time he saw the end in front of him and welcomed it, the path fragmented and scattered smaller and smaller pieces of him in all directions.

"You know," he said, pointing his glass at Martin, "a long time ago, a good friend pointed out that allowing the past to run my future was ruining my life, but it wasn't until today that I realized that if I don't find a way to get beyond this, I will kill myself." He laughed bitterly and finished the rest of his drink in two swallows. "Neither my parents, nor good old Uncle Frank are, excuse me, were, worth the trouble of such agonizing."

He closed his eyes, searching for courage, for the very breath to speak. This thing, this burden, demanded all of his energy. He said a silent prayer hoping that God would at least answer this one prayer because this was his last chance. If he didn't succeed, the gun was loaded and waiting.

He leaned back on the couch and looked up at the ceiling, resting the empty glass on his thigh. He closed his eyes and let the past fall over him. "Let's just jump into the deep end, one week before my twelfth birthday."

The swift turn for the worst began with his choice of absolute defiance at what would be his last piano competition in 1962. Uncle Frank and his teacher had insisted on a complicated Mozart concerto, one that never appealed to Michael. He had made up his mind to do his best to meet all of Frank's aspirations when it came to academics, but music was his and his alone. Music lifted his spirit, taking him to a place where pain and disappointment gave way to hope. If he didn't have music, he had nothing.

He walked on stage knowing if he played what was in his heart instead of the program, he probably would not win and the consequence of losing meant submitting himself to Frank's rage. Defiance of Frank's wishes was one thing, losing would be much worse.

Frank stood off stage, watching intently as he sat before the grand piano. Winning was personal to his uncle, anything less than first place would be greeted as absolute failure. Frank fed on the power and control he wielded and this contest was especially important to him. The prize of fifteen-thousand dollars wasn't the goal. He needed the world to see Michael's accomplishments as the direct reflection of his devotion, his tutelage, ultimately his own brilliance.

Michael placed shaking hands over the keys, took a deep breath and played Claire de Lune with a passion borne in anger and loss of hope, a musical litany to the child he was never allowed to be.

When they awarded him first place, Frank watched on from the sidelines. The smile on his face looked genuine to everyone but Michael and finally he understood his uncle's interest wasn't about winning first place after all. The whole thing was about owning him, living through him. He wasn't a living, breathing child to Uncle Frank and his desires and hopes were of little concern.

Frank was silent as they left the auditorium and on the cab ride to meet old friends of Frank's for dinner. Michael watched with growing dread as Frank swallowed drink after drink. His speech became urgent, louder, and the bitterness Frank usually contained so well seeped into his attitudes. Michael found it curious that no one seemed to notice his uncle's decline in character. In fact, no one except him ever seemed willing to see the real Frank O'Mara.

Back in their hotel room, Michael undressed in the bathroom, bathed and put on his pajamas slowly, stalling for time. On the other side of the door, Frank turned on a hockey game, a sign that his mind might be on other things. Michael hoped his uncle would soon drift off to sleep, but when he opened the door, Frank insisted he join him in a champagne toast to their victory. Michael buried the idea of resistance with other arguments and sipped the bitter champagne.

Soon, he was dizzy and Frank guided him to the bed. He lay there staring at the ceiling, with the room spinning, drunk for the first time and Frank started to unbutton his pajama top. He pushed clumsily at Frank's hands.

"Be still," Frank said, slipping the shirt from Michael's shoulders.

Michael opened his eyes and tried to focus. "Please, leave me alone."

His uncle thumped his forehead with the knuckles of his right hand, "Ungrateful bastard."

Frank yanked his pajama bottoms away and swung him over the edge of the bed, raining blows to his lower back, buttocks, and thighs with a wooden hanger, like always carefully striking the flesh where it wouldn't show. Michael struggled violently and Frank grabbed his hair, bending his head back so Michael had to look at him.

"You earned this."

Finally, Frank lifted him back to the bed and began to rub lotion into the raised welts. Michael's stomach tightened and he shut his eyes tightly to avoid looking at Frank.

"That's it, Mikey, just relax. Uncle Frank will take care of you."

Franks hand began rubbing the lotion on Michael's genitals. "That feels good now, doesn't it?"

Michael started to shake, drowning in rage and shame, tears rolling out of his closed eyes.

Frank leaned forward raining kisses over Michael's eyes and face, stroking him all the while.

"Sweet, sweet tears," Frank murmured.

Frank climbed onto the bed and started to roll him to his side. Everything in Michael rose in defiance.

"No," he said. He wanted the word to come out strong, but the sound was weak, like a plea.

"Hush."

Frank continued to force him around and Michael grabbed the headboard clinging to it desperately. Frank straddled him and started punching. Random blows fell over Michael's back and head. Finally, a blow landed between his shoulder blades and knocked the wind from his lungs. While he gasped for air, Frank's weight pinned him to the bed.

The first thrust ripped him like a dull knife. He groaned and Frank covered his face with his hand, the fingernails digging into

Michael's cheek. The angry assault pushed the remainder of precious air from Michael's lungs and darkness came quickly.

When he woke, Frank lay next to him snoring. He quietly crawled out of bed, locked himself in the bathroom and sat under the shower for a long time, letting the hot water beat on his body, hoping he could wash the filth away.

The next morning over a breakfast Michael was forced to eat, Frank smiled paternally.

"Don't play with your food, Michael. We are on a tight schedule this morning."

Michael swallowed a small bite of toast that scraped his dry throat. "Aren't we going home now?"

Frank stared for a long moment, the paternal smile slipped and his gaze cold now. "You know we are going to have your picture taken for the Christmas cards. Don't test my patience, not after what you pulled yesterday."

Frank stepped into the dressing room and helped him slip on an altar boy's cassock then walked him to the photographer who guided Michael to a spot before a dark blue canvas and posed him with a candle in his hands and combed his hair.

"Ready?"

He managed a nod and the photographer lit the candle. "Be careful to hold it away from you."

"And remember to smile," Uncle Frank said.

While Michael stared into the lens of the camera, a trickle of blood ran down his leg and into a shoe. A sudden wave of nausea rocked him.

The photographer smiled at him and sighed. "Sweetie, you have the blue eyes of an angel. Can you smile for me?"

Michael sank to his knees and vomited.

Frank grabbed him by the neck, pushing him down the hall, shoved him into the men's room then stepped inside and locked the door where he yanked the cassock over Michael's head. He grabbed a handful of paper towels, wet them and wiped Michael's face roughly then shook him hard. "Why are you being so defiant today?"

Michael closed his eyes and fought another wave of nausea. Frank pinched the flesh of his thin chest between a thumb and fore-finger and twisted.

"You are going to get dressed and go back in there with a smile, understand me?"

He swallowed hard and managed to nod.

The photographer eyed them both, her sympathy not lost on Michael. She positioned him on a small platform, handed him another candle and patted his cheek tenderly.

"You don't have to smile," she said gently. "Just look right into the camera lens, all right?"

Michael heard Frank stirring in the darkness beyond the bright lights.

Later, on their way back to Brooklyn, he leaned against the door of his grandmother's big Lincoln, resting his forehead against the cool glass as the world slid by the window.

Frank's hand gently grazed his cheek.

Michael scooted away, closer to the door. His heart beat so hard stars danced in front of his eyes.

Frank surveyed him with an odd, unpleasant detachment. "Name one person who cares about you other than me."

Tears welled in Michael's eyes and he lowered his head.

Frank's voice infiltrated his prayer. "You know I love you."

The edges of his vision were black, as if he were living inside a tube. He turned his head slowly, summoning courage. Frank smiled and held a hand out.

Michael stared at his hand, looked up at Frank's smiling face and his stomach turned sour.

"God meant for you to be mine," Frank said ever so softly.

Back at home, Frank set the trophy on the kitchen table before Michael's father and grinned broadly. "Look what your boy did this weekend."

Ed grunted and rose for a cup of coffee.

Frank tried again. "Evidently you don't understand. This was a major competition."

Ed turned on him, "I understand only one thing. You're turning my son into a pansy and I want it to stop. The education is one thing, but I want this fagoty piano playing to stop now."

Ed looked down on Michael, his face a mask of disgust. "Just look at him." He grabbed Michael's collar, pulling him up in the chair. "Sit up, Genius."

"You should be proud, Ed."

His father turned his attention to Frank. "Don't come into my house and lecture me. I didn't have it easy like you did. I had to work from the time I was fifteen."

"Here we go with the poor-me routine again. I'm not going to apologize for being the youngest in the family."

Michael managed to slip away as the old argument began between his father and Frank.

He stepped out the back door and around the corner, to the alley and sidewalk. Soon he was running hard until he was beyond their sight, away from their reach. He spent the night hiding in the park, cold, hungry, and jumping at every sound. Near dawn he reluctantly started toward home, but saw the church and a few people streaming in to early mass. He slipped inside and knelt in the shadows of the back pew, lost in prayer when a hand touched his shoulder. He looked up into the kindly face of Father Patrick, the elder priest in the church, a man whom Frank mocked behind his back.

Father Patrick's smile slipped. "What is it?"

"I..." With all of the agony of the last eight years balanced on the tip of his tongue, he glanced around, knowing Frank was probably near.

Father Patrick cupped his chin in the palm of his hand and lifted his face gently. Tears filled Michael's eyes and he swallowed hard.

"There you are!" Frank said from his left. "You've got the whole family looking for you!"

Frank grabbed him by the back of his collar and pulled him out of the pew.

"No need to be so rough," Father Patrick said.

Frank eyed the older priest with barely suppressed rage. "This is family business."

Frank took him out of the view of others and marched him down the corridor to his personal living quarters and closed the door.

Frank shook him roughly. "What did you say to him?"

Michael stood five feet away, trembling, with no answers.

"Well?" Frank grabbed his face and dug his fingernails into Michael's cheek.

"Nothing, I..."

Frank slapped him hard. "Don't lie to me!"

Michael backed away, hot tears streaking down his face.

Frank matched him step for step. "You little bastard, after all I did for you."

He backed into the wall and Frank kept coming. Absolute panic rose in Michael and he charged, knocking his uncle flat on his back. He ran out the door and down the hall toward the back door with Frank on his heels. Outside in the garden a hoe rested against the brick wall and he grabbed it, swinging at his uncle and connected with both shins, bringing him down again.

Frank sat back on the ground and Michael held the hoe firmly.

"If you ever touch me again," he said breathlessly, "I'll tell Father Patrick everything."

Neither of them was aware that Father Patrick had stepped outside and witnessed Michael's statement.

Father Patrick looked at Uncle Frank, his face flushed and angry. "What is going on here?

Michael tossed the hoe into a garden of roses and walked away, leaving Frank to whatever lie he might choose.

He opened the back door at home and found his father at the table, smoking and scowling at the paper.

"Where the hell have you been? Your mother's worried sick."

Since his mother didn't seem to know he existed most of the time, Michael doubted the truth of his father's statement. Ed rose, towering above him, loosening his belt.

"Go downstairs."

There was little doubt about what would happen in the basement with the belt swinging in his father's hand.

Ed followed a few steps behind and closed the basement door, "Where were you?"

Michael turned at the bottom of the steps. "I was just walking."

"Turn around and drop your pants."

Michael turned, wondering if his father's blows would be equal to Frank's. He let his pants drop and for a moment nothing happened. Then his father grabbed his shirt and lifted it, pulled him around, looking at his back and chest.

"Where the hell did you get all these bruises?"

"Uncle Frank."

"What did you do?"

He was smart, everyone said so, he should have known to keep his mouth shut, but he hurt so much, he went ahead and told the truth, hoping his father would rise to the occasion.

At first, his father's reaction to his statement was hard to interpret. He stared at Michael, sat down on the bottom step and stared some more.

"You make me sick," he said finally.

All hope for anything better in this relationship vanished. His father's face flushed red and he rose again, drawing back his hand. Michael's eyes filled with tears and he lowered his head just as his father's big fist knocked him off his feet.

At breakfast the next morning, his father informed him it was his turn to mow Grandma O'Mara's small back yard. He walked the three blocks to her house and opened the garage door to get the mower. A stench flooded his nostrils and he backed away, peering into the dark, until his eyes adjusted and his mind registered the horror. Frank's body hung motionless from the rafters at the center of the garage. His eyes bulged out of his head and his black tongue protruded out of his mouth. His face was swollen and discolored.

Michael backed away, looking down the alley toward the street just as his brother Bobby and a few friends walked by laughing and talking, happy on this spring day, completely oblivious of him, of this horror. He turned back, praying he wouldn't see Frank again.

"Ah, Michael, I thought I heard someone out here..." his grandmother's voice stopped mid sentence and she uttered a low cry.

He turned and caught her as she fell.

"Get your father," she said quietly, leaning against the garage door, clutching her chest.

Ed stared at his dead brother for a moment then turned and grasped Michael's shoulder, digging his thick fingers into the flesh.

"That should be you."

Tears swam in Michael's eyes as he choked on his father's words. His father slapped him, knocking him backward.

"Don't start any of that crybaby crap. Get over there and stand under his feet while I cut him down."

He inched along the concrete floor while his father got the ladder. Finally, he stood just in front of Frank's shoes. His father opened the ladder then shoved him forward.

"I said under. Put his feet on your shoulders so you can bear his weight."

Michael held his breath and moved forward, touching the dead man's shoes, while his father climbed the ladder and cut the rope. The body swung loose and his father wrapped an arm around the waist. One of Frank's cold hands brushed across Michael's face and he bit back the cry that rose in his throat.

His father eased Frank's body down to the concrete floor and took a deep breath as he straightened his back. Finally, he looked at Michael.

"Get out of my sight."

That night, after a hard day at the bottle, Ed O'Mara slammed into his bedroom and pulled him from the bed for the first time. He grabbed a handful of Michael's pajama top and yanked him down the stairs, punching and cursing him every step of the way. At the edge of the basement stairs, his father shoved him and he tumbled down the full flight.

"Frank told Grandma O'Mara you'd been making trouble for him with Father Patrick."

Ed took two quick steps to the thick leather strap and lifted it from a hook on a support post. Turning, he eyed Michael with clear rage. "I'm going to make you wish it was you hanging in that garage."

"Dad, please I didn't tell Father Patrick anything..."

"You killed a priest!"

After Ed's energy finally ran down, he grabbed him by a foot and dragged him across the floor where he tossed him into a storage box that was once used for coal.

Ed slammed the door and snapped the lock shut then popped it with his fist. "God will never forgive you."

When the light went out and the upstairs door closed, Michael crawled into a corner and curled into the fetal position.

In the early morning hours, he was certain something there in the dark called his name, cloth whispered over the bare concrete, cold air chilled him, and that dead hand reached for him again.

The next morning, his mother stuck a key in the padlock and swung the door open. She gasped at the site of him all bloody and bruised and turned away quickly, pausing at the foot of the stairs, looking only at the open door at the top.

"Clean up then go over and cut your grandmother's grass."

"Good God," Martin muttered, drawing him back to the present.

Michael got to his feet and went to the windows, looking out at the Manhattan skyline. There were other, smaller details he could tell, but his strength was gone. The glass of scotch slipped from his fingers, bursting into a thousand tiny pieces on the white marble floor. He leaned against the door frame and slid to his knees. Martin hurried over and put a hand on his shoulder.

"I'm so tired, Martin."

Chapter 22

Michael ducked and stepped out of the plane. The pilot said they were expecting snow and the heavy clouds in the distance confirmed the information, but a blizzard wasn't about to get in his way. He had traveled a million miles and wasn't stopping now. He rented a car and by the time he left Jackson big flakes drifted lazily from the skies.

The last few months had been hard. Martin had taken him to a hospital where he suffered through alcohol withdrawal for days. There were times during those long hours that he wished he had taken the easy way out and put a bullet in his head. He spent the rest of the time entertaining a psychologist Martin introduced him to.

He turned onto the gravel road and the yellow glow from the kitchen windows flooded him with relief. Sam opened the front door and waited on the porch as he climbed out of the rented car. He stood looking up at Sam, the snow swirling around in a heady wind. He felt he owed an explanation for this sudden appearance, but words failed him.

Like the warmth of the kitchen light guiding him home, the steady favor in Sam's brown eyes never disappointed him. "It's good to see you, Boy."

Nellie pulled the door open wider and squinted out at them. Seeing Michael, she immediately took him into her arms and held him against her softness until Sam gently patted her shoulder.

"It's cold out here, Nell. You can hug him just as well inside."

They didn't ask questions and, as always, the unconditional affection of these two kind people eased the despair that plagued him. That night, Michael once again fell asleep feeling safe.

After a few days, while Nellie was away, he told Sam everything. Sam listened without interruption and when he finished, Sam quietly tapped the ashes from his pipe then looked at him squarely.

"Time to come home."

Tears clouded Michael's eyes and the best he could do was nod.

Six months later, he flew to New York to settle that life. He walked into the offices at Nathan B and Kelly met him at the elevators with a broad smile, offering her hand.

"I'm not sure you'll remember me. I was your administrative assistant."

Michael laughed and ignored her hand, opting for a hug instead. "I've missed you too."

He draped an arm around her shoulders as they walked back to their suite of offices.

"So," Kelly said, "does Mrs. Bartholomew know you're back?"

"We talked yesterday. She had nothing but praise for you."

"What I'd really appreciate is a raise. Do you think you could swing that for me?"

"Would you settle for a six-figure income?"

"Right," she laughed.

"I'm serious. Your boss has resigned and recommended you for the job. There's even talk of compensation for the hell he put you through this past year."

Michael's next bit of business was with Christine and the lawyers. They finally hammered out a divorce agreement and she agreed to sign the papers. Christine got the house and he agreed to pay two million up front and thirty-five thousand dollars per month until Katie was eighteen, when she would receive a trust. The only part that really mattered to him was his visiting privileges with Katie.

Martin followed the waiter through the crowded restaurant fully expecting to find an empty table, but Michael was already there. Michael rose and smiled.

Martin shook his hand then clapped him on the back. "On time, I'm impressed."

"I've been on time occasionally in my life."

Martin seated himself and took a hard look at his friend. "Peace looks good on you."

"I owe it all to you."

Martin shrugged and picked up a menu. He was just grateful Michael had finally turned a corner.

"No, Martin, I really mean it. Thanks for sticking with me. I'd be dead if it wasn't for you."

Martin met his gaze and understood the days of dodging the truth for this man were over. "I'm so very glad I could help," he said.

The last person on Michael's list was Bobby. Bobby's wife took their children out, leaving the brothers to talk in peace.

Michael joined Bobby at the kitchen table. "I can't stay long," he said. "My flight leaves at six. I just wanted to say goodbye. Of course, you've got an open invitation to come out to Wyoming whenever you want, my treat."

Across the table, Bobby shuffled his feet and repositioned himself on the chair. "We need to talk."

"What's on your mind?"

Bobby looked away for a minute then took a deep breath and got to his feet. "I think I have a right to know what happened. Do you expect me to keep pretending the rest of my life?"

"Pretending?"

Bobby struck the table with his fist. "What did that letter mean to you?"

Shocked by his brother's sudden emotional outburst, Michael took a minute before responding. "Come on, Bobby, you all knew what happened."

"I told you a thousand times, I don't know anything! I know you used to wake me up screaming like somebody just ripped you open. I know Dad beat you and beat you until I thought I'd die if I had to witness it one more time. What I don't know is why."

"Didn't you read the article?"

Bobby nodded impatiently. "Debbie showed it to me. What was all that about? What went on between you and Uncle Frank?"

"Too much."

"Stop being so vague, damn it."

Michael took a breath and gave him a shortened version of what Frank did to him. While he talked, Bobby backed up a few paces, as if to put space between him and the reality he thought he wanted to hear, but now found too much to bear.

Finally, after Michael finished, Bobby spoke, his voice soft. "Didn't you tell anyone what Uncle Frank did to you?"

Michael looked out the window at the old neighborhood. Three blocks away were his parents' home, his grandmother's house and the garage where Frank hung himself. Suddenly his vision blurred. He blinked and tears fell down his face.

"I told Dad," he said quietly.

Bobby ran a hand through his hair and sat down again with a sigh. "I'm so sorry."

Michael wiped his face and looked down at his empty coffee cup. They sat in silence for a few minutes, both lost in the past. Finally, Bobby cleared his throat, shifted his weight and changed the subject.

"Mom asked me to talk to you," Bobby began quietly. "She wants you to know how much she regrets what happened. She hopes you'll find it in your heart to give her a few minutes of your time."

"No."

"Hey, you weren't the only one who was terrified of him, you know."

He looked across the table, remembering a time when he still believed there was affection for him in his mother's heart, but that was so long ago.

"I don't owe her anything," Michael said quietly.

"Maybe if you talk to her, you could find a way to forgive her. Her generation was tough on women. What was she supposed to do? She had six other kids, no job skills..."

Michael held up a hand. "I realize all of that, but what you are asking me to do is walk backwards. I told you, Bob, I won't be the family scapegoat. I didn't cause Mom's problems. It wasn't me."

"I didn't say you did," Bobby snapped.

Michael got to his feet, towering over his smaller brother. "But you expect me to listen to her side, like I owe her. Well, I don't. She abandoned me Bobby. If I had died the last time Dad kicked the shit out of me, she would have justified it and moved on through her catatonic life." He paused, taking a breath, unable to tamp down his anger any more. "If she wants forgiveness, let her talk to God. Maybe He listens to people like her," he finished bitterly.

Bobby stared at him for a long moment, an obvious change coming over him. He softened his tone, "I don't think Mom expects you to forgive her."

Michael sighed, suddenly tired beyond his years. "I don't want to punish her."

"I know you don't, but maybe it would help you to just tell her how you feel. Maybe you owe her that."

While Bobby knocked, Michael waited at the bottom of the steps of his parents' home with a lump of panic pulsing in his chest. Once again, he wanted to run from this place. Their mother opened the door and smiled at Bobby.

"Since when do you knock?" she said.

Michael watched his mother hug Bobby and old resentment rose in him.

"I brought somebody with me, Mom." Bobby stepped to the side and she gasped.

Her fingers flew to her mouth and her eyes filled with tears. "Michael," she whispered.

"I can't stay long," he said quickly.

The only difference in the house was a few pieces of furniture and some new paint. He looked into the living room, his gaze drawn to the mantel and all the pictures where he found a picture of Katie right next to the one of him as an altar boy. Resentment toward Christine rushed over him again.

Forcing his eyes away, he found his mother watching him. Her once-dark hair was almost completely silver. She was thinner and seemed fragile. He looked away and drew in a long breath.

She cleared her throat. "Come into the kitchen. I'll make some coffee and we'll talk."

Bobby wrapped an arm around his mother's shoulders and walked her to the kitchen. Michael followed down the long, dark hallway, until he reached the basement door and stopped. For four long years, one way or another, he descended those thirteen steps to face immeasurable suffering down there in the dimness.

He shifted his attention to the marks on the doorframe where his mother had measured all seven of them as they grew, their names and birthdays recorded beside the pen marks. The last entry for him was his birthday, June 2, 1962, the day he found Frank swinging from the rafters. He grazed the date with a fingertip and dropped his hand.

The kitchen didn't remind him so much of the past. Bobby poured three cups of coffee and brought them to the table while their mother plunged ahead.

"I won't offer excuses for not protecting you, Michael. There aren't any. I was your mother, and that was my job, but I failed you. I can't tell you how it feels to live with such a burden every single moment of twenty-two years."

Michael couldn't believe the irony. She still had no idea what he had been through. This conversation was about her.

"You were a sweet child, so gentle," she continued. "It was so horrible to watch what they did, to know I couldn't stop it without sacrificing everything else. I had hard choices. I know you don't understand it, because when I look back now it seems insane even to me, but I saw it that way then. If I could do it over, I'd change so many things, but I can't. I'll understand if you can't forgive, if you want nothing to do with me. I just wanted the opportunity to tell you that I deeply regret my part in what happened to you."

Michael watched and listened without moving. Finished, she cried openly. He sipped his coffee and glanced at the clock, waiting until she had calmed down before speaking.

"Sometimes when I look at my daughter," he began, "I can't help but wonder what makes a person hurt a child, turn their back on them, or find any reason to withhold love."

"I'm sorry," she said, sobbing into a handkerchief.

"You were as bad as they were," he said. Out of the corner of his eye, he saw Bobby flinch and right now he didn't care. "I never understood the withdrawal of your love or the alienation. You gave me to Frank, but I felt like I didn't belong anywhere."

He paused for a breath. The lump in his chest was expanding making it difficult to breathe. "You stood by in silence while they tortured me," he finished softly.

He stopped and took a shallow breath. His heart pounded so hard, he found it difficult to speak.

He cleared his throat, gathering strength. "Forgive me if I can't separate it all yet. For me, you're still on their level."

Her hands rested on her lap and Michael saw tears drop onto them. He drew in another long, hard breath and glanced at Bobby. Bobby had folded his arms over his chest and stared at the distant wall, away from the two of them.

Michael simply couldn't be here one minute more and stood. "I have to catch a plane."

His mother rose slowly and for the first time in over twenty-five years he received an embrace from his mother. As she cried against his chest, he just held on, longing for Nellie, understanding the road ahead much better now.

Chapter 23

Michael shifted his weight in the saddle and pushed the dark brown Stetson higher on his head, affording himself a better view of the concrete pouring into the wooden forms. This was the last portion of a foundation for the home he always envisioned. The builders estimated the project would take nearly a year, but that was fine with him. He was content just being back in Wyoming for good.

His home would rest on a high plateau with a view that stretched to the horizon, the perfect location for a boy who spent most of his childhood begging God to help him disappear.

In Sam and Nellie, he had found the much-needed nourishment of love. This endless land provided another kind of nourishment. In this high place, God had answered a battered child's pleas for mercy.

The day he brought Christine here, a profound sense of betrayal had overcome him and on that day he understood that the only person he wanted to share this with was Beth. He might try to love a thousand women, but no one could take her place. That knowledge had created the worst loneliness of his life.

Before reading the letter from Uncle Frank, guilt had dominated all of his other emotions, smothering any good that came his way. He believed he was responsible for Frank's suicide and deserved the punishment his father so willingly provided. Then that damned suicide note from Frank, courtesy of his father, injected his weary defenses with new venom. One piece of paper, so few words, represented so much.

Frank's cruel words were not an apology. The miserable excuse for a suicide note simply provided both Frank and his father with the final opportunity to torture him. Even at death's door, they chose to blame him.

The threat he had issued to Frank had come from a terrified boy with no real power. Still, he had accepted the responsibility for his uncle's suicide. After reading that vile note, the world tilted upside down, hurling him into a hole so deep he nearly vanished.

Finally, he had loaded the gun and stuck it in his mouth. As he pulled the hammer back, Beth's words rocketed out of the past and hit him hard. He was clinging to those words like a drowning man when Martin walked in the door and God finally answered his prayers.

Telling the truth to Martin had set him on a journey which liberated him from misdirected responsibility, but letting go of the rage would probably take the rest of his life.

He had written a long letter to Beth, attempting to explain what kept him away from a commitment to her. He explained his conviction that if she knew the real Michael, she would understand he didn't deserve love.

He never considered telling her the truth before that day. Guilt insisted he keep the secret, even when that silence meant losing her. Not even his father's worst beating compared to the agony of that penance.

In the letter, he told her everything about his life, including Uncle Frank. Telling Martin the truth had been terrifying. Telling Beth that same truth shredded what remained of his battered dignity. He never wanted her to know him that way. Still, he put each miserable word on paper and mailed the letter. Two months had passed and Beth hadn't responded. Knowing she finally had the facts offered a small amount of solace. Accepting her silence would be another agonizing task.

Thinking of Beth always twisted his insides into knots. He pulled the Stetson down and turned the horse toward Sam and Nellie's.

The previous week, he had flown back East to collect Katie for her summer visit. The minute the cab stopped in front of his former home in Connecticut, Katie flung the door open and rushed to him. He knelt to embrace her and the joy of those little arms around his neck was incomparable.

Christine stepped into the open doorway and a shaft of sunlight illuminated her face. Her blond hair was paler than he remembered and she seemed lighter than air, as if she might float away in the sunbeam. Though she was more beautiful than ever, any attraction to her was gone.

She shielded her eyes from the sun with a delicate hand and studied his face. "Would you like to come in?"

"I'm sorry, I can't. Our plane leaves at two."

Unmistakable disappointment flickered in her blue eyes, reminding him of old times.

"Maybe when I bring Katie back," he said.

Christine nodded quickly and turned for Katie's suitcase.

Katie didn't leave his side and except for a brief nap on the plane didn't stop talking until they arrived in Wyoming when she ran for Nellie's open arms.

He would have Katie for six weeks before returning her to Christine. On paper those six weeks sounded like a lot of time, but when it came to living them they always flicked by too quickly.

Today was his thirty-fifth birthday and he dreaded what waited back at the house. There had been too much whispering, too many strange silences and odd looks. Nellie was planning something.

He opened the lower field gate and walked the horse to the cool interior of the barn. He began to loosen the saddle just as Sam entered the other end.

"How's the work going over there at your place?" Sam asked.

"They have just about finished the foundation."

"You best hurry. Nellie's got supper done."

"Already? It's only four."

"She wants to go to town for some deal at the church. Hurry up now. Red and his bunch should be here any minute."

Michael lifted the saddle and placed it on the top rail of an empty stall. He removed the bridle and sent the horse trotting to the field behind the barn.

"Hey! I hear you're looking for a summer hand."

Michael turned and distinguished only a woman's silhouette in the doorway. She stepped farther into the barn where he could see her and he smiled broadly.

"Claire, what a wonderful surprise."

She embraced him and held on for a minute before pulling back to examine him closely. "My goodness, Cowboy, you just get better and better looking. I guess that wicked city did you some good after all."

"How long are you staying?"

"A couple of days. I have to be in Geneva next Wednesday. I'm doing some shots for a calendar."

Nellie started ringing the dinner bell and Sam fell in step with them. They were halfway to the house when a van approached.

Michael glanced at Sam. "Who's this?"

Sam squinted at the approaching vehicle. "I have no idea."

Claire grinned and wrapped her arm around Michael's waist. "You'll just have to wait and see."

Nellie and Katie waited on the porch. Kevin slipped out of the driver's side and all three boys jumped out of the back. Audrey was the last to emerge.

Michael quickened his steps and embraced Audrey first. "This is a pleasant surprise."

"Well, hey," Kevin said. "We were sitting around trying to decide who we could drive crazy on this year's vacation and guess who was first on our list?"

"It's good to see you too, Kevin."

"Come on inside everyone, dinner's ready," Nellie said.

Michael frowned. "Aren't we waiting for Red and Mary?"

"Mary is on her way, but Reds tied up in town." She waved a hand at him. "Come on, the food's getting cold."

After eating a full meal, Michael, Sam, and Kevin went to the front porch. Kevin lit a cigar and Sam stoked his pipe as dust rose in the distance again. Michael watched in silence, until Red's truck appeared followed by a long line of unfamiliar vehicles. Michael looked to Sam and waited for an explanation.

Sam shrugged after a moment. "Nellie's throwing you a birthday party."

"I hate my birthdays," Michael said.

Kevin slapped him on the back. "I got a feeling this ones gonna change all that."

Bobby and his family were the first to emerge from a rental car. Bobby hugged Michael with enthusiasm and stood out of the way as Martin and Gail approached. Kelly and her new husband opened the doors of a third vehicle and waited their turn.

Nellie invited all the members of her church and some of the local people who knew Michael. Kevin had somehow persuaded the old roadhouse band to come all the way from Amarillo for this one night event. The band set up in the barn and struck up their first song as the sun began to set in the clear June sky.

After their first set, Don, the band leader, looked to Michael, "Why don't we get the birthday boy up here for a song or two?"

Michael started to shake his head, but Kevin gave him a little shove toward the band and started applauding. Michael decided not to argue the way he had in the past and moved behind the electronic keyboard.

Don stepped close, lowering his voice, "Angel's Blues?"

"Absolutely not."

He remembered several of the band's songs pretty well and started the opening of one of their more upbeat songs. Don smiled and moved back.

Bobby pushed to the edge of the group and stood nearby watching intently. Michael glanced his way and Bobby saluted him with a nod of approval and a broad smile.

After a few songs, Michael moved away from the keyboard and refused to play anymore.

"It is my birthday," he reminded Don with a pat on the back.

He had no desire to ever drink alcohol again and quenched his thirst with a large glass of iced tea. The band began a slow song and he turned to watch as couples started to dance. Katie bobbed back and forth with Kevin's youngest son. Even Sam and Nellie took a turn.

A finger tapped his shoulder lightly. "Excuse me."

His heart recognized her voice two beats before his brain and started a crazy, pounding rhythm that left him breathless. He turned quickly and when she smiled, the rest of the world melted away.

"My name is Beth," she began. "Well, actually my name's Elizabeth, but everyone calls me Beth. I was named after my mother and grandmother, only Grandma went by Betty and Mom was called Elizabeth. Of course, Kevin still insists on calling me Bethie, which makes me feel like I'm still five years old, but you, Michael O'Mara, can call me anything you want."

Michael smiled slowly as she spoke. His body ached from holding back the embrace he wanted to give her. He never needed her more. Tears danced in his eyes.

"I can't believe you're here."

"Come on," she said, taking his hand, "I think I still remember how to slow dance."

Kevin whistled loudly as they moved to the dance floor.

Beth looked up at Michael and grinned. "You're face is red."

"Being this close to you makes me think embarrassing thoughts."

"Hey, don't tease me Michael Anthony."

"I'd never do that," he laughed. Beth deliberately stepped on the top of his foot and he winced in pain.

After a moment's recovery, he looked down into those dark eyes. "Where have you been hiding all evening?"

"In a hotel room in town waiting for a ride. I rode up from Utah with Claire. Oh, by the way, remind me later and I'll tell you this interesting story she shared with me about a young man and an engagement ring he never got around to using."

"I couldn't, Beth…"

She waved away his defense. "Let's get back to my day. Kevin was supposed to come back and get me around five. Without consulting me, he decided it would be best for me to make my appearance at the party after every one else arrived. So, I've been sitting there in my little, bitty motel room, waiting and waiting for him to come back for me. Were you surprised?"

"Well," he paused to clear his throat. "The last time we talked you said you hated me. Since you always mean what you say, I figured I was out of luck, particularly when you didn't arrive with Kevin and his family. I figured you were in Texas since this is your daughter's birthday as well."

"She's with her father this year."

Kevin laid a big hand on Michael's shoulder. "Excuse me."

Beth frowned at Kevin. "Can't you see we're talking?"

"I thought you might want to know..." he grinned broadly and waved a hand at the silent band who were conferring over their next tune, "the music stopped."

Embarrassed, Michael and Beth looked around them as Bobby crossed the room to introduce himself.

"I'm Michael's brother, Bobby," he said.

Beth shook Bobby's hand and shot a quick, hard look at Michael. "I didn't know he had any brothers until just recently. It's a pleasure meeting you, Bobby."

"You too," Bobby glanced at Michael then back to Beth and grinned. "Mind if I ask a quick question?"

"No, go right ahead."

"Did you really break his nose? I mean, you're so tiny and all."

Again, Beth threw a look at Michael. He stepped back, holding up his hands in a gesture of innocence. "Talk to Kevin."

Beth looked back to Bobby. "His nose was already broken. I just tapped it."

"Some tap," Michael said. "You brought me to my knees."

"Oh, I remember now," she said. "That happened way back when you still believed you could predict the future." She patted his chest and there was fire in her eyes.

Bobby grinned at Michael, "Looks like she still knows how to clock you pretty good."

Michael sighed, "Every time."

Bobby discretely slipped away as Beth turned to Michael.

"You had it coming," she said, looking away at the open barn door.

"Everybody's wrong sometimes, Beth."

"Sometimes? It's been seventeen years. Add up those hours and I'd say that's a monumental wrong."

"One hundred forty-nine thousand and forty," Michael clicked off easily.

Beth threw her hands up in frustration. "What can I say to you? How can you be so smart and completely stupid at the same time?"

"I was born lucky," he said with a little grin.

Beth moved close, as close as she could get without actually touching him, and fixed him with a cocky smile. "You...have yet to get lucky."

Michael's shifting expression apparently pleased her. He understood her perfectly. She smiled broadly as his face relaxed into an easy smile.

"Are you enjoying yourself, Beth?"

"Are you uncomfortable, Michael?"

He released a long, uneasy breath and laughed.

She took his hand. "Let's take a walk."

They walked down the sloping field to the fence and stood in silence for a moment, taking in the beauty and the cool night air.

Michael reached out and gently lifted a strand of her hair. "Did you get my letter?"

She nodded and kept her eyes on the field and the grazing horses. "Yes, Michael, that's why I'm standing here."

Beth sighed and put her arm around his waist, leaning against him. "How could you ever leave this place?"

He followed her gaze to the moonlit valley stretching before them and pointed to the right. "I'm having a house built right over there."

"So you intend to stay?"

He nodded and fought the old need to keep his feelings to himself. "I was down there today looking at my house being built and it occurred to me, in this place, God finally answered my prayers."

She took a quick step back and frowned at him.

"What?" He asked.

"Open your eyes wider, Michael. God's been answering your prayers for a long time."

"Well, yeah, I've had some luck..."

She shook her head and put a finger on his lips. "I read your letter, did you?"

"I wrote the thing..."

"I just met Martin. He treated you in the hospital and cared enough to take you in, didn't he?"

Michael nodded, getting her point.

"What about your brother, Bobby? He stood up against your family to save your life. And what about my sweet brother picking you up in that snow storm, wasn't that a miracle? Not to mention Red, Nellie and Sam who obviously adore you and gave you a place to call home and the first real peace you ever knew. Last, but not least, Katie, how precious is she?"

She stared at him, her expression and tone softening. "And then there is me, loving you for seventeen years."

She stretched up on her toes and kissed his lips softly. "God's been right there all along," she whispered.

Red appeared in the door of the barn. "Hey! We're ready to sing Happy Birthday and cut this cake. Get your butt up here, boy."

The evening was a happy blur. He was by Beth's side whenever possible and his mind wasn't on looking after Katie or the social amenities of this birthday. He wished it was over so he could just be with Beth.

At ten, he took Katie to the house and tucked her in bed. On his way back to the barn, he crossed through the living room and glanced through the picture window and there on the deck sat Beth rocking slowly in Nellie's old chair, her serene face lovely in the glow of a full moon.

Michael decided to allow her this privacy and continued out the back door, but the closer he got to the barn and the party, the slower he walked. Halfway to the barn he turned back, quickening his steps.

Beth didn't seem at all surprised to see him standing there at the foot of the stairs. She glanced over, offering a serene little smile before turning her attention back to the view. "I love it here."

"Beth..." he began, but paused to clear the longing from his throat. "I need you to know that I meant every word I said that day at Kelsey's bar seventeen years ago."

She rose from the chair and came to the edge of the stairs. She looked deep into his eyes and for once Michael put up no barriers.

"Say it again," she said quietly. "Let's see if we remember every word the same way."

He stepped up on the bottom step and looked up at her. His voice was soft with emotion, but he spoke the truth without hesitation.

"I want you more than anyone I've ever met. I want to be together forever. I don't want to face life without you one more day." He paused for a breath and finished softly. "I love you."

A small cry escaped her lips and she lowered her head.

"I'm through running, Beth. I'll be right here if you ever want to give us a try."

She took her time responding, making him wait and wonder. Finally, she raised her head, smiled widely and opened her arms.

Michael would never remember how he got on the deck, but would swear he didn't touch the last two steps. He wrapped his arms around her, lifted her easily, and kissed her with seventeen years of longing.

6565131R0

Made in the USA
Charleston, SC
08 November 2010